MW00873817

1st Edition

STAY UP TO DATE

Join the conversation and get updates on new and upcoming releases in the Facebook group called "JN Chaney's Renegade Readers." This is a hotspot where readers come together and share their lives and interests, discuss the series, and speak directly to J.N. Chaney and his co-authors.

https://www.facebook.com/groups/jnchaneyreaders/

He also post updates, official art, and other awesome stuff on his website and you can also follow him on Instagram, Facebook, and Twitter.

For email updates about new releases, as well as exclusive promotions, visit his website and sign up for the VIP mailing list. Head there now to receive a free copy of *The Other Side of Nowhere.*

https://www.jnchaney.com/the-messenger-subscribe

Enjoying the series? Help others discover *The Messenger* series by leaving a review on Amazon.

HEAVEN'S DOOR

BOOK 8 IN THE MESSENGER SERIES

J.N. CHANEY

TERRY MAGGERT

CONTENTS

THE MESSENGER UNIVERSE KEY TERMS

The Messenger: The chosen pilot of the Archetype.

Archetype: A massive weapon system designed for both space battle, close combat, and planetary defense. Humanoid in shape, the Archetype is controlled by a pilot and the Sentinel, an artificial intelligence designed to work with an organic humanoid nervous systems. The Archetype is equipped with offensive weaponry beyond anything known to current galactic standards, and has the ability to self-repair, travel in unSpace, and link with other weapons systems to fight in a combined arms operation.

Blobs: Amorphous alien race, famed for being traders. They manufacture nothing and are known as difficult employers.

Clan Shirna: A vicious, hierarchical tribe of reptilian beings whose territory is in and around the **Globe of Suns** and the **Pasture**. Clan Shirna is wired at the genetic level to defend and protect their territory. Originally under the control of Nathis, they are space-based, with a powerful navy and the collective will to fight to the last soldier if necessary.

Couriers: Independent starship pilots who deliver goods—legal, illegal, and everything in between—to customers. They find their jobs on a centralized posting system (See: **Needs Slate**) that is galaxy-wide, ranked by danger and pay, and constantly changing. Couriers supply their own craft, unless they're part of a Shipping Conglom. Couriers are often ex-military or a product of hard worlds.

Fade: A modification to the engine. It is a cutting edge shielding device that rotates through millions of subspace frequencies per second, rendering most scans ineffective. If the Fade is set to insertion, then the ship will translate into unSpace, where it can go faster than light. The Fade is rare, borderline illegal, and highly expensive. It works best on smaller masses, so Courier ships are optimal for installation of the Fade. One drawback is the echo left behind in regular space, an issue that other cloaking systems do not have. By using echoes as pathway markers, it is possible to track and destroy ships using the Fade.

Golden: A transhumanist race of beings who are attempting to scour the galaxy of intelligent life. The Golden were once engaged in warfare with the **Unseen**. They are said to return every 200,000 years to enact a cycle of galactic genocide, wiping out all technologically advanced civilizations before disappearing back from which they came. They destroyed their creators at some unknown point in the distant past and are remaking themselves with each revolution of their eternal, cyclical war.

Globe of Suns: A star cluster located in the far arm of the Milky Way Galaxy. It is an astronomical outlier. Dense with stars, it's a hotbed of Unseen tech, warfare, and Clan Shirna activity. Highly dangerous, both as an obstacle and combat area.

Kingsport: Located in the Dark Between, these are planetoid sized bases made of material that is resistant to detection, light-absorbing, and heavily armored. Oval in shape, the Kingsport is naval base and medical facility in one, intended as a deep space sleep/recovery facility for more than a thousand Unseen. The Kingsports maintain complete silence and do not communicate with other facilities, regardless of how dire the current military situation.

Lens: Unseen tech; a weapon capable of sending stars into premature collapse at considerable distance. The Lens is not unique—the Unseen left many of them behind in the Pasture, indicating that they were willing to destroy stars in their fight with the Golden.

Ribbon: Unseen tech that imparts a visual history of their engineering, left behind as a kind of beacon for spacefaring races.

Sentinel: A machine intelligence designed by the Unseen, the Sentinel is a specific intellect within the Archetype. It meshes with the human nervous system, indicating some anticipation of space-borne humans on the part of the Unseen. Sentinel is both combat system and advisor, and it has the ability to impart historical data when necessary to the fight at hand.

Shadow Nebula: A massive nebula possibly resulting from simultaneous star explosions. The Shadow Nebula may be a lingering effect from the use of a Lens, but it is unknown at this time.

Unseen: An extinct and ancient race who were among the progenitors of all advanced technology in the Milky Way, and possibly beyond. In appearance, they were slender, canine, and bipedal, with the forward-facing eyes of a predator. Their history is long and murky, but their engineering skills are nothing short of godlike. They commanded gravity, materials, space, and the ability to use all of these sciences in tandem to hold the Golden at bay during the last great war. The Unseen knew about humans, although their plans for humanity have since been lost to time.

unSpace: Neither space nor an alternate reality, this is the mathematically generated location used to span massive distances between points in the galaxy. There are several ways to penetrate unSpace, but only two are known to humans.

Pasture: Unseen tech in the form of an artificial Oort Cloud; a comet field of enormous size and complexity. Held in place by Unseen engineering, the Pasture is a repository for hidden items left by the Unseen. The Pasture remains stable despite having thousands of objects, a feat which is a demonstration of Unseen technical skills. The Lens and Archetype are just two of the items left behind for the next chapter in galactic warfare.

Prelate: In Clan Shirna, the Prelate is both military commander and morale officer, imbued with religious authority over all events concerning defense of their holy territory.

1

SOMETHING DRIPPED on Dash as he ducked under the tangle of vines. Whatever it was had the unusual quality of being viscous, warm, and putrid all at once. It mingled with the sweat dripping from his forehead, prompting him to wipe at it with a sleeve before it managed to get in his eyes.

He glanced at the ooze glistening on his sleeve, a wry grin on his face. "Another gem of a planet."

Fortunately, the biochemistry of terrestrial planets seemed to always adhere to a moderate range of things like toxicity and corrosive properties. The exceptions were the bizarre outliers called death worlds, but this planet wasn't one of those.

As far as they knew.

Well, the goo might not be obviously poisonous or toxic, but as they walked on, the scent intensified. "Certainly doesn't smell like a Golden facility," he said, wrinkling his nose while holding the vines up for Leira and Wei-Ping to duck under. Four sailors from the

Retribution trailed along behind them, a column that ended with a softly swearing Ragsdale.

"Smells like life," Leira said.

"And death," Wei-Ping added, screwing up her own nose. "You sure about this, boss?"

Dash leveled his weapon into the darkness ahead of them. "As sure as we can be, given the details of Sentinel's scans." He looked back along the line. "Those haulers coming along behind?"

"Yeah, they're right here, Dash." Ragsdale stepped aside, wiping his brow with a filthy cloth. They'd been hiking uphill for an hour now, toward a cave system that apparently contained a potent Dark Metal signature. With the Shroud ramping up production, every kilo of the precious stuff mattered, so here they were, striking into the heart of an alien jungle more than thirty light years away from the Forge.

With a soft, grinding rumble, the hauler units advanced, working their way across the rough ground then stopping to wait for their human companions to continue forward. The AI-assisted haulers clung to the ground, their combination of bulbous wheels and gravity polarizers capable of carrying heavy masses in nearly any combination of gravity and terrain. Since the Archetype, or any of their other mechs, would have to excavate tunnels to break into the cave system, the little haulers were a better option—for the moment, anyway.

Dash stepped into the cave mouth. He could see a few meters, and then it was nothing but impenetrable darkness. He lowered his goggles and toggled between low light and thermal imaging; the first gave him only a few more meters of visibility, while the second showed virtually no temperature variations at all.

"Looks like we've got to light the lights," he said, snapping a

small lamp on his pulse-gun, and another on the side of his helmet.
The others did likewise, as did the haulers, whose powerful lights
threw the darkness far down the tunnel.

Dash tensed. If anything lived in these tunnels, it was probably
used to darkness—which meant it probably wouldn't take kindly to
being bathed in sudden brilliance.

But nothing roared, or shrieked, or lunged, or even moved. He
saw wet rock, and that was it.

"A pleasant surprise. Okay, let's go," he said, and started
forward.

The tunnel was narrow enough that they needed to stay in
single file, which was both good and bad; it meant that any threat
was constrained the same way, but it also meant that anyone but
Dash would have trouble safely taking shots at anything. He trusted
Leira, Wei-Ping, and Ragsdale but didn't know the crew they'd
brought along from the *Retribution* well enough to be fully confident
they wouldn't accidentally shoot him in the back. It made a spot
between his shoulder blades start to itch under his body armor—just
another distraction to add to the list that already included heat,
sweat, scrapes, and a twisted foot from plunging into a hole filled
with scummy water.

Dash caught himself. Focusing on anything other than the way
ahead was a good way to get jumped by something. Or worse.

"Sentinel," he said. "How far ahead do you make that signal?"

"Approximately forty meters," the AI replied. "It appears that
the tunnel branches about fifteen meters ahead of you. You must
follow the way to the right."

"Got it, thanks."

He carried on. That spot between his shoulder blades still
itched, but now he was starting to feel far more exposed and

vulnerable to the darkness ahead—especially when they reached the branch Sentinel had mentioned and they turned to pass the way leading to the left. It looked no different than the path to the right, but as it fell behind, the thought of leaving that dark portal gaping into the only way they knew back to the surface made a few more anxious itches start up. Dash was comfortable in space because there, he could see what was coming.

This was different.

They reached a tight bend to the right. They should have maybe another fifteen meters to go. The tunnel widened, the roof rising, meaning they could spread out a bit.

Dash turned to pass instructions to spread out, just in time to see the first of the *Retribution's* sailors raise his pulse-gun and seem to aim it directly at Dash.

What the hell?

"Dash, get down!" the man shouted. Driven by instinct, Dash did, just as pulse-gun bolts snapped over his head. Behind him, from what was the way forward, a sudden, pervasive hum erupted, then it immediately swelled to a harsh buzz. Dash yanked himself around just in time to see segmented legs dangling from a chitinous mass, held up by what seemed to be a multitude of beating, membranous wings. A thin, slimy tube darted toward him, and that was all Dash needed to see; he swivelled his pulse-gun straight and fired, point blank.

The searing bluish bolts slammed into the chitinous horror, blasting out chunks and spattering yet more stinking goo over Dash. More shots struck it as the others opened fire. The creature abruptly reversed, backing up in a frenzy as the drone of its wings became a torrent of teeth-aching noise that splashed against the rock around him. He fired again, his shots slamming home, part of a fusillade that now poured into the thing.

The wings suddenly rattled and clashed as they beat, no longer smoothly coordinated. The thing wobbled then hit the ground with a heavy clack. It writhed and flopped, wings beating in spasms as it scraped against the rocky floor. It took another pair of well-aimed shots to finally make it go still.

Dash levered himself to his feet, sucking in breaths of humid air that tasted like that horrific stink. "What the hell was *that?*"

"Big, ugly, and really, really smelly," Wei-Ping said, her pulse-gun still held against her shoulder. "And hopefully also dead."

Leira played her light across it. "Okay, that's it."

"That's what?" Dash asked, glancing away from the now-steaming corpse.

"That's a spider. A *giant* spider. And it has *wings*." She shook her head. "There are spiders. With wings. I'm never stepping foot on a planet again."

"Me either," Ragsdale said, grimacing. "Had a spider incident in my bunk once."

"What happened—" Leira said, but Ragsdale waved her off.

"Too soon."

Leira just returned a knowing nod, and they continued their descent, keeping their guns trained on the fallen monstrosity as they gave it the widest berth they could.

"SO THAT OBVIOUSLY DOESN'T BELONG here," Dash said.

The rest of them nodded, their pulse-guns raised yet again, this time at the thing lying in the cave.

It was a probe, obviously of Golden origin. Four meters long, roughly cylindrical, about a meter in diameter, and showing damage suggestive of violent entry into the cave. It must have either decelerated during its plunge from orbit or been slowed enough by its no doubt fiery passage through the atmosphere. Whatever the reason, the probe had hit hard enough to smash through into the cave complex, but not so hard that it created an impact crater.

"I wonder what brought it down," Ragsdale said. "There's no signs of obvious damage from weapons fire or anything like that."

Dash shrugged. "Maybe it's got information stored that would tell us. A small data core isn't out of the question."

Leira walked partway around it. "I doubt it's been here since the Unseen-Golden war. She nudged a vine dangling into the cave through the hole smashed in its roof, which was now firmly plugged with tangled vegetation. "If it was, you'd think it would have been completely buried, like that ship on Gulch, and not just coated in dust and leaves."

Dash shrugged again. "Maybe it was brought down because of whatever strife is happening inside the Golden right now. In any case, like I said, maybe there's some data in it that will tell us. Right now, we really just want to recover it."

Leira raised an eyebrow. "You really aren't curious about what happened here?"

"Sure I am. But let me say one thing—spiders. With wings."

"Okay, good point. Let's get this thing loaded up and get it the hell out of here."

Given that the probe theoretically was accessible from above, Dash considered just having Sentinel bring the Archetype in, and recovering it that way. But the AI warned him that the network of caves and tunnels eroded into the rock made the ground unstable, and probably not capable of supporting the mech's weight; even just clearing the thick jungle growth above them risked collapsing the cave and burying the probe.

"Okay," he said, slinging his pulse-gun. "Looks like we're going to have to do this the old-fashioned way. Let's get the haulers in here and get them started cutting this thing apart."

They moved aside as the first of the machines partly rolled, and partly floated into the cave. It was equipped with a powerful cutting laser. Dash and the others pulled back out of the cave while the hauler did its job. A dazzling flash lit the tunnels—and then, nothing.

Dash frowned at Leira. "That was quick."

"Dash," Sentinel said. "I have detected a power surge from the probe. It appears to be attempting to activate its drive."

Dash blinked. "Where the hell does it think it can go?"

Ragsdale, peering around the corner into the cavern, looked back. "I don't think it plans to go anywhere." he said, his eyes suddenly wide. "If it manages to fire up a fusion drive in here—"

"Oh, shit," Wei-Ping snapped. "Let's haul ass!"

But Dash shook his head. "No time. Sentinel, how long?"

"Unknown. Likely less than one minute until its drive has fully cycled up to ignition."

Dash sighed. "Nothing's *ever* simple, is it?" He gestured to Wei-Ping. "Take your crew out of here. We'll—"

Wei-Ping snapped out a curse. "Like you said, no time." She hurried into the cavern containing the probe.

Now it was Dash's turn to curse as he lunged toward the probe. Leira followed, while Ragsdale organized the others to watch out for things like flying spiders, and otherwise wait to see if they were about to be incinerated.

7

Wei-Ping clambered past the hauler, which sat motionless, its laser-cutter still deployed, apparently awaiting further instructions. She moved to the back of the probe and studied it.

Dash pushed in beside her. "What are you looking for?"

"Access plate. I've done enough salvage of this Golden tech now to—yeah, there it is," she said, dropping to her knees and examining the probe's underside.

She yanked a universal tool off of her belt and jammed into a recess. She pried, straining, then pried again, and the plate popped off.

Dash peered into the opening. Modules—lots of modules. It was typical Golden tech, based on an array of modular components of a generalized design, each seeming to be able to adapt itself to whatever purpose was needed at the moment. It was a flexible, robust design, and tough to deactivate. Every time you yanked out a module, the others just adjusted. Worse, they could keep communicating among themselves remotely. Conover and Amy had faced a similar problem trying to shut down a Golden drone that had crashed into the Forge and hacked the station to bring down many of its defensive systems.

Wei-Ping just began yanking out modules and handing them to Dash and Leira. "Get rid of these. Take them as far away from here as you can."

Dash called Ragsdale, who quickly arranged the *Retribution*'s sailors into a chain. Each soldier tossed modules to one another, moving them as far back up the tunnel as they could.

"Sentinel, are we making any difference?"

"None that I can detect. I would caution that you have no more than thirty seconds left, and perhaps as little as twenty."

Wei-ping yanked out more modules, but Dash snapped, "Screw

this." He stood and moved to the back of the probe, then he jammed his pulse-gun into the exhaust port and started firing, shot after shot, emptying the weapon's power cell.

The seconds ticked by.

Finally, Sentinel simply said, "Ignition is imminent."

Dash fumbled with a fresh power cell for his weapon, but he realized they were out of time. He looked at Leira—

I wonder if my eyes are as wide as hers?

He braced himself for a blinding flash of light, and then—

Nothing.

Literally nothing. Nothing happened.

"Uh, Sentinel?" he said. "Got an update, by chance?"

"The probe has initiated its fusion drive. You should now be bathed in superheated plasma. I am assuming that's not the case."

"Yeah, there's actually very little superheated plasma," Dash said, trying to will his heart, which had been pounding like a pulsar, to slow down. "In fact, I'm not even sweating more than I was a minute ago. Wie-Ping, do I have eyebrows?"

She looked at him, mildly stunned. "Um. Yes?"

"Excellent. Then we clearly haven't been incinerated." He looked at Wei-Ping's hands, which were still holding a pair of modules she'd yanked out of the probe, and her eyes were as wide as everyone else's. He shrugged. "I figured that shutting down the probe wasn't going to work in time, but it can't really light a drive that doesn't work, right?"

"Uh, Dash, that's a fusion drive," Wei-Ping replied. "You know, something designed to take the sort of temperatures you'd find in a star? What makes you think you disabled it with that little gun of yours?"

He shrugged once more. "Hey, I'm going to choose me being

the hero and having exactly the right answer to solve the problem. Makes for a better story over drinks."

Wei-Ping just grinned and shook her head. "Whatever. We're all still here, definitely not puffs of vapor, so it's all good." She gave him a searching look. "Even with *those* eyebrows."

"Are you saying I'm hairy?" Dash asked her, holding a hand to his heart. "I'm masculine. You know, *rugged*. Like a dignified mountain or something."

"Sure. A mountain. Let's go with that," Wei-Ping said.

"Definitely rugged," Leira said. "In any case, now that the excitement is over, can we just salvage this damned probe and get out of here? Or do I need to remind everyone about spiders. With *wings*?"

2

Dᴀsʜ ᴄʀᴏssᴇᴅ his arms and looked at the probe they'd recovered, which was now laid out in three pieces on the floor of one of the Forge's fabrication bays. They'd had to cut it apart so the haulers could pull it out of the cave, but it remained intact enough that Custodian could determine, and then point out, that it was quite different from the usual Golden probe they'd encountered.

"This version has a surprisingly sophisticated translation drive," Custodian said. "It is capable of fast jumps over long distances, more akin to a large ship than a simple probe."

Dash scratched an ear, thinking. "Any idea what it was for? I mean, besides intel?"

"It mounts what appears to be a standard sensor suite, and a single weapon similar to a pulse-cannon, but its specific purpose is unclear," Custodian said. "I am attempting to access data still contained in the probe's aft section."

"Let me guess," Ragsdale said. "It's encrypted."

"It is, but that is not the issue. Rather, the data has been corrupted, mainly during the probe's recovery."

"When we cut it into pieces, you mean," Leira said.

"Yes."

Viktor and Conover, who'd been studying the probe up close, and with more than a little amazement at the thing's strikingly complex and advanced design, both looked up. "It would have been nice if you could have brought it back in one piece," Conover said. "We might have been able to learn more about it."

"Did I mention spiders with wings?" Leira said. "Giant ones?"

Conover made a disgusted face. "Yeah, okay, that's a good reason to hurry."

Viktor stood. "Still, thirteen hundred kilos of Dark Metal. That's quite a prize," he said.

Dash nodded. "Yeah, it is. And that leads me to my next question, something to ponder while Custodian tries to access the data aboard it. What are we going to do with it? I can think of about ten different uses for it."

"Only ten?" Viktor said.

Dash nodded. "Exactly. We need to stay on top of our prioritizing."

"We should keep a chunk of it for the Shroud to turn into Q-cores," Ragsdale offered. "Its capacity ramps up a little more each day, and those Q-cores you brought back from that gas giant shows how damned useful those things are."

Dash had to nod at that. The two Q-cores—quad power cores, arranged in a way that made them synergistically much more powerful than four individual cores would be alone—had dramatically increased the Forge's capabilities. Not only had its manufacturing capacity increased, but so had its offensive and defensive power. But it still had a long way to go to *fully power up*.

The mechs were in the same state. They could all be made much more powerful by adding power cores. And the Shroud, even when it was finally running flat out, could only produce cores so fast, and then only depending on the Dark Metal available. That left them hunting down cores, like they had in the early days of the war, or trying to retrieve them from the depth of gas giants, where the Golden had apparently stashed an unknown number of them. Dash and the Archetype had proved that possible, but only at terrible risk.

"Actually, Dash, I've been thinking," Conover said. "We've still got that carrier we seized from Sur-natha in our last big battle. I know we haven't done much with it yet—"

"I think we've actually been considering just scrapping it for its components, in fact," Leira put in.

"We have, but I have another suggestion," Conover went on. "Suppose we refurbish it instead and put a squadron of *Makos* aboard it?"

Dash gave Conover a thoughtful stare. The *Mako* was a proto-type fighter, able to be equipped with a range of weapons, including one of their most potent weapons of all, known as the blast-cannon. It could also use a direct, neural interface with its pilot, greatly increasing its capabilities, and it was suited for use in space or atmo. They'd only built one plus the original, though, and hadn't followed up with any more, as they hadn't had any particular role for such a small vessel that wasn't itself translation-capable.

"I thought of that," Dash said. "But it would be a big job. Between fixing up that carrier and making a bunch of *Makos*—that's going to take a *lot* of time and tie up a *lot* of our resources."

"It will, but we'd have something that could project a *lot* of power, where and when we want it projected there. It would be strong enough, in fact, that it could probably function as a task force all by itself."

Dash crossed his arms again. Custodian had said that Conover had the makings of a capable, even a skilled tactician. He could see the soundness of the reasoning and found himself nodding.

"Good points," he said.

"You sure about that, Dash?" Viktor said. "I agree that Conover makes some good points, but we'd have to shelve about six or seven other projects to make this happen, at least in any decent amount of time."

Ragsdale cocked his head. "So why not use some of this big score of Dark Metal to improve the Forge's manufacturing capacity even more, and then use the rest to build *Makos*. And while that's going on, focus on getting that carrier spaceworthy again."

"Sounds like a decent plan, actually," Leira said. "Imagine deploying a squadron of Makos with blast-cannons. That's a force to be reckoned with for sure."

Even Viktor had to nod. "It would mean we'd have in-atmo capabilities, without having to rely on the mechs."

"It also means we have to train up pilots for the Makos," Ragsdale said. "Which means we'll need to *find* pilots for them."

"True," Leira replied. "But we're getting more and more people telling us they want to join the cause."

"Tell me about it," Ragsdale muttered. "As if vetting people wasn't hard enough." When he realized everyone had turned to look at him, he shrugged. "Why do you think I volunteered to come along on that little jaunt of yours to the jungle planet? I needed a break from combing through personnel files, outstanding warrant lists, security bulletins—"

"So, instead, you got to encounter a giant flying spider and risk being incinerated by an alien probe," Leira said.

"*Still* better than sitting for eight or ten hours at a terminal, trying to figure out if the fact someone lied on a resume five years ago is because they really wanted the job, or because they were up to something else," Ragsdale shot back.

Leira smiled. "Anyway, one thing the Makos will do is actually make things easier, when it comes to employing people. Benzel and Wei-Ping have the fleet fully crewed again—and let's face it, not everyone is suited to fly a mech."

"Plus mechs take a lot to build," Conover said.

Dash had followed the conversation as it bounced around. "Okay, let's do it," he finally said. "Conover, I'm giving this over to you to head up. Work with Wei-Ping and Benzel, because the labor's going to come from their fully crewed ships, which means anyone we recruit in the meantime can replace them. You can coordinate with Ragsdale and Harolyn about the person-power side of it. Custodian can start harvesting this Dark Metal and doing whatever needs to be done with it to expand the Forge's fabrication facilities so we can get rolling."

"Will do, Dash," Conover said.

"It is fortuitous that, just as you have arrived at that decision, I have something to report regarding data I have been able to retrieve from the probe," Custodian suddenly put in.

"Oh? And what's that?" Dash asked.

"The data is fragmentary and incomplete, but it is sufficient to confirm that this probe originated in a system approximately two-hundred light-years away from where you located it, in a star system named Beacon."

"Okay—and what's there?"

"According to the only existing stellar survey, an unremarkable K-class, yellow-orange, main sequence star, around which a desert planet, a single gas giant, and an extensive asteroid belt orbit."

"Huh." Dash looked at the others, who all just stared back with blank expressions and shrugs.

"Okay, is there anything to indicate where the probe was before that?" Dash asked. "Where it came from?"

"That is the unusual aspect of this. There is nothing to indicate it was ever anywhere prior to Beacon. It is as though that is the system where it originated."

Dash frowned then asked Custodian to show them a star chart, with Beacon highlighted. A holo-image appeared; for a moment, they all stared at it.

"Still doesn't mean a thing to me," Viktor said. "I've never had reason to go that far spinward—in that part of the arm, at least."

It didn't mean anything to Dash, either. However, he noticed a symbol appended to the system that indicated there was an entry in the Aquarian Collective's database. Dash asked Custodian to call it up, but the comet miners' entry didn't have much to say beyond it was a no-go zone for their prospecting and resource-harvesting operations.

"Huh, I wonder why," Dash said. "Custodian, call up Al'Bijea and see if you can conference him into this meeting by comm."

While they waited and the others poked around the remains of the probe, Leira sidled up to Dash.

Dash looked at her, raised an eyebrow, then gave her a sly grin. "What? Right now? Woman, you're insatiable."

She curled her lip. "You wish." But she turned immediately serious. "Dash, about that project, getting the carrier refurbished and the *Makos* built—I'm a little concerned."

"It really does seem to be the best use of our resources, Leira——"

"No, that's not what I'm talking about," she cut in, shaking her head. "I'm concerned about you putting Conover in charge of it."

"Oh? Why? The kid——" He stopped. "No, wait, I said I wouldn't call him that anymore. Conover is bright, organized, and methodical. I think he's a good choice."

"Sure, I agree, he's bright and organized and methodical. But he's also, what, not even twenty yet? Or, if he is, he just turned it." She lowered her voice. "I agree we shouldn't call him a kid, but in a lot of ways, that's exactly what he is, Dash. That's an awfully big, complicated, and important project to be giving to him——especially solo. Why not have him and Viktor work on it, like we've done in the past."

Dash shook his head. "We can't treat Conover like a kid anymore, Leira. Not because of his age, or even because of his skills and accomplishments. It's because we can't afford to have him *be* a kid anymore. We just don't have that kind of luxury. I've got other things for Viktor to do. Conover can't be an understudy anymore. Hell, we've given him a mech to strap on and go fight the Golden."

Leira still looked doubtful, but Dash persisted. "I've been having some...let's call it alone time with Custodian. He thinks that Conover has the potential to be a strong and capable leader. So do I. In fact, he might be pivotal in this war." He sighed and stuck his hands in his pockets. "The worst part is that he's even going to get the chance in the first place. This war could go on for a long time."

Leira sagged a bit. "Yeah. I know." She gave a weary shrug. "And you're right about Conover. And that's the problem, I think."

"What?"

"That you're right. I wish you weren't, because if we expect

Conover to become a pivotal leader, like you say, then this war really *will* be going on for a long time."

A holo image opened, showing Al'Bijea sitting at his desk on the Aquarian Collective's home ring world. The dapper leader of the comet miners smiled.

"Hello, Dash. Custodian says you wish to speak to me. It is something, I assume, that can't wait until our meeting on the Forge in"—he glanced at something just off-screen—"three days?"

Dash nodded. "Freya's making a special batch of that spicy plumato wine you like so much."

"Excellent!"

"You're right, though, I do have something I'd like to talk to you about. Custodian, please transmit the details of the system to Al'Bijea."

The Aquarian again looked at something, presumably another display, just off-screen. "Ah, yes. Beacon."

"I didn't see you call up any info on it," Dash said. "Which means you recognize it right off the top of your head."

"Which means it's important, somehow," Leira added.

"Indeed it is," Al'Bijea replied. "We have declared Beacon—and all star systems in that cluster—to be out of bounds to our surveyors and harvesters." He leaned back. "I assume you consider it important as well, or you would not be asking about it."

"We've recovered the remains of a Golden probe"—Dash waved toward the debris—"that seemed to originate in that system —not just pass through it, but actually originate there."

"Ah. Well, that's a matter of concern, then."

"Yeah, a little bit. Why have you marked it a no-go zone?"

"There is a large shipyard there, run by a private consortium.

They build legitimate ships, mainly two or three classes of mid-sized freighters—but they also build more, ah, specialized vessels."

"Pirate ships?" Leira asked.

"Somebody talking about me?" Benzel's voice boomed. Dash turned to see a grinning Benzel and Wei-Ping approaching.

Dash filled him in, and Benzel nodded. "Yeah, heard of it. They're called…um…" He looked at Wei-Ping.

"The Telorum Syndicate. We talked to them about buying a couple of ships but could never settle on a fair price," Wei-Ping replied. "It comes from *pax superiore vi telorum*, an Old Earth phrase."

Everyone—even Al'Bijea—just stared at Wei-Ping.

She shrugged. "What? I know things. I'm not just another pretty face, you know."

"Maybe not even that," Benzel quipped, and got a hard shoulder punch from Wei-Ping for it.

"So what does pax superior…whatever it was you said, mean?" Dash asked.

"Yeah, whatever language that is," Leira said.

Conover spoke up. "It's an old language called Latin. It means, roughly, *peace through superior firepower*."

This time, Wei-Ping scowled. "What, he says something weird and offbeat, and everyone just goes, yeah, okay. But I do it, and it's a moment of freaking wonder?"

Benzel stared at her. "Yes. Yes it is."

She punched him again.

"Anyway," Dash said. "If we can return to the matter at hand, I gather what we're saying here is that this Telorum Syndicate builds more than freighters."

"They do," Al'Bijea replied. "Like Benzel and Wei-Ping, we had negotiations with them over the purchase of upgrades to our survey vessels, mainly to protect them from the likes of Benzel and Wei-Ping." He gave an apologetic shrug. "Sorry, my friends, but you did have a reputation."

"Damned right we did," Benzel said.

"Unfortunately, the negotiations did not go well, and we parted on less than amicable terms. We have chosen to simply steer clear of the space near the Telorum shipyards—which is unfortunate, because there is a particularly rich Oort Cloud around the Beacon system."

"So they build ships for pirates, mercenaries, that sort of thing," Dash said. "Basically, warships."

"They do," Al'Bijea replied. "And very good ones. During our initial meetings with them, they gave a presentation that included a recording of a live action between one of their ships, called"—he glanced off screen again, this time apparently listening to someone—probably his ubiquitous and apparently all-knowing assistant, Aliya—"the *Spearpoint*, yes. It was engaged by three ships of apparently equal capability, and several smaller ones. It fought all of them to a draw, destroying several of the smaller craft, and then retiring from the battle only a little worse for it. It was probably somewhat embellished, of course. It was a sales pitch, after all. But our own investigations showed it wasn't embellished very much."

"I can understand why you don't want to risk running afoul of these guys," Viktor said.

"Indeed."

Dash frowned. "How have we never heard of this Telorum Syndicate before? If they make such damned good warships, they should have been on our scanners right away."

"Because they're discreet about it, to the point of being outright secretive," Al'Bijea replied. "And they don't make very many such ships."

"Yeah, that's their thing. To most people, they just build freighters," Wei-Ping added.

"Well, they're on our scanners now," Viktor said. "Especially if they built and launched, or even just helped build and launch a Golden probe."

"Think we're looking at another group of Golden minions?" Leira asked. "Another Clan Shirna?"

"Maybe," Dash said. "But we need to find out, so it looks like we're taking a little trip to Beacon. We need to know what's going on there, and if they're in league with the Golden. If they're not, then we need to see about recruiting these guys to our cause."

"And if they are?" Leira asked.

"Then they die."

3

THE ARCHETYPE DRIFTED FAR outside the Oort Cloud Al'Bijea had described as rich, although to Dash it was just a vast multitude of hunks of rock and ice. The distance, and the plethora of objects between them and the inner system, meant their task force—the four mechs, plus the *Herald* and the *Snow Leopard*, each of which carried a *Mako* in its hold—would be invisible to the Telorum Syndicate's scanners.

Invisible, that is, as long as they weren't using Golden tech and could detect their Dark Metal signatures. But there'd been nothing to suggest they could; the stealth drone they'd sent in to do reconnaissance had detected no activity to suggest they were getting ready for a confrontation.

"That shipyard's pretty damned impressive, I have to admit," Leira said. "Be a shame if we have to destroy it."

"Agreed," Dash replied. "But we either leave here having done just that, or having these guys come on board with our cause, willing to help us out."

"What if they decide not to take sides and just sit it out?" Amy asked. "You know, stay neutral."

"Nobody's neutral," Dash replied. "Not in this war."

The silence that hung off the end of his words rang with ominous, unstated meaning.

He studied the probe's telemetry. The shipyard was impressive, a massive array of free-orbiting platforms, arranged to be able to work on six keels simultaneously—four up to about the equivalent of light cruisers in size, and the other two probably up to heavies. They were modular enough to be rearranged as needed, though, so the Telorum facilities could probably handle one, or even two battleship or carrier-sized projects, if it came to it.

Surrounding the shipyard were more modules—habs and workshops and storage pods, plus a swarm of small support craft, construction tenders, and tugs. All of it orbited on a trajectory inclined off the ecliptic plane by about twenty degrees and inside the system's extensive asteroid belt, probably to minimize the chances of collisions with stray rocks. It all came across as very professional and purposeful.

It would, indeed, be a shame if they had to destroy it.

"There's a lot of comm traffic," Conover said. "The probe's picking up at least thirty channels in use."

"Takes a lot of coordination to run an operation that big," Benzel replied.

"I get that," Dash said. "But there must be a main channel, one they use for inbound traffic control. Sentinel, see if you can figure out—"

"It is this one," Sentinel replied, highlighting a comm channel designation on the heads-up. "This channel appears to be reserved for traffic control."

"Good. Open it up."

"Done."

"This is a message to the Telorum Syndicate from the Cygnus Realm. We would like to enter your system and meet——"

The threat indicator lit up. Dash frowned. Four missiles had just popped out of unSpace and now raced toward the Cygnus task force.

"Oh, for——" He targeted the dark-lance and destroyed one; Amy got one more, and Leira the remaining two.

"That wasn't very friendly," Amy said.

"No, it wasn't. And, unfortunately, I think it also answers our question about whose side they're——"

Eight more missiles appeared and came rushing in at them. At the same time, the drive signatures of two ships lit up, about a quarter revolution spinward of the Cygnus task force.

"They've got some defenses hidden out here in the Oort Cloud, it seems," Benzel said.

Dash glared at the heads-up. "I suspect you're right."

The four mechs opened up in unison, blasting the eight incoming missiles to fragments. As the last one died, a gruff, male voice crackled across the comm.

"This is Bercale, Overseer of the Telorum Syndicate. Piss off, Golden scum!"

Dash blinked at that. The signal had come from a ship he recognized as probably one of the *Spearpoints* Al'Bijea had described. It was now breaking away from a fueling station near the shipyard and accelerating toward them. It would be able to translate in about ten minutes, which meant they had that long to avoid a decisive battle.

"Everyone wait here," Dash said, then powered up the translation drive. He translated the Archetype to within dark-lance range of the approaching Telorum ships, an easy thing to do this far outside the system's gravity well. The ships immediately launched three missiles each, which Dash methodically destroyed with the dark-lance; he then disabled both ships with precisely targeted shots, leaving them otherwise intact but adrift.

He switched back to the comm. "Bercale, the only thing golden about me is my aim. If you don't stand down, I'll come and put the next one right through the viewscreen on that ship of yours and down your throat."

"Bullshit. Only a Golden has that much Dark Metal in their sig. Bercale out." The Spearpoint accelerated hard, and several other ships raced to follow it.

"Huh. Hadn't thought of that," Dash said.

"To be fair, we had no reason to believe they could detect Dark Metal, at least not without the assistance of Golden technology," Sentinel said. "But his derogatory reference to the Golden, which seems to be the reason he is insisting on attacking, implies that he considers the Golden to be an enemy. Given that, I would suggest that perhaps a more diplomatic approach is in order."

"Like what?"

"A nova-gun shot into a cluster of asteroids would be a display of power and would also clutter the field, giving you time to discuss less violent options with Overseer Bercale, who appears quite agitated."

"He does, and I like that idea. I don't want to just get into a fight, because there's obviously more going on here than meets the eye." Dash turned his attention to the tactical display. "So, let's start off by getting closer." Again, he spooled up the translation drive and shifted the Archetype to a point above the ecliptic plane in the path of Bercale's *Spearpoint*.

"Okay," Dash said. "Got a solution...and firing."

The nova-gun shot detonated among several large asteroids on the inner edge of the belt girdling the system. The dazzling flash and pulse of energy faded, leaving a cloud of debris slowly radiating out from the aiming point. Dash then fired the distortion cannon several times, pulling the rocky fragments into a trajectory that would put them on collision course with the *Spearpoint.*

"Okay, Bercale," Dash muttered. "You either have to veer around those rocks or shoot them out of the way. But notice I didn't shoot at *you—*"

Bercale's voice came over the comm. "You didn't shoot at me."

"Fancy that. It's almost like we're trying very hard not to be your enemy."

"Who the hell did you say you were again?" Bercale asked.

"My name is Newton Sawyer, but everyone calls me Dash. And I'm the leader of the Cygnus Realm."

"I've heard of you guys. Heard you were some mercenary outfit, all kinds of high tech. That mech of yours, though—that wasn't built by humans."

"You know what? I would love to talk to you face-to-face. If you can put off trying to kill me for a little while, maybe we can do just that."

"And why the hell should I trust you? Mechs like that are only used by the Golden, and if you are a mercenary band, then you might be working for those bastards."

"Believe me, we're not. Very much the opposite, in fact."

"And why should I believe that?" Bercale asked.

"Because I'm asking you to, nicely. I mean, I can fly around and disable some more of your ships, maybe even shut down that dock-yard of yours, but I don't want to. I really just want to talk."

There was a long pause. Dash sincerely hoped this man wasn't going to be unreasonable and turn this into a fight that Dash truly didn't want—

"I'm going to have my forces stand down, in place, but keep their weapons charged up. You can come aboard my ship, and we'll talk. And if I don't like what I hear, you'll be leaving my ship via an airlock, without a suit."

Dash opened his mouth, ready to snap something defiant back, but he didn't. He actually got Bercale; he'd probably have said much the same thing in the man's place.

"By the time we're done talking, I expect that either I'll be pulling you out the airlock with me, or we'll be sharing a drink," Dash said.

"We'll see," Bercale replied, but Dash thought he could hear a bit of a smile in his voice even across the comm.

DASH AND LEIRA followed a pair of crew wearing Telorum Syndicate livery along a spartan corridor aboard the *Spearpoint*, to a compartment just behind the bridge. Inside, they found a heavyset man with a greying beard and a ponytail sitting behind a small desk. He kept pale grey eyes locked on them as they entered, his intelligent gaze hard, but also curious.

Bercale nodded to the crew, who nodded back and stepped out into the corridor. The door closed behind them. Dash noticed that Bercale and his crew all sported nasty-looking, snub-nosed laser pistols; Bercale's had been conspicuously unstrapped and sat loose in his holster. Dash had made sure his pulse-pistol, and Leira's, were firmly strapped in.

Dash stuck out his hand. "Overseer Bercale, I'm Dash. This is Leira, my second-in-command."

Bercale nodded, shaking Dash's offered hand, but in an entirely non-committal way. "Second-in-command of the...Cygnus Realm, right?"

"That's right."

"Well, Dash and Leira, tell me something—why shouldn't I just blast what are obviously alien mechs to scrap, now that you've left them unpiloted?"

"Sentinel," Dash said. "Let's show Overseer Bercale here that the Archetype and Swift are very much not unpiloted."

As prearranged, Dash's instruction prompted Sentinel to fire the distortion-cannon close enough to the *Spearpoint* to make its effects felt. Bercale's ready room suddenly and briefly surged hard to one side, making them all sway.

"Is that sufficient?" Sentinel asked.

"I don't know," Dash replied, his gaze on Bercale. "Was that sufficient? Because if it's not, I've also got this." He nodded to Leira, who pulled a data-pad out of a belt pouch and activated its holo-imaging function. A 3D image of the Forge appeared, with the Archetype a small but recognizable point beside it for scale.

"Well, this, and my fleet, and sailors, and every other weapon we have, but you get the picture," Dash said.

Bercale narrowed his eyes at Dash for a moment. "Yeah, it's sufficient from where I sit. And speaking of sitting—" He gestured at a chair across the desk, and another jammed up against the bulkhead of Bercale's cramped ready room.

Bercale stared at the holo-image. "That thing's real, huh?"

"We live aboard it," Dash replied, sitting as invited. "So, yeah, I'd say it's real enough."

Bercale shook his head then grinned.

"I guess the only thing left to say is… welcome aboard."

4

THE SHOWERS WERE SMALL, circular, and separated by walls that gave the entire room a sterile, charmless feeling. Under punishing spray, everyone got clean—and then some—before dressing in their individual areas, kept separated by an opaque plastic divider. Even the steamy air smelled lightly of disinfectant.

"So they had some sort of plague here?" Leira asked, pulling on the disposable boots she'd been given. "Is a decontamination shower enough?"

Dash pulled a set of coveralls on, thinking about the implications of the process. "Apparently some ship coming in for upgrades carried a fever and started spreading it to the dockworkers before they even knew it was here. They got it under control, but everyone has to go through decon before they can visit the shipyard."

They finished getting dressed, all of them decked out in disposable coveralls and footwear. Their own clothing would stay on the "contaminated" side of the decon protocols, but Dash had had them specifically bring their sidearms through, having them passed through a UV box to clean them. He didn't at all like the idea of them going completely unarmed. Even if they trusted Bercale and his people, there was still the matter of the apparent, and as yet unexplained involvement of the Golden in all of this. They might have agents here who'd jump at a chance to kill off the Messenger and his most senior people.

Dash slid his pulse-pistol into a cargo pocket on the coveralls. "Okay, folks, keep your weapons handy, but be discreet about it. We *are* guests here, after all."

Conover, whose face was a study in the word *relieved* now that he'd pulled on his own coveralls, looked up from sticking a foot into a clean sock. "What do we say if they object to us walking around armed?"

"Eh, they let us bring our weapons through to the clean side of decon," Amy said, stamping her foot into a boot. "They obviously aren't that worried about it."

"Well, except for the fact I never actually asked about our weapons, just our comms," Dash said, then shrugged. "Like I said, keep it discreet."

When they were all finally dressed, they made their way out of decon and into the reception compartment. Garish signs on the walls cautioned that from here on, this was an industrial site, requiring various forms of protection in designated areas, as well as how to report injuries and safety issues. There was a sign every meter, and in some spaces, *two* signs proclaiming doom if a person was caught without a helmet.

A dock worker waited for them, his face showing all the charm of a clenched fist.

I thought there were five of you," the man said, then he glared at a data-pad. "I was told there'd be a Newton Sawyer—"

"Please, Dash is fine."

The man raised his glower for a moment then made a hmph sound and looked back at the pad. "Leira, Conover, Benzel—"

"You're missing Benzel," Dash said. "He's staying in immediate command of our ships."

The man curled his lip. "Fine. Whatever. Anyway, you can follow—" He stopped abruptly, and his scowl deepened. "What the hell is that?"

Dash followed the man's glare. Conover had pulled his pulse-pistol partway out of his pocket, apparently trying to get it to sit less awkwardly. He looked up and hastily shoved it back out of sight. But the dock worker took a step toward him.

"Is that a freakin' *weapon*?"

Conover went wide-eyed, but Dash intercepted him. "It is. I okayed it for my people, so if you have any questions, you can ask me."

The man nodded once. "Fine—*Dash*, was it? Well, *Dash*, what the hell makes you think you can okay *anything* around here, much less bring weapons into the shipyard?"

"Not sure if you're aware of it, but we're in a war," Dash replied. "That's why we're here, in fact."

"I don't give a shit," the man snapped. "You can hand over your weapons *right* freakin' now."

Dash smiled. "Look, why don't you call up Bercale—"

"And why don't you just do what I tell you to, *Dash*."

Dash met the man's eyes. The hard, uncompromising gleam in them told him everything he needed to know. This man was some minor official with designs on being a major official, and he was full of unfulfilled ambition as a result. He was probably a perennial personnel issue for Bercale, the sort of worker who fomented strife and unrest among his co-workers, projecting what he thought was leadership but was really just insolent bullying.

Dash knew the type only too well. Reason was not this man's style; in fact, he no doubt perceived it as nothing but weakness.

So, a change of approach was in order.

Dash's smile didn't change a fraction. "Okay, I get it. We have to hand over our weapons. Here, you can start with me."

The man held out his hand.

Dash looked at it, then back at the man. "And, now you can close that hand of yours on nothing, because nothing is what you're getting from me, or the rest of my companions here."

The man's face reddened, and he opened his mouth, but Dash just kept smiling and cut him off before he could speak. "Not a damned thing."

The dock worker shoved his data-pad back into a belt pouch, gave a slow nod—

And lunged at Dash, a meaty fist already swinging.

Dash had seen it coming and ducked, then he grabbed the man, spun him around, and jammed him against the nearby bulkhead. He yanked the man's own weapon, a snub-nosed slug-pistol, out of his holster and tossed it behind him, then he pulled the man's comm away.

The dock worker tried to drive himself backward, but Leira appeared on one side of him, Amy on the other, both smiling.

"You really don't want to fight back," Leira said. "Dash has never quite figured out how much he can bend someone's arm without breaking it."

To make the point, Dash levered the dock worker's arm upward behind his back, making him groan. He raised the comm and tapped the transmit control on it.

"Hey, Bercale. You there?"

"Who's this? Dash?"

"Yup."

"You should be on your way to see me. Problem?"

"You might say that. One of your guys here is being a bit of a mad dog and has kind of—oh, what's that old saying? Gone off the farm? Anyway, he wanted us to surrender our sidearms and wouldn't take no for an answer."

Bercale laughed. "Considering the firepower you guys have sitting outside, I think we can let a few pistols slide. Who are you dealing with?"

Dash moved the comm in front of the man's face. "It's Witman," he groaned. "Bastard attacked me!"

"Yeah, Witman. Figures it was you. Hey Dash, if you want to punch him a couple of times, go ahead."

"Hey—!" Witman started, but Dash cut him off.

"Nah, that's not necessary...yet."

Dash released Witman, who gave him a venomous glare. At one time, that might have worried Dash—Witman was a big guy, probably a scrapper, and knew his way around a fight.

But so did Dash.

And somehow facing the existential horror of the Golden put thugs like Witman into a very minor perspective. So he just shrugged back into the teeth of the man's hostility.

"Anytime you're ready to take us to Bercale, we're ready to follow."

Still glowering and muttering, Witman led them into the dock-yard's control center. Dash, Amy, and Leira made sure to offer him bright smiles the whole way. Part of Dash's smile was genuine, though, as he noticed Conover was still conspicuously trying to sneak glances at Amy, and yet not look at her, both at the same time.

THEY MET Bercale in a much more expansive office than his ready room on the *Spearpoint*. It was, nonetheless, cramped, because Bercale had filled it with all manner of junk. Amy immediately seemed to feel right at home, exclaiming over the profusion of parts, circuits, pieces of conduit, and crates of bolts and other fasteners. As Dash sat down, he figured that a significant portion of a full spaceship was probably stacked around him.

"So, tell me about the Cygnus Realm," Bercale said.

"Sure, I'll tell you all about the Cygnus Realm," Dash replied. "Just as soon as you tell us how you even know about Dark Metal, much less how you can detect it, and why a Golden probe seems to have originated in or near this system."

"The Golden are kind of our mortal enemies," Leira put in. "We're fighting a no-holds-barred war against them, so we get naturally curious when we find anyone who might be collaborating with them."

Bercale clearly bristled at that. "There's no damned collaboration going on with those Golden assholes—"

"So we gathered," Dash cut in, holding up a conciliatory hand. "Just from the fact that you thought we were Golden and immediately opened fire on us. But the question still stands."

Bercale's scowl faded. "Well, it's pretty simple. We were approached by a group called Clan Shirna a few months back. They wanted to buy some spaceships from us. Made a damned good offer, too, and left a down payment with a sample of Dark Metal and a detector for it."

At the mention of Clan Shirna, Dash exchanged a look with Leira. "So what made you say no?"

"They claimed Dark Metal was their invention. That was obviously bullshit, so I did some digging and didn't like what I found. I eventually confronted them over it, and they started ranting about the Golden, how if you weren't with them, then you were against them, blah, blah." Bercale steepled his fingers and smiled. "They went out of their way, incidentally, to paint you guys as a bunch of mercenary thugs."

"I bet they did," Dash said. "That's because we've kicked their ass, over and over."

"As in, they don't exist anymore," Conover added.

Bercale's eyebrows raised. "Okay, I think, at this point, we need that talk about your Cygnus Realm, and what's going on."

"Fair enough." Dash began to talk.

"—WHICH brings us to pretty much right now," Dash said. "You see why we were concerned about this system and, well, to be honest, about you guys, the Telorum Syndicate."

Bercale waved a hand. "You can call us the Local Group. That's the name we use. We're a three-system consortium, with our shipyard the hub of what we do." He leaned back. "And now, just give me a moment to digest what you've just told me."

Dash waited. He knew Bercale was a sharp man, someone not easily deceived and able to see right through bullshit. That had been

Clan Shirna's mistake, thinking they could simply bluster and boggle their way past Bercale to get what they want. Dash had been one-hundred percent honest about everything, which meant he didn't have to try to *appear* sincere, because he was offering the real thing.

Finally, Bercale sat forward again. "Okay, so I believe you. There's a war going on, the Unseen really exist-- and are fighting it. Or, rather, you guys are fighting it on their behalf."

"That's what it amounts to, yes," Dash replied. "Like I described, I fell into the role of Messenger—literally fell into it, in fact, on that comet in the Pasture—and, well, here I am, and here we are."

Bercale gave a rueful smile. "You know, I've taken great pride in the work we've done here, the ships we build. And, yes, we some-times build them for—let's call them not very nice people."

Dash shrugged. "There are those who'd say I'm not a very nice person, so whatever."

"Anyway, the best work we've done here pales in comparison to what you did at your Forge? Yeah, compared to what you seem to do there, we might as well be using scrap lumber and sheet plastic to build our ships."

"Well, it's pretty hard to compare anything to two-hundred thousand year old, super-advanced alien tech, so I wouldn't worry about it."

"Besides, your ships seemed to be enough to ward off the Gold-en," Leira put in. "I mean, you basically told them to go shove an asteroid up their butt via their Clan Shirna minions, and you haven't heard anything from them since, right?"

"True enough. The only trouble is that probe you found, the one that seemed to originate here, seems to date from sometime after we ran off Clan Shirna. But I can guarantee you it had nothing to do with us."

"It's my turn to believe you," Dash said. "I don't think for a moment that you've been collaborating with these Golden jerks."

"But the probe did still seem to originate here, or close by here," Conover said.

"Which means you might have some Golden lurking nearby," Amy added. "They're sneaky bastards that way."

"And if that's the case, now that I know the Golden are super-aliens who could probably run right over top of us, then I'm really glad you guys are here."

"Which brings me to the next order of business," Dash said, and Bercale nodded.

"You want us to join your Realm."

"That's up to you. Even just an alliance would be good."

"Hell, even a *let's just politely leave one another alone would* be good," Leira said.

Dash resisted giving her a look; he was really hoping for more than that, but Leira apparently knew just the right thing to say, because Bercale grinned and pointed at her.

"That, right there, is what sets you apart from those Clan Shirna asses: no demands, no veiled threats, just a respectful conversation." His grin widened. "You guys are definitely winning me over, here." But his eyes narrowed. "All that said, though, I have to admit that the idea of you becoming a major power in the arm is kind of a stretch. You've obviously got the power, but you just don't seem to have the numbers to make it stick."

Dash nodded. "You're absolutely right. And that's why we're looking for allies, or anyone who wants to join us in any capacity, really."

"Well, you definitely don't have history on your side. I mean, why so small?" Bercale asked, waving at the stars.

"By which I take it you mean, why aren't we planning to take over the whole damned galaxy?" Dash asked, his voice dry.

"Something like that," Bercale said, laughing, then he waved again, ending the gesture with a contemplative tap of a star map on his desk. His laughter died. "Empires. Clans. States. Hell, things like us, our Local Group—call it whatever you want, but it seems no one's been able to form a single government that can stand up and fight against the Golden or their minions."

Dash narrowed his eyes. This man had just hit on something he'd been starting to ponder himself. He'd only discussed it with Custodian, and hadn't even raised it with Leira yet because he was still getting his own thoughts wrapped around what it implied.

"You know, I think you just answered your own question without realizing it," Dash said. "Think about the past few centuries. Every time a union or empire has gotten too big, what happens?"

"They split apart. Civil war, mostly. Like the Praxis, or the Unified Arm. Hell, even the Reborn Faithless turned their ships on each other out in the Aquila Rift—" Now it was Bercale's turn to narrow his eyes back at Dash. "Wait. Are you telling me it wasn't just the natural order of things?"

"Civil Wars aren't always started from within. I've been digging a little since we formed our realm," Dash said, realizing that Leira, Amy, and Conover were all watching him as well, having not heard any of this before. As much to them as to Bercale, he went on. "Because I've been curious about this myself, frankly. Guess what I found?"

"A pattern?" Bercale asked. Yes, he was sharp for sure.

"Yup, a pattern. Almost the same thing happens every time. The way I see it, it starts and empires and such end in one of two ways: they're allowed to progress to a point where their tech is interesting, and then they're harvested by the Golden for that tech and whatever else those bastards want, or—"

"They're blown to dust and ash," Bercale finished.

Dash nodded. "Welcome to history. Now you understand my mission."

"Which is?"

Dash offered a smile he reserved for things that were anything but funny.

"The death of every Golden in the universe," he said. "And then? And then, I'm going to erase their legacy, one memory at a time, until there's nothing left of it."

5

DASH FOUND himself impressed by the Local Group's shipyard, despite having been exposed daily to the fully automated wonder of the Forge's fabrication facilities. Putting aside super-sophisticated alien tech, the ship-building operation here in the Beacon system was truly a wonder to behold. Not only did the Local Group produce their own classes of ship like the *Spearpoint*, and other warships, they built custom-designed ships of almost any size or purpose to order.

"The largest was a bulk super carrier we built to haul and refine hydrogen into deuterium," Bercale said as they walked along a glassed-in access tube connecting two work modules. "A thousand meters long, and almost three-quarters of a million tonnes. Took every worker, fabricator, hauler, and dock module we had."

"Impressive," Dash replied. "I'll bet it was an impressive price tag, too."

Bercale grinned. "You want the best, you pay for it."

They reached a junction and turned toward a docking port with a waiting shuttle. Bercale ushered them in, then sat at the pilot's station and deftly thrust away from the docking port. After a quick safety briefing, he launched into a running chatter while expertly piloting them among myriad haulers and fabricators going about their business, lugging components among the docks, or dead-heading back to warehouses for new loads.

"It looks like you've got a lot of work," Amy said. "There must be, what, a dozen ships under construction here?"

"Thirteen," Bercale said, nodding, then gesturing ahead. "See those two asteroids ahead of us, lashed together with gantries? That's our newest addition. We've set up another five construction docks on them. They're fixed size, up to about fifty thousand tonnes, so we can only build smaller ships there, but it frees up the modular docks for bigger projects."

The collision alarm sounded, making all of them except Bercale jump. He just glared out the viewport then pointed at a vac-suited figure riding a hauler. The figure, whose face was hidden behind a reflecting faceplate, waved back.

"We've only had two fatal accidents in almost twenty years of working here," Bercale said. "Another couple of dozen injuries." He glanced back and shrugged. "Still have close calls, but that's to be expected when you have this much heavy work going on."

"I'm surprised you don't have everyone out here wearing vac-suits," Leira said.

"Including us," Conover muttered.

Bercale grinned again. "All our yard shuttles are double hulled, plus you've got those quick-seal emergency suits under your seats. More to point, though, you've got me flying—"

He turned back to the controls then gasped and rolled the

shuttle hard. Conover yelped, his eyes going as wide as thruster ports. Dash, Leira, and Amy all just smiled.

"Was wondering how long it would take you to do that," Dash said.

Bercale turned back, laughing. "Eh, it's a good way of sorting out who the real spacers are."

"What do you mean?" Conover asked, then he looked at Dash, still breathing hard. "What's he talking about?"

"No collision alarm," Dash replied. "Plus, he just rolled the shuttle. If it had been a real emergency, he'd have pitched and yawed and burned like crazy."

Amy grinned and touched Conover's shoulder. "Back on Passage, if we had noobs on board, we used to put the yard shuttles into an end-over-end tumble and pretend we'd lost control." She suddenly waved her hands about and uttered a blatantly fake shriek of panic. "Oh, no, we're all going to die!"

Conover scowled. "That seems pretty irresponsible."

"Irresponsible as hell," Dash agreed. "And childish. Still funny, though."

Conover's scowl remained, but it softened a bit as Amy slid her hand onto the back of his neck and left it there.

They reached the paired asteroids and docked again. Bercale continued the tour, describing how they had five identical short-haul transports under construction for a commercial consortium that served a five world republic called the Downside Cooperative. They were located near the bottom of the galactic arm, relative to the galactic ecliptic plane, a region of space sparse of star systems. Dash made a mental note to get in touch with the Downsiders and find out if they had any unusual activity to report—anything that might hint at the Golden trying to flank the galactic arm in a vertical sense.

That led his thinking, and eventually the conversation, back to more pragmatic matters, as they continued the tour.

"Bercale, how would you like to come and visit the Forge?"

"If you hadn't asked, I would have for sure. In other words, I'd love to." Bercale stopped at a panoramic view across the asteroids and the gantry that connected them. "I assume you're also going to ply me with—what did you call it? Plum-something?"

"Plumato wine," Amy said. "And it's *awesome*."

"Anyway, I gather it's part of trying to get us into an alliance with your Cygnus Realm," Bercale said.

Dash shrugged. "Not going to deny it. My main aim coming here was to make sure you weren't making ships for the Golden."

"Not a freakin' chance," Bercale muttered.

"Yeah, I get that now. But if we can persuade you to—"

"Dash, I need your attention," Sentinel cut in.

Dash frowned. She might be an AI, but Sentinel was starting to develop a *tone* to her speech, and this one said bad news was incoming. "Go ahead.'

"I have detected two signals inbound, currently beyond the system's Oort cloud. They are using active sensors, resulting in strong emissions that identify them as Harbingers."

Dash glanced at the others. "Shit."

"Harbingers?" Bercale asked. "I take it those are something that belong to the Golden, or someone you're not happy to see, anyway?"

"Remember you mentioned Golden mechs?" Dash said. "That's what these are."

"Well damn. Guess we've got a fight on our hands."

Dash nodded. "Looks that way. Sentinel, you and the other mechs come to my current location. We'll mount up here."

"I'll get the Spearpoint brought over, too," Bercale said. "Along with whatever else we've got fired up and ready to deploy."

Dash's instinct was to tell Bercale not to worry about it, but this was his shipyard, after all, and he'd want to defend it. Moreover, based on his initial reaction to the arrival of the Cygnus force, he wasn't afraid of a firefight, even with the Golden. If he wanted Bercale as an ally, then he shouldn't start their relationship with a suggestion he wasn't up to the job of fighting their common enemy.

So, instead he just nodded and smiled. "Glad to have your help," Dash said—and he meant it.

———

"Okay, Dash," Bercale said over the comm. "I've got the *Spearpoint* underway, along with a light cruiser of our own design we keep on station, a frigate that we need to trial for a client anyway, and a corvette that's still not completed but has a full array of weapons. I'm afraid that's all we've got to bring to the fight."

"That's more than sufficient, Bercale, believe me. I put you guys"—Dash examined the tactical display—"about fifteen minutes behind us. Just make your best possible speed, and if you can watch our backs for other threats as you close, that'd be great."

"Will do, Dash. In the meantime, go get those Golden bastards."

"That's the plan. Dash out."

Dash turned to the threat indicator. The two Harbingers had entered the Oort cloud but were now paralleling the general orbital trend of the literally billions, perhaps trillions of rock and ice fragments that comprised it.

"They're keeping their distance," Leira said. "Maybe it's just a reconnaissance mission."

"And maybe finding us here has given them incentive to keep their distance," Amy put in. "And they're damned right about that!"

"Maybe," Dash said, but he kept his eyes narrowed on the threat indicator. The two Harbingers were still banging away with active sensors, turning themselves into beacons of emissions. But they weren't closing. That suggested to Dash that they wanted to attract attention, and were maybe even trying to pull the Cygnus mechs out to the edge of the system.

"Amy, Conover, I want you guys to fall back and take up station with Bercale. When he finally closes, I want you to keep hanging back, even if he decides to get into the fight."

"You think something's up, don't you?" Leira said.

"Just being cautious. You and I should be more than able to handle a couple of Harbingers, especially since these seem to be the lighter models. I wouldn't put it past these assholes to try to get all four of us decisively engaged and then strike at Bercale's ships and his shipyard while we're way the hell out on the edge of the system."

"Much as I don't want to miss the fight, I think you're right, Dash," Conover said. "This has all the makings of a dislocation operation."

"A what now?"

"Sorry, I've been spending a lot of time reading military theory lately. Dislocation ops are where you try to cause your enemy's strength to be where it shouldn't. You use, you know, deception and feints and the like to pull his forces out of position."

Dash had to nod at that, but more broadly, at the words Custodian had spoken in the isolated part of the Forge when they were talking about future commanders of the Cygnus Realm.

Conover has abilities that, given time, will develop and allow him to thrive as a commander…in fact, he may have the greatest potential of all of your current allies.

That seemed to be true a little more every day, but Dash took no joy in it.

"I think you've nailed it, Conover. In the courier game, we called it sleight-of-ship, but I like your term better. More dignified. Anyway, you and Amy fall back, and brief Bercale on what's going on. I've got some things to do in the meantime."

"Things?" Conover asked.

"Two, to be specific."

———

DASH WHIPPED, snapped, and spun the Archetype among drifting chunks of rock and ice, snapping out the occasional shot from the dark-lance. The Harbingers were proving extremely elusive, though. They seemed to be anxious to avoid outright battle, and instead dodged and weaved their way through the Oort cloud. To what purpose, Dash didn't know, but he was suspecting more and more that the dislocation operation Conover had mentioned was exactly what these Harbingers were up to.

"Dash, Bercale here. We've changed our trajectory to head those bastards off. Unless they just turn and burn back out of the system, we should intercept them at—see the dwarf planet at the coordinates I just sent? Right near there."

"Clear. Amy, Conover, you guys keep hanging back in over-watch. We'll call you in if we need you."

"Got it, Dash," Amy said.

"Leira, angle your trajectory toward the outer edge of the Oort cloud. You'll lose some distance on these guys, but you'll be better placed to cut them off if they make a—shit!"

Dash lunged in the cradle, the Archetype slewing hard to avoid a chunk of rock that had abruptly been redirected by a collision with an even bigger chunk of rock.

"You okay?" Leira asked.

"Yeah. I know these Oort clouds and asteroid belts aren't really as crowded as they're made out to be, but a big hunk of rock is still a big hunk of rock," Dash replied.

"I hear you. And I'm reorienting my trajectory now."

Dash watched as the Swift began to subtly edge outward, away from the inner system. The Harbingers now had Dash chasing them from directly astern, Leira working toward one flank, and Bercale working toward the other. If they didn't break off soon, they'd be run down.

Which meant the next move was up to them.

It became apparent a few minutes later, when the two Harbingers suddenly decelerated hard and snugged themselves up close to the dwarf planet. A thick cloud of rocky, icy debris surrounded it, gradually pulled toward it by a strong gravitational tug. The larger it got, the more stuff it attracted, which meant it might someday be a full-fledged planet. In the meantime, though, it fuzzed out the Harbingers' sensor returns; a moment later, their active sensors stopped radiating, and both of the Golden mechs effectively vanished into the cloud of debris.

Dash opened his mouth to ask Sentinel to reacquire the Harbingers from their Dark Metal signatures, but she was already on it.

"The two Harbingers are maintaining a close position relative to the dwarf planet," she said, updating the threat indicator. "However, their locations are only approximate. Firing solutions based on these data will be much less than optimal."

"We're probably going to miss if we shoot at them."

"Isn't that what I said?"

Dash chuckled. "No, but that's okay. I get it. How much effect would the distortion cannon have?"

"It would disrupt the orbits of the debris currently in the vicinity of the dwarf planet. Its gravitation is relatively weak."

"Perfect."

Dash accelerated, closing rapidly on the dwarf planet and its halo of rock and ice. Leira angled back in from the opposite side, closing the Harbingers in a pincer attack.

"Okay, Leira, stand by," Dash said. "I'm going to try to spook those assholes out of there."

The Archetype passed through a thickening cloud of fine debris, gravel- and pebble-sized mostly. The mech's shield was able to deflect the vast majority of the material; what leaked through clanged off the armor, doing only superficial damage.

Sentinel calculated an aiming point for the distortion cannon that would wreak the most havoc on the otherwise sedate revolution of the debris cloud around the small, icy planet. Dash fired.

Then he fired again. And again.

Chaos rippled through the debris, as the powerful gravitational pulses from the distortion cannon slammed through it. It roiled and rippled, like vast schools of fish abruptly swerving and changing direction the way they were prone to do.

"Come on, boys," Dash muttered. "Get the hell out of—"

The Harbingers suddenly accelerated, driving directly toward Dash.

He was ready for it and switched his fire from the distortion cannon to the dark-lance. The Golden mechs loosed missiles as they charged; Dash ignored them and kept his fire focused on the lead Harbinger. Dark-lance shots slammed into it, blasting off chunks of glowing armor. It was a far cry from the first time he'd used the weapon against a Harbinger, when the shots had simply seemed to glance and skip off its Dark Metal armor. The weapon had long since been upgraded to make it far deadlier, and now the Harbinger paid the price. It tried to deploy its chest cannon—its most powerful attack—but a dark-lance burst ripped through its torso.

Seconds later, a massive explosion blew the mech apart.

"So much for easy salvage," Dash muttered.

The second Harbinger abruptly turned hard and accelerated away, apparently trying to make a break for it. Leira snapped out a shot as it passed, and Dash loosed a fusillade of dark-lance fire that damaged it, but didn't stop it. He cursed, because now he did have to turn his attention to those incoming missiles—

Which began to explode, one after another. Dash glanced at the tactical display and saw another barrage of projectiles erupt from the *Spearpoint* and race toward the remaining Golden missiles at incredible speed.

"Bercale, I definitely owe you a glass of plumato wine for that. What the hell are those?"

"We call them Vipers," Bercale replied. "They're something new, dedicated anti-missiles, optimized with AI-driven proximity detonators and a shit ton of ball-bearings as projectiles. They won't do much to a ship—or a mech, I guess—but they seem to work pretty well against missiles."

"I'll say," Dash said. "A lot longer range than our point-defense systems, too. We *definitely* need to talk. In the meantime, though— Benzel, you in position?"

"Any time, Dash."

"Okay, you're on."

Dash watched the tactical display. Two new icons abruptly popped onto it, directly in the path of the fleeing Harbinger. One was the *Herald*, the other the *Snow Leopard*, and both had just dropped out of unSpace.

They opened fire, the *Herald* bathing the Harbinger in pulse-cannon fire, while the *Snow Leopard* fired her railgun. Energy bolts and hyper-velocity slugs ripped into the Golden mech, tearing chunks out of it. The mech tried to maneuver, but that only slowed it down, letting Dash close and take a clean shot with the dark-lance. That blew it apart.

The threat indicator went dark.

Dash glanced over the status summaries of the other mechs, the *Herald*, and the *Snow Leopard*, and saw that everything was green. "Bercale, how about you? Any damage?"

"Some minor stuff from collisions with fragments, but nothing serious."

"Okay, well, those anti-missiles of yours are pretty damned sweet. I think we've found our first thing to negotiate about. Oh, and sorry about not leaving anything for you guys to shoot at."

"Hey, don't worry about us being late to the party. Watching you guys at work was just a sight to behold. I'm just damned glad we were able to de-escalate things when you first showed up, because—and I hate like hell to admit this—but you would have dealt us some serious damage."

"So would the Golden," Dash replied.

"I get that, yeah, which means I guess we need to talk about accessing some of that sweet tech of yours to even things out."

Dash smiled. "How about we meet you back at your shipyard,

and we'll work out the details. We'll bring Benzel along this time, because I think he's got a surprise for you."

"Oh, what's that?"

Benzel answered. "Four bottles of plumato wine. One to share, and three just for you."

"If this stuff is as good as you say it is, we might not stop with one," Bercale said.

"If that's the case, then you'd better get ready for us to spend the night," Dash said.

Bercale laughed. "Oh, believe me, it wouldn't be the first time we had guests who needed to recover from some intense negotiations."

"Offer accepted. Start pouring."

6

"Okay, everyone," Dash said, stepping to the raised platform at the front of the Command Center. "It looks like we've got ourselves a new ally. Bercale says the Local Group is definitely in, as far as helping us with the war effort goes."

"I thought they were called the Telorum Syndicate," Harolyn said.

"That's apparently just their business name."

"So Local Group is to them, what Dash is to you," Harolyn quipped.

Dash smiled. "Something like that. Anyway, we've got their ships and, more importantly, their ship-building and repair capacity going for us. And even more important than that, we've got a powerful ally, consolidated into three systems, sitting a lot closer to the galactic core. Harolyn, you and Ragsdale work with Viktor and Custodian about doing a tech transfer. We're starting with some anti-missile tech they've got and, in return, they need to bulk up both their offensive and defensive capabilities. I'm thinking shield and pulse-cannon tech would be a good start."

"I would like to raise the matter of food production," Al'Bijea put in.

Dash turned to the dapper Aquarian leader. He'd arrived at the Forge the day before, looking to increase the volume of food shipments they were importing—both from the Forge, and from the *Greenbelt*, the farming ship they'd taken from the Verity.

"Is there a problem?" Dash asked. "Freya hasn't said anything to me about not producing enough food."

"There is a problem, but that isn't it," Al'Bijea replied, turning to his ever-present assistant, Aliya, who held a data-pad where he could see it. "The problem, my friends, is that you are producing too much food. Even with the increase we've requested, Freya believes your storage capacity for surplus food will be exhausted in about three weeks. Then, we will have to begin eating much more, or it will simply end up having to be recycled."

"Yeah, Freya asked to see me about something, and I put her off until later today," Dash replied. "It was probably this."

"Indeed. Anyway, it would seem that the Local Group has a large population aboard space-borne platforms and relatively little food production of their own. I suspect there is an opportunity to exchange foodstuffs with them, in return for additional build and repair capacity in their shipyards."

Dash nodded. "Great idea. Al'Bijea, how about you work with Freya on the details of the surplus then approach Bercale with the proposal?"

Al'Bijea blinked. "You want me to do that?"

"Yeah. You're the ones who had a somewhat rocky start to your relationship with Bercale and his people, right? This would be a great chance to smooth that over—ensure harmony among all our allies, that sort of thing."

The Aquarian gave Dash an impressed look. "That is an excellent suggestion. You, my friend, are very good at this diplomacy thing. I believe you missed your calling."

Dash chuckled and waited for the rest of those gathered to join in, but no one did. In fact, he caught a few people just nodding.

"Okay, my particular life paths not taken aside, let's—"

"Messenger, there is an incoming message from Bercale. It is urgent," Custodian cut in.

Dash frowned as his gut tightened. Had the Golden struck back already?

"Put him on."

A window opened in the big holo-image. Bercale's face looked grave.

"Dash, we just lost the two ships that accompanied the *Spearpoint* out to confront those Golden mechs. The *Spearpoint* herself took heavy damage."

Dash cursed. "Can you hang on until we get there?"

"It wasn't an attack," Bercale said, shaking his head. "Or, it wasn't the type of attack you're thinking of. As near as we can tell, some sort of mines with delayed initiators attached themselves to our ships while we were out in that debris cloud. We didn't detect them because they're tiny—as in, maybe the size of your fist. They pack a hell of a wallop, though." He shook his head. "Lost four people. Guess that screws up our safety record, huh?"

"Not at all," Dash said. "Those deaths were no accident. That was an attack." He sighed. "I am so sorry, Bercale—"

"Dash, the only ones who need to be sorry here are the Golden. Because you're right, this was an *attack*. We think that the whole section of the Oort cloud is contaminated with these damn things, which means all our shipping has to be diverted above or below the system's ecliptic until we can figure out countermeasures. But that's not my big worry. Your mechs were in the Oort cloud, too."

"Yeah, they were. Custodian—"

"I have already scanned the mechs. There are, indeed, foreign objects attached to both the Archetype and the Swift. The Talon and the Pulsar are clean. I have informed the *Herald* and the *Snow Leopard* about the threat."

Dash stiffened. "Okay, we need to get those mechs cleaned."

"I have suppressed the initiators of the attached mines through a broad-spectrum dampening field. Unfortunately, it also suppresses most of the functionality of the Archetype and the Swift."

"So we can't launch them," Dash said.

"No. Moreover, I cannot guarantee that the devices' initiators will remain suppressed, as they are of a type—indeed, a basic nature—that is unknown to me. It would be useful if one could be preserved for study—"

A burst of noise erupted from Benzel's comm. He turned away to converse with whoever it was; Dash and the others just waited.

When Benzel turned back, his face was grave. "That was the *Herald*. They just got hit with an explosion that knocked her reactors into safe mode. She's out of action, at least for now."

Dash balled his fists. *Shit.* "Anyone hurt?"

"Three injured," Benzel said. "No one killed, thankfully."

"Okay, if we can't launch those mechs, then we need to get those mines off them asap," Dash said. "Custodian, can you use maintenance remotes to do it?"

"They are also affected by the dampening field. As I said, it is a broad-spectrum effect. I judged it as—the expression is, I believe, *better safe than sorry*, correct?"

"It is, yeah." Dash started for the door, glancing back over his shoulder as he did. "Thanks for the heads-up, Bercale."

"No problem, Dash. Good luck."

Leira fell into step beside Dash as he walked. He turned to her and opened his mouth, but she pre-empted him. "My mech, my mines to get rid of."

The way she said it told Dash it was pointless—indeed, dangerous—to argue with her.

They really were rather similar, he thought, and he knew it as the bare truth.

As if to underscore their peril, shortly before they reached the docking bay, one of the mines attached to the Archetype detonated. The blast thumped through the Forge, pulsing through the deck under Dash's feet. Grimly, he and Leira carried on, stopping just outside the docking bay. The blast doors remained closed.

"Sentinel, how much damage did that blast do?"

"The Archetype suffered moderate damage to the structure and actuator systems of its left leg. The docking bay also suffered moderate damage, mainly to the deck. As a positive side effect, however, the blast also destroyed all but one of the mines that had attached to the Archetype."

"Tybalt, what's your status?" Leira asked.

"The Swift has experienced superficial blast damage only. However, three mines remain attached to it."

"We've got to get those mines off those mechs and chuck them out of the bay," Leira said.

Dash nodded. "Between the two of us——"

"The four of us," Ragsdale said, hurrying to join them, Viktor right behind him.

"Guys, I appreciate that, but——" Dash began, but Ragsdale cut him off.

"We're wasting time. Amy and Conover wanted to come, but I wouldn't let them. We can't risk all four of our mech pilots at once. But we can risk Viktor and me."

"For that matter, Dash, you should stay——" Viktor started to say but was cut off by Dash.

"Ragsdale's right. We're wasting time. Custodian, open the doors and let's get to work."

The blast doors opened and they immediately raced inside, heading for the mechs.

It wasn't a scene of devastation by any means, but the damage to the bay plucked at Dash as he ran toward the Archetype. Scorch marks across the bay's deck and bulkheads were cut by lurid streaks of bright, bare metal where fragments had plowed furrows and blasted craters in the tough alloy. It was jarring to see damage like this in a place he'd come to think of as a special part of home—the last place he saw before departing on every mission, and the first place when he returned. The insidious nature of this new weapon especially angered him. They'd developed stealth mines themselves, but they wrought their violence out in the battlespace; the Golden didn't unknowingly bring them back home with them, where they could wreak havoc where they lived.

Even among their families, if they *had* such a thing.

"I've got the Archetype," Dash shouted. "You three take care of the Swift!"

The others shouted back their assent, and Dash peeled off, veering toward the Archetype.

"Sentinel, where's the mine?"

"On the top rear of the right shoulder."

"Can you crouch the Archetype down?"

"No," Sentinel replied. "Custodian's dampening field has taken all of the actuators off-line."

"Shit." Dash stopped and craned his neck up at the mech looming high above him.

"Same problem over here, Dash," Leira shouted. "We can't reach two of these mines without a gantry!"

"No time for that!" Dash looked around for inspiration, keenly aware of the gravity of the situation. Any second, one of these mines could detonate and kill them all.

Gravity.

"There we go," Dash snapped. "Custodian, can you kill the artificial gravity in here?"

"Yes. Stand by."

"Everyone brace yourselves for zero-g!" Dash shouted. A few seconds later, there was suddenly no *up* or *down*, just freefall. Dash swallowed the wrenching disorientation that bubbled up from his gut, grabbed the Archetype's leg, and pulled himself along it, hand over hand. Glancing over, he saw the others doing the same.

He reached the Archetype's back and kept going. "Sentinel, how far?"

"Five meters ahead, and twenty-five degrees to your right—"

"I see it," Dash said, pulling himself that way. He reached a smooth expanse of armor that gave him no obvious handholds; on the far side, just three meters away, he saw what looked like an ordinary rock stuck on the exterior of the mech. As Bercale had said, it was no bigger than his clenched fist.

With no handholds, he'd have to improvise. "Okay, Dash," he muttered. "Let's see how good you are in null-g."

He launched himself directly toward the mine. This wasn't vacuum, so air resistance immediately began to slow him down; he pushed himself along a few times, keeping himself moving. As soon as the mine came within reach, he grabbed it, desperately hoping that if it had any anti-tamper devices, they were inert, too—

He slammed to a halt. The mine wouldn't come unstuck.

It left him weightless and hanging onto a mine that could turn him to a spray of bloody chunks before his nervous system could even register it. For a moment, he flailed around, before getting his feet planted on the armor. Still gripping the mine, he pulled.

Nothing. It remained stuck fast.

"Sentinel, anything you can do to help me out here?"

"I have consulted with Custodian. If the strength of the dampening field is increased sufficiently, it should cause the force locks on the mines to deactivate. There is still a mechanical anchor, but you should be able to overcome that."

"But?"

"The containment field over the mouth of the docking bay will also deactivate, and the bay will explosively decompress."

"Shit." Still clinging to the mine, Dash turned and looked back over his shoulder at the Swift. Leira, Ragsdale, and Viktor had each grabbed a mine but were now stuck in the same position he was. "You guys hear that?"

"Yes!" Leira shouted back. "I'll take that sort of explosive event over the alternative, thanks!"

"Okay, everybody, hang on! As soon as you can pull the mine free, just fling it and let it get carried out with the air!"

"We've got it, Dash!" Ragsdale shouted. "Let's just do it!"

"Custodian, go ahead!" Dash shouted.

"Stand by—in, three, two, one."

The world turned to a thundering gale.

Dash yanked at the mine; it resisted, and then it came free. Only then did he realize that he'd been holding onto the mine with both hands, and now that it had come unstuck, so had he. He desperately clutched at the Archetype, but his fingers just skidded across the smooth armor, and then he was being flung away, carried by the rush of escaping air toward the infinite black vacuum beyond.

Well, shit. This is how I die, huh? Definitely never saw *this* coming…

He found himself shrouded in pale vapor, the moisture in the air condensing, and then freezing into ice fog as the pressure dropped. He saw the Archetype rushing away from him. Then it was lost in mist and there was nothing he could—

A hurricane slammed into him, hard. He closed his eyes but couldn't breathe. The avalanche of air blasting him in the face was simply too strong to catch any breath from it. But the wind started slowing, sound getting muffled, distant, and then he couldn't breathe because the air was getting too thin, too tenuous. He must have been pulled outside, he must be in space, and this was it, the end.

Except something hard and solid banged into him, and then there was silence. The air seemed to thicken, filling his lungs a little more fully each time he gasped in a breath. It took a moment, but he finally realized he was lying on the hard deck of the docking bay, and that wind had stopped. Groaning, he levered himself to his elbows and looked around.

He saw Ragsdale. And there was Viktor. Both were levering themselves back to their feet. But he couldn't see Leira. Where was Leira?

"Uh, hello down there."

Dash looked up. Oh, *there* was Leira, clinging to the Swift's shoulder high above them.

Dash stood. "Custodian, what happened?"

"Only Leira was able to maintain her grip when the bay decompressed. I was able to prevent you and the others from being carried into space with the escaping air by means of tractor fields."

Dash took in a long, deep breath, then let it out. "Okay. Good work, you know, stopping us from dying. How about the mines?"

"They were all ejected by the escaping atmosphere. I was able to use the point-defense systems to destroy them before they could detonate."

Ragsdale suddenly cursed. Dash found him looking down at his feet. One of them was missing a boot.

"Damn, this is my favorite pair, too. Had them for years." He scowled at Dash. "That's it. If I didn't hate the Golden before, I do now. They'll *pay* for this."

"Damned right they will," Dash said. "And sooner, rather than later, the Golden will get *exactly* what they deserve."

"Before that, how about we figure out a way to get me down from here?" Leira called from her lofty perch.

Dash looked up at her then nodded. "Ragsdale, Viktor, find something to hang onto. Custodian, let's cut the gravity again so Leira can get back down."

"And make it fast," she said. "I, uh—" She lowered her voice. "I *really* have to go to the bathroom."

Dash couldn't resist. "Should have gone before we left."

"Know what, Dash?" she called down. "*You'd* better grab something to hang onto. Your ass is going back out into the black."

"Big threats from a tiny bladder," he answered.

"Weirdo."

He smiled. "Kinda."

7

Dᴀꜱʜ ʟᴇᴀɴᴇᴅ against a console in the Control Center and looked up at the oversized image of Bercale. "What we're proposing is to deploy robotic versions of three of our standard minelayers, repurposed into minesweepers, and use them to clean your system of any mines. They'll also scour and save any Dark Metal or other useful materials they happen across. Custodian, the AI who runs the Forge, figures we can have that conversion done in a couple of days. Give it another day to get them to you and working, so you've got about three days to watch out for those damned mines."

Conover nodded. "Which means that you shouldn't allow any traffic even close to your system's Oort cloud for at least that long, plus however long it takes for the minesweepers to do their job."

"It's a pain in the ass," Bercale replied. "But I think we can live with that, at least for now. We have to give the whole Oort cloud a wide berth, which means entering and leaving the system well above the plane of the ecliptic, and—" He stopped and grinned. "Well, you folks are spacers, so you know what that all means."

"Sure do," Dash replied. It meant longer transit times and more fuel used for all traffic to and from Beacon. Over the long-term, that would add up. "Like I said, we'll get working on this right away. I'm going to pass you over to Harolyn and Wei-Ping to talk about the details of the trade and military-assistance deals we'd like to open with you."

"Sounds good. I guess your ultimate goal, once this system is cleaned up, is to base some forces here permanently?"

"That's what we're thinking, but we're still talking it over. You're a lot closer to the galactic core, which is where we think the Golden threat is greatest. That puts you right on the front lines of this thing. So it makes sense to base a force there now, to help protect you, and as something we can build around later to launch offensive ops."

"Again, sounds good. Just keep me posted on that."

"Will do. In the meantime, here's Harolyn and Wei-Ping."

Dash nodded at the operator on the duty console, and she tapped a control, redirecting Bercale's signature to Harolyn and Wei-Ping in the ready room.

"Messenger," Custodian said. "Since the moment would now seem opportune, could you and Leira please attend the fabrication level? There is a matter I would like to discuss with you."

Dash glanced at Leira, who shrugged. "I think I've got a slot open in my social calendar," she said.

"Be right there," Dash replied to Custodian, then he left with Leira, heading for the elevator that would take them to the Forge's fabrication plant.

"I HAVE TO ADMIT, that seat looks pretty damned comfortable,"

Leira said, studying the exposed cockpit of the Mako.

Custodian had brought them to one of the fabrication bays adjoining the main plant; it was, in fact, the very one within which they'd cornered some Verity who'd slipped aboard the station aboard the wreckage of one of their ships. That had led to a running firefight through the fabrication plant, a security breach that had left Ragsdale with more than a few sleepless nights. Now, when larger fragments of derelict ships were brought aboard, they were thoroughly scanned, with any apparently sealed-up void spaces being cut open with plasma torches while still in space.

Now, though, it held the nose and cockpit modules for three of the new *Mako* fighters under construction. The rest of each craft had yet to be completed—or probably even started. Dash still hadn't quite divined the sequence Custodian used to assemble things; it seemed haphazard, just stuff being built in what seemed to be some randomly arbitrary way. But he knew it wasn't. Custodian absolutely optimized the efficiency of the fabrication systems, which meant that he constantly accounted for the combined effects of production capacity, availability of different types of resources, the time it took molded components of various sizes and shapes to cool and harden, and probably dozens, if not hundreds of other factors. It might seem counterintuitive to switch back and forth between jobs, but the end result was everything being made faster.

Dash had literally no reason to complain, having learned to trust the Unseen AIs in a way he never would have even just a year or so earlier.

Still, Leira was right about the *Mako's* seat. It looked *damned* comfy.

But he shrugged. He couldn't really complain about the cradle systems used by those of them piloting the mechs.

"I've spent—oh, crap, a few *days* at a stretch in that cradle, and I can't say it was ever really *un*comfortable," he finished.

"Sure, because the Meld makes you believe it's comfortable," she replied. "That doesn't mean it is."

He smiled at her. "But if you believe it's comfortable, then isn't it actually comfortable?"

She arched an eyebrow. "Look at mister philosophy here. Oooh, perception is reality. I think, therefore I am. If a thruster fires and there's no one to hear it—"

"Just saying."

"Yeah, well, sometimes it creeps me out. Thanks to the Meld, somehow our bodily functions are all kind of suspended, too—which, when you think about it, raises all sorts of awkward questions."

"Which is why I don't think about it. Anyway, Custodian, if you just wanted to go over the status of the construction projects underway, you didn't really need to bring us down here."

"I did not. This is, instead, a preface to another matter I wish to discuss. First, though, I wish to establish that we are currently meeting our production targets, the fleet is being both expanded and upgraded according to plan, and losses in battle have been light enough that they have not significantly set that plan back."

"So what's this other matter?"

"If you proceed to the far end of the fabrication plant, and pass through the door I have opened there, you will see."

Dash exchanged an intrigued glance with Leira then they set off, leaving the bay and walking past the ceaseless activity of the primary smelters. Glowing streams of metal sluiced into molds, while articulated robotic arms lifted components and structural pieces out of others, the air around them shimmering with waste heat. Newcomers here found even getting too close to the purposeful mechanical chaos intimidating, but Dash and Leira had both long since accepted that an accident was virtually impossible; you'd have to try to get hurt here, and even then, Custodian would probably be able to prevent it. So they simply strolled through the automated bustle, which adjusted its activities to accommodate them being there.

They reached the door Custodian had indicated. It led through another fabrication bay—this one currently holding a pair of almost-completed pulse-cannons meant to replace two of the *Herald*'s, which were destroyed when the Golden micro mine detonated. They passed through the bay and along a short corridor, then they reached a smaller door Dash realized had not yet been unsealed. There were a lot of those aboard the Forge, since large portions of it were still not powered up. But this one slid open as they approached.

Dash glanced at Leira. "Looks like we've got a whole new part of this place to explore."

"It still has that new-Forge smell," Leira replied as they stepped through.

Custodian directed them to another elevator, which took them down into the "south polar" region of the Forge. Dash knew there were still areas below the fabrication level that hadn't yet been activated, but this one seemed different.

"Yes, this area has only recently been powered-up, with life support only just having stabilized," Custodian replied to Dash when he noted this. "There are additional habitat facilities—"

"There's what we need," Leira cut in, smiling wryly. "More space to accommodate all the people we don't have."

Dash gave an exaggerated leer. "More beds to break in."

"If you are able to take a moment from making suggestive remarks about your biological imperative for procreation—"

"Hey!" Leira snapped. "Stop listening in on our private chats, Custodian!"

Dash shrugged. "It's kind of what he does," Dash said. "Kind of what he has to do, to be able to respond to us, right?"

"I guess, but—"

"If it assuages your concerns, I have absolutely no interest in your biological imperatives, except insofar as they may affect the efficient operation of the Forge," Custodian said. "Now, if I may continue—"

"Go ahead," Dash said, grinning at how Custodian had actually sounded annoyed.

"In addition to a hab, there are also ancillary medical, storage, and food handling and preparation facilities. More to point, however, is that additional fabrication facilities are now online—which means you face a decision regarding how they are employed."

Custodian directed them to a compartment that opened onto the Forge's exterior, with viewports opening onto the station's "south pole." It gave a panoramic view across the gently curved sweep of the massive hull, a smooth expanse broken by the protrusions of miscellaneous things. Dash had no idea what all of the sundry masts, and towers, and spheres, and various polyhedral shapes were all for, but he presumed Custodian knew and would bring it to his attention if it was important for him to know.

A holo-image appeared off to one side of the chamber. It was split, showing two different images. One was a sleek and obviously massive ship; the other, a toroidal shape that Dash recognized from his surreptitious meeting with Custodian in the isolated part of the Forge apparently meant only for the Messenger to enter.

"What are we looking at?" Leira asked.

"Well, that is an Anchor," Dash replied, pointing at the toroidal object.

Leira gave him a blank stare. "And that means…?"

"It's sort of a sub-Forge. An independent station meant to control a region of space, while acting as a base for Unseen forces—or our forces."

Leira gave Dash a curious look that said, *how do you know this, and what else do you know that you haven't said*, but she evidently decided that was a conversation that could wait and just nodded.

"That is correct," Custodian said. "The complete schematic, as well as the schematic for the carrier, were only just unlocked and made available with the activation of this part of the Forge."

"So I gather the decision we have to make is which of these things we want to build," she said.

"Again, correct."

"Tell me about this carrier," Dash said.

"It is the largest design contemplated by the Creators for actual construction and deployment, although there are references to even larger concepts, which have not yet been made available to me. It is meant to not only be fully combat capable on its own, but to act as a mobile base for various designs of fighters."

Dash held up a hand. "Okay, let's put a pin in the carrier thing for a moment. What about the Anchor, or whatever we end up calling it?"

The carrier schematic vanished, replaced by a data summary of the Anchor's schematic, including both capabilities and resources required.

Leira read them and shook her head. Dash whistled.

"Holy crap, building one of these things is going to need a *stag-*

gering number of components. Between alloys, Dark Metal, sheer fabrication, and construction effort, this would take every bit of fabrication capability we've got."

"And then some," Leira said.

"The demands are, indeed, high," Custodian said. "However, they are mitigated by the fact that construction is meant to be undertaken not by the Forge, but by a fabrication hub operated by an AI. It will be necessary to construct the core here, but then it can be detached and allowed to simply proceed with ongoing assembly of the Anchor. As long as it has a supply of raw materials—for example, from comets and asteroids, which can be refined *in situ*—it will continue to work independently."

"So we turn it loose and it will just do its own thing?" Leira asked. "This AI is, what—basically a copy of you?"

"In essence, yes. The AI will use the construction hub to first build a framework and then add habs and other facilities as raw materials are made available."

"How long will it take to complete?" Dash asked.

"If construction is not interrupted, and a steady supply of adequate raw materials remains available, approximately six months."

Leira crossed her arms. "Six months. And this much raw material. Even building one of these things looks like it's going to take as much effort as fighting the whole damned war."

"The Creators believed that they were—and therefore, are—a necessary component to the overall war-fighting strategy regarding the Golden. The deployment of Anchors will not only increase the reach of our forces, but they will help to ensure that areas that are cleared of Golden influence remain that way."

Dash nodded. "We could sure use one of these at, or somewhere near, Beacon." He rubbed his chin. "How long would it take to get one of those construction hubs built and up and running?"

"Approximately two weeks."

Dash looked at Leira. "I say we go ahead. Custodian can start work on a hub"—he peered at the data on the holo-image—"and we should still be able to keep almost all of our other production going. That's especially true if Al'Bijea can help us ensure a supply of comets and asteroids and the like for the hub to use as raw materials."

Leira stared at the image thoughtfully and finally nodded. "Yeah, I agree. Much as I'd like us to keep building lots of ships, eventually we need to extend our reach and influence away from the Forge."

Dash nodded back. He could actually think of another use for the Anchors, but he didn't want to bring it up—at least, not yet.

"Okay, then, Custodian," Dash said. "You can go ahead and start work on a construction hub for our first Anchor. And I gather that that was the decision you said we would face—either building one of these or the carrier." He looked at Leira. "That carrier would be nice, I admit, but—"

"They are not necessarily mutually exclusive," Custodian cut in, as the display switched back to the image of the carrier.

"Okay, so just how big is this carrier?" Dash asked.

"There are two versions. The dual-strike version is slightly longer, at nine-hundred and fifty-eight meters—"

"What? Are you serious? How the hell are we going to find that much metal? Even our robotic mining units can't keep up with that kind of demand, to say nothing of the Dark Metal we need," Dash said. Never mind the construction hub for the Anchor, this would consume *all* of their fabrication capacity.

"What's the dual-strike version do? Can we save material by making the other one—and, well, what's the difference?" Leira asked.

"The Alpha Carrier has atmospheric attack capability. Simply stated, it carries offensive airships that can fight anywhere, as well as four heavy-lift orbital troop ships. With the Alpha design, it is possible to land no fewer than six hundred armed troops anywhere on a planet within minutes. The Alpha-Prime, or A-Prime design, is forty meters shorter in length, but it has nearly double the space-born fighter complement, with two wings of twelve Mako-type craft, plus eight craft the Unseen designated as *Denkillers*," Custodian said.

"*Denkiller*? Sounds ominous. More punch than a *Mako*, I take it?" Dash asked.

"The *Denkiller* is a ship designed around a specific design of railgun that has the ability to translate its projectiles through the Dark Between, effectively making it a zero time-of-flight weapon. It has heavy armor, twin core engines, and a crew of four. It was intended to clear any battlespace of working technology with one pass," Custodian said.

"Okay, so what's the catch?" Dash asked. "Or the weakness?" Either way, there had to be one—or more.

"Its acceleration is relatively low, and the craft does not turn well at high speeds. To save mass, it favors heavy armor forward, with its nose constructed of forty centimeters of hardened ceramic-alloy composite. However, it is lightly armored in the rear. Nonetheless, in more than sixty sorties against the Golden, only fourteen *Denkillers* were a complete loss."

Dash smiled. He couldn't help it. The idea of a ship that lethal made him a little giddy. "And we can build these now?"

"We can, with one caveat," Custodian said.

"Let me guess—materials and power," Leira muttered. "The bane of our dreams."

"I have a partial solution," Custodian said. A map flickered into existence adjacent to the carrier schematic. Dash recognized the edge of it, but not the stars toward the center.

"Is that toward the galactic core?" Leira asked.

"Yeah, it is," Dash answered, trailing a finger over the map. He stopped at a small red circle that was above the galactic ecliptic and more than three hundred million klicks from its star, which was either a galactic outlier or a rogue interloper from deep space passing through. "I imagine your solution is here?"

"That is correct," Custodian said. "For materials, that is. As for power, we need a consistent source of Q-Cores. I have not yet located a source anywhere in the available data, meaning that beyond the Shroud, we are forced into retrieving cores from where the Golden have hidden them in gas giants."

"And what, we're going to attack?" Leira asked. "For materials alone?"

"I do not recommend that at all. In fact, I believe the term is, you have to see it to believe it, if my records are correct," Custodian said.

"Huh." Dash looked sidelong at Leira. "Well now we *have* to go and check this out."

Leira sighed. "So much for time off." But she shrugged. "Eh, no rest for the wicked, as they say. How about we go now?"

"No time like the present," Dash agreed. "Sentinel, Tybalt, bring our rides around. We're going sightseeing."

8

"Dash, I am sharing this with Tybalt and Leira," Sentinel said, as data blinked to life on the Archetype's heads-up.

"I have it as well," Tybalt said. "I do not have a cause, however, for these anomalous readings from the star."

"So, what is this?" Leira asked. "Are we witnessing a star on its way to going supernova?"

The two mechs were keeping station some five hundred million klicks away from the system's primary star, a blue giant. Data pouring in through the mechs' sensors compiled a stellar picture that was unusual, if not alarming.

"It appears so, but there are anomalies within the anomalies," Tybalt said. "Our combined records go back far enough to contain an extensive sampling of stars in their later stages, but spectral data indicate that this star is young—too young to be exhibiting some of the heavier elements resulting from more advanced stages of fusion. The inconsistencies are alarming."

"How alarming?" Dash asked. "Do you mean, 'holy crap, this thing is about to explode, and we need to run away' alarming?"

"There is no indication that that degree of alarm is warranted, no."

"Okay, good. So, is there a pattern you can work out?" Dash asked.

"There may be, but if so, the sequence would take longer than we can reasonably wait—" Sentinel abruptly paused, then went on. "I am detecting an abrupt increase in luminosity, as well as other emissions—" she said, then a dull flash emanated from the general vicinity of their target.

"What the hell was that? I mean, I'm not exactly a stellar expert, but shouldn't we have detected some sort of spectral shift? Either blue or red? It's just—" Leira trailed off.

"It's a fixed point," Dash said. "But the star isn't. Or at least part of it isn't, am I right, Sentinel? Tybalt?"

"Correct. That anomaly surged across the entire EM spectrum just as the star's output shifted. The entire sequence took less than three seconds, real time," Sentinel said.

"Which means it's Golden tech, because that's faster than light," Dash finished. "That means it's a Lens, or something like it, but it's not being used to destroy the star."

"Then what is it being used for?" Leira asked.

"Maximum stealth," Dash said. "Let's go take a look."

The two mechs accelerated toward the star, but with their emissions dampened as much as the AIs could manage. It wouldn't eliminate their signatures, but it would make them harder to detect by anyone or anything not specifically scanning for them.

As they got closer to the star, they realized that the anomalous emissions they'd detected were, sure enough, coming from a point nearby, and not the star itself. Dash cut the Archetype's drive and had Leira do the same with the Swift, so both mechs now just coasted toward the star. It buried whatever emanations did come from them in the background ruckus of the blue giant, but it degraded their own sensors, too.

"If I may suggest, Dash, we will shortly be deep enough into the star's corona that it should be safe to reactivate the drive without giving our position away," Sentinel said. "We can then change our trajectory into an orbit around the star, which will cause us to pass between it and whatever is producing the anomaly."

"So if they look at us, they'll literally have the sun in their eyes, while we'll see them against the background of space. Perfect," Dash said. "Let's do it."

The Archetype accelerated, changing its trajectory, then decelerated until its velocity allowed the star's gravity to capture it. Together with the Swift, it fell into a fast orbit of the massive star. Despite being a good hundred million klicks out from the searing, blue-white incandescence, the Archetype's hull temperature began to slowly rise.

"We can safely maintain this orbital distance for approximately thirty minutes, whereupon the heat buildup will begin to threaten the stability of key systems—"

"No problem, Sentinel. I don't think we're even going to need that long," Dash said, eyeing the heads-up and the imagery starting to solidify on it as the mech swung along in its orbit. "There," he said. "That part of the image, right there, lower-right quadrant— can you clean that up, magnify it some?"

The image suddenly expanded. Flickers of interference rippled across it, spillover noise from the raw stew of energetic stellar particles now bathing the mech. It looked like rings. Were they ring worlds, like the one built by the Aquarians? As soon as he thought it, though, Dash knew it wasn't that. These rings were far too small.

"Sentinel, can you improve that imagery at all?" Dash asked.

"Dash," Leira said. "Tybalt's recommending that we separate, put as much distance between us as we can. He and Sentinel can then combine their imagery, and we should get a clearer picture."

Dash frowned. "I don't like us getting too far apart."

"Well, it's either that, or we raise our orbits and try to get a better view."

"Which means they might see us, yeah." Dash glanced at the threat indicator. Other than the unknown item, there seemed to be nothing else in this system to menace them. The star apparently had only a single planet, a small rock. This further suggested it was a rogue, just passing through from some intergalactic origin. Any other planets the star might have had were lost during the cataclysm that flung it out of its birthplace. So, aside from that, and anything that might happen to have been lurking on the far side of the star, there was nowhere else for anything *to* hide.

"Okay, let's do it," he finally said.

Leira acknowledged, and the Archetype decelerated, letting the Swift pull ahead. Decelerating meant dropping its orbit around the star, which meant falling closer toward its hellish surface—which also meant accumulating more heat, faster. But the Archetype, being bigger and sturdier, was up to it. Just in case, though, Dash had Sentinel increase the power of the mech's shield to ward off the worst of the particulate emissions from the big star.

Time passed, and Dash watched the imagery. There were two rings. And a dull, reddish glow emanating from at least one of them. And that was all—

No, wait. The image was starting to focus, details resolving, a more coherent picture coming into view.

"What the hell is that?" Dash said, his voice just above a whisper.

The fact that neither Leira nor either of the AIs answered told Dash they had no insights either.

There were, indeed, two rings, each a little less than a kilometer in diameter. They were oriented parallel to one another, their centers aligned, and apparently held in that configuration by either a gantry structure or massive cables. Several small ships, or stations, seemed to be keeping watch around each of the rings, which were maybe a klick apart.

"There is nothing to match this structure, or device, or—" Sentinel finally began, then paused. "There is no match to this in the available data."

Dash shook his head. Whatever this thing was, it was sitting out here on the edge of intergalactic space, all alone. He wondered if it might be some ancient artifact, perhaps even something that had nothing to do with the Golden or their ongoing conflict—maybe, he thought, it was something truly anomalous and alien, dragged along by the rogue star from wherever it originated. That could make it hundreds of millions, even *billions* of years old.

"Something's happening," Leira said.

Dash snapped out of his thoughts. Sure enough, that dim flicker of reddish glow was intensifying.

"I am detecting a variety of increasing emissions in the red end of the visible light spectrum, and well into the microwave and radio bands," Sentinel said.

"So it's some sort of communication device?" Dash asked. "Like a radio relay?"

"Unknown. And now the emissions are increasing across the entire EM spectrum."

"There are also gravitational distortions, suggestive of a translation underway," Tybalt said.

Dash just kept staring. *What the hell?*

A sudden, dazzling flash of energy pulsed away from the enigmatic rings, sweeping over the Archetype and causing the heads-up imagery to briefly flicker and wobble. When it cleared, Dash saw that a ship now sat between the two rings. It had the squat, boxy lines of a cargo craft, like a barge. And now some of the small objects that had been keeping station swarmed in around it, apparently—

"They're loading cargo, it looks like," Leira said.

"Yeah, they are," Dash agreed.

"That flash of energetic discharge corresponds with the anomalous readings we detected earlier," Tybalt said.

"Yeah, that was this gate, or whatever it is, probably sending a barge on its way. Now, this new one has arrived to be loaded with who knows what?" Dash replied.

In short order, the loading operation had apparently completed, and the drones withdrew. Some of the larger modules keeping station nearby must be warehouses of some sort, Dash thought. But what was stored out here? And why was it being loaded in such a specific and seemingly cumbersome way?"

The reddish glow once again spooled up, before terminating in another powerful burst of broad-spectrum energy. When it faded, the barge was gone.

"Dash, we can stay in orbit here and keep speculating on what this is, or we could just get closer."

"We do risk being detected that way," Tybalt cautioned.

Dash glanced at the Archetype's stats—especially its hull temperature. "Yeah, well, we need to pull away from this star soon anyway." He bit his lip for a moment, thinking. "Okay, what the hell. I really want to know what this is, in case it's something important, something we really want to understand. That means I don't want to just destroy it. So we do need to get closer—as close as we can, in fact, without being detected."

Sentinel and Tybalt calculated the maximum distance they could raise their orbits while still remaining reasonably certain their own signatures would be lost against the glare of the star. Dash and Leira accelerated their mechs, closing on the strange structure they'd found.

Once more, in the next couple of hours, the paired rings received a barge, containers were loaded on it, and then it flashed away again.

"Wonder if getting assigned to a place like this is for the real screw-ups," Leira said.

"That's if there's anyone actually here at all," Dash replied. "I suspect this might all be automated." He looked at the vast gulf of nothing extending away from the star, its nearest neighbor over three hundred light years away. "At least I hope it is, because this would suck as a job, you're right."

"I would need plumato wine," Leira replied. "Lots and lots of plumato wine."

"I believe that we have recorded all of the useful data we are likely to," Sentinel said. "Do you wish to continue observing, withdraw, or attack?"

Dash bit his lip again. His inclination was to approach it and to engage with it, on the off chance it was somehow friendly, or at least neutral, or attack and destroy it if it was Golden. But if it was something they could use—

He blinked as the threat indicator suddenly lit up. A second later, something slammed hard into the Archetype.

THEY WERE FORTUNATE the mech's shield had been ramped up to an overpowered state; it absorbed most of the incoming energy then began immediately to radiate it away. Warnings still flashed across the Archetype's status indicators, as various systems—fortunately, none of them critical—either went off-line or rebooted. Dash immediately flung the mech into a hard turn, rolling and yawing through a rapid series of evasive maneuvers as he did.

"Leira, status!"

"I'm in the clear—no, wait, I've got one inbound on me, too!"

"One what?"

"Harbinger," she snapped back. "Three of them, two coming your way from starward—shit, gotta go."

Dash hunted frantically across the tactical display. He saw two flickering, inconsistent signals tracking him. Indeed, they had managed to get starward of them, turning their own use of the star's racket as camouflage against them. But there was more to it than that. The sensors fought to resolve the two Golden mechs, their active emissions slipping and sliding off the Harbingers like wet hands trying to clutch a bar of soap.

"Sentinel, what's going on here? Why are these things so hard to pin down?" he asked.

"They are employing some form of stealth technology. It is making them extremely difficult to resolve."

"What about their Dark Metal? Can you see that?"

"Even against the neutrino background of the star, there should be some sort of signal. But I am detecting nothing."

"Invisible Harbingers," Dash muttered. "I'm not a fan."

The threat indicator lit up with new contacts—missiles, inbound. Fortunately, they weren't stealthed up the same way, so the Archetype's fire control immediately got hard locks and firing solutions on them.

"Okay, they brought something new to the fight, but so did we," Dash said. "Let's try out Bercale's spiffy new anti-missiles."

As a goodwill gesture, Bercale had sent them a load of fifty of their Viper anti-missiles. Dash had had Custodian and the other AIs load them into the Archetype and Swift, and revise their fire control systems to accommodate them. He'd wanted to field test them, and now he had a chance.

He fired ten of the Vipers and watched them flash away at an incredible acceleration. Seconds passed, and then they began to detonate in rapid succession as their proximity sensors detected their targets. Shrapnel tore through the Golden projectiles, destroying all of them in just a few seconds.

"Yeah, I'd say that works," Dash said, then he followed up with a missile barrage of his own, followed by a series of dark-lance shots. Both had trouble getting and keeping firing solutions, though, and Dash finally had to resort to some old-fashioned brain power. It was a skill he'd had to pick up, because the *Slipwing's* balky fire controller was offline as much as it was on. He missed three times in rapid succession, before scoring a hit on one of the Harbingers, which flitted through the manual sighting reticle on the heads-up like a dust mote dancing on a gusty breeze. The enemy mech staggered under the hit, and its sensor signal immediately firmed up.

"At least some of their stealth capability seems to rely on a physical coating, or something similar," Sentinel offered. "Now that it has been damaged, the exposed alloy is much easier to detect."

"Easier to detect is good," Dash said, letting the fire control system take over the targeting again. The solution was still far from perfect, and it took three more shots, but he finally disabled the Harbinger, leaving it coasting along, apparently dead.

The second Harbinger, though, hadn't been idle. Dash's missiles had all failed to lock, and although they'd distracted the enemy mech, it still managed to close and loose a shot from its chest-cannon. The weapon's power depended on range, so it was deadlier with diminishing distance; it caught the Archetype with a potent blast that took down the shield and knocked several more systems offline, including the distortion cannon. The Harbinger followed up with another salvo of missiles, but Dash was able to launch a wave of Vipers in return. He then ignored the missiles and concentrated on the Harbinger.

The firing solution was weak, less than thirty percent hit proba-bility. Dash cursed, flicked back to manual, and tracked the Harbinger by eye.

"A little left," he muttered. "Little more—damn." His shot missed. The Harbinger, in the meantime, had accelerated hard, trying to flank him; he kept turning the Archetype in place, trying to track his elusive quarry.

"Dash—" Leira started, but he cut her off.

"Busy!"

A series of explosions rippled across the display as the Vipers again took down the incoming Golden missiles. Dash ignored it.

Wait. *Missiles.*

"Sentinel, those first missiles we fired, that all missed. Are they still active?"

"They are, but they have no target locks and will shortly self-destruct."

"Can we send them at this Harbinger?"

"They are unlikely to lock."

"I don't care. Just do it."

"Complying."

The telemetry from five of the missiles he'd fired at the first Harbinger showed them coming back to life. They rotated in place then accelerated, aiming themselves in the general direction of the Harbinger. Sure enough, what stealth system was in place prevented them from locking—but it still caused the enemy mech to change its random evasions and begin jinking mostly in one direction.

Dash watched the target reticle closely, nudging it, until it intersected the Harbinger.

He fired, loosing an overcharged shot from the dark-lance that briefly took it offline, while it recovered.

It didn't matter, though, because the over-powered beam punched clean through the Harbinger. It shuddered under the impact; worse for it, the damage allowed the missiles to suddenly lock, and they immediately raced in to attack. The Harbinger's point defense tried to respond but only took out two of the missiles; the other three staggered their attacks to avoid destroying one another. Three times, the Harbinger was hit by their detonating warheads. When the last cloud of plasma dissipated, the Golden mech was nothing but wreckage.

"Dash?"

"Go ahead, Leira."

"You okay?"

"Yeah, I'm good." He glanced at the threat indicator. "Looks like you got your Harbinger."

"Yeah. Once it took damage from the nova gun, it was easy to get a firing solution."

"So whatever stealth system these things are using has its limits. Good to know."

"It's still worrisome, though," Leira replied. "It gives them a huge first-strike potential."

"Tell me about it." Dash studied the heads-up. The Archetype had taken moderate damage, and the distortion cannon was still off-line. The Swift was in similar shape. So they could both still fight—but an ambush from more Harbingers could change that.

"I don't want to stick around here any longer than necessary," he said. "Let's scavenge what we can, get as much data as possible, then get the hell away. Leira, you've got overwatch. Keep your eyes *really* peeled for anything that might be a stealthy Harbinger."

"Believe me, *everything* is suddenly a Harbinger, until I know for sure otherwise," Leira replied.

THE BIG BLUE star dwindled away behind them. Dash agonized over leaving the gate alone and operating. He hated to just destroy it, because they still had little idea what it was for and if it included tech that they might want. However, it might be a key linchpin in the Golden war effort, so leaving it alone and operating might be leaving the Golden with a crucial capability.

"You know, the fact that they deployed three Harbingers with a new stealth tech to guard this thing is telling. Let's face it, if it hadn't been us that found this place, and someone else had, they'd have almost certainly been slaughtered," he said.

"And we only found it because Custodian happened to get some unrelated data points to logically converge," Sentinel replied.

"Yeah, being this remote suggests the Golden really didn't want this found," Leira said. "That points to it being something important."

"Okay, so let's disable it, but not destroy it. I also want to bring back some of the wreckage from those Harbingers so we can study that stealth tech, whatever it is," Dash finally decided.

"Study? Or borrow?" Leira asked,

"Steal, more like. And only the best part."

"Good," she said.

Aside from point-defenses, the transfer station—because it clearly was an intermediate point between two places—proved essentially undefended. A single dark-lance shot to what seemed to be the power source for each of the rings made them go dark, their emissions dropping to virtually zero.

"That'll take them offline for now. We can head back to the Forge and send a task force back here to study this thing in more detail. Then we'll salvage whatever we can," Dash said.

"The Golden may come back to fix this thing in the meantime," Leira cautioned. "And they might station a much stronger force here to protect it."

"True, which means it will have to be a capable task force. We'll talk to Benzel and Wei-Ping about it—"

"Dash, I have an observation," Sentinel said.

Dash glanced at the tactical display. All clear—just the big star falling away behind them, the derelict transfer station marked with an icon. So it wasn't something about their immediate situation—

"Go ahead," he said.

"I have been giving close consideration to the data we gathered here, along with previous data we've collected. I've also analyzed the readings collected from the transit station while it was operating. I have to conclude that we have been wrong in our assumptions."

Dash frowned at that. "What do you mean?"

"We have suspected that the Golden are located near or in the galactic core. But this transfer station suggests that they have connected at least two, far-flung locations in the galaxy. It would appear that there is also a Golden presence in the outer reaches of the galactic arm, particularly along its periphery above the galactic plane. This transfer station may be part of a network that allows for rapid travel and communication between these two enclaves. I would caution that this is a preliminary observation but—"

"But, I get it," Dash said, his tone grim. "We have Golden on both sides of us. In other words, the Forge is surrounded."

9

THEY HAD RELEASED the components of the wrecked Golden Harbingers to Custodian, who tractored them into a fabrication bay, and then both Dash and Leira had returned their mechs to their home docking bay. By the time the two of them had made it back to the fabrication level, they found a crowd—most of the senior officers, in fact—had already gathered there to give this new and unsettling Golden stealth tech a look over.

"So what have we got?" Dash asked as he approached, Leira at his side. Conover, Amy, and Viktor were all crouching or kneeling beside a slab of leg armor, poring over a coating on the alloy so black it just seemed to be a hole in space. Dash couldn't see a single reflection or highlight on it anywhere; in fact, he'd never before seen anything so absolutely black. It was, he thought, disturbing, almost difficult to look at, giving the eye nothing to settle on, no points of reference at all.

"Not sure," Viktor said. "Custodian's doing some detailed scans now. It's some sort of coating, but really, really thin."

"It's also really, really hard," Conover said. "Whatever it is, it has the potential to be almost impervious to most forms of energy. Worse, it works like a superconductor, instantly absorbing any energy impinging on it and spreading it across its whole surface area." He gestured at it. "Go ahead, try touching it."

Dash did, but only briefly, before yanking his hand away. "What the… that's bloody *cold*!"

Conover nodded as he stood. "It would keep pulling heat from your hand and distributing it across its whole surface area until it, and you, were the same temperature."

"Wait, are you saying I could have frozen myself to death by doing that? Warn me next time, if you don't mind."

Conover smiled. "Don't worry, Dash, I'm not trying to kill you. You'll notice it's a little warm in here. I had Custodian bump up the heat. This stuff would only get to an ambient temperature. That might still be enough to send you a little hypothermic, but I figured you'd pull your hand away before that happened."

Dash gave Conover a sidelong look. "You sure it's that, and you're not after my job? Assassinate your way to the top and all that?"

"Me, be the Messenger? Yeah, no thanks."

Dash stuck his hand under his armpit to warm it up. "Okay, so if this armor is impervious, how come we were able to defeat those Harbingers?"

"Because this stuff isn't properly bonded to the alloy of the Harbinger's hull," Amy said. To prove it, she chipped at it with the edge of an insulated tool. The black material flaked away, revealing the dull gleam of metal. "The seams weren't covered properly, either. But that's the only reason you guys got any sensor returns at all, and why, when you hit them with your weapons, the stealth coating just came off."

Viktor nodded. "If this stuff was properly applied and completely enclosed the mech, or the ship, or the missile, or whatever it was used on——"

"Then they'd be totally invisible to us," Benzel said, his arms crossed, his tone grave. "We'd never be able to get firing solutions."

Dash thought about the manual targeting he'd done with the dark-lance during the battle. It struck him that he had only been able to find the Harbingers because of the weak sensor returns from their exposed seams. If it hadn't been for that, he'd have never known where they were to line up eye-balled shots on them.

"This is a disturbing development," Ragsdale said. "It's a good thing you guys ran into this before it had been perfected."

"Either that, or it can't be perfected, and this is as good as it gets," Harolyn offered.

But Dash shook his head. "That's starting to sound like wishful thinking. Wishful thinking makes you dead. We have to assume the worst case, and that the Golden are going to be able to perfect this." He rubbed his chin. "It doesn't explain why we weren't able to detect their Dark Metal, though. You can't stop neutrinos, like at all, except with Dark Metal, but that's the point of how we detect it."

"I believe I can offer some insight in that regard," Custodian said. "I have reviewed the data collected by Sentinel and Tybalt during the battle. It would appear that the Harbingers were generating neutrino emissions, specifically in order to defeat Dark Metal detection. Only a careful analysis showed that the characteristics of the neutrinos they emitted were slightly different than those of the star."

"Is that something we can reliably use to keep up our ability to see things like this?" Leira asked. "Can our Dark Metal detectors discriminate the difference?"

"Currently, no," Custodian replied. "The difference is only discernible once a certain threshold level of data has been collected and is then thoroughly analyzed. The process requires, I would estimate, between fifteen and thirty minutes to complete."

"Well, that's *way* too long," Dash said. "A whole battle usually doesn't last that long." He took a deep breath and released it. "So we have a problem."

"We do," Leira agreed.

"I would suggest that, although this is a problem indeed, it is not insurmountable," Custodian went on. "This stealth technology does appear to have its limits. I have examined the bonding process between it and the alloy substrate of the armor to which it is applied. The bonding is inherently weak *because* of the properties of the stealth coating. It may not be possible to apply it to all surfaces and seams."

"That sounds like wishful thinking again," Dash said.

"I am incapable of what you call *wishful thinking*, Messenger," Custodian replied, once more managing to sound a little put out. "I am extrapolating conclusions based on available evidence. And, as it stands, the evidence suggests that the process of applying the stealth coating is complex and unreliable. So, this is either a new and experimental effort by the Golden, or they have retrieved an older process and are attempting to improve it."

"There's another possibility," Conover said. "It might be something a Golden ally has resurrected."

Dash looked at him. "What makes you say that? If we're going with the evidence we have, then what would suggest it's an ally?"

"Custodian, can you bring up the image you showed us just before Dash and Leira got here? The one showing the marks?"

A holo-image appeared. Dash frowned at it for a moment, before realizing it was an extreme magnification, virtually a microscopic image. Except for several roughly parallel grooves, it was absolutely featureless.

"The only way Custodian could detect those grooves was by some super-accurate gamma-ray imaging. It took the really short wavelength to resolve these details, which have been false colored to let them show," Conover said.

Dash stared. Four grooves, approximately parallel. He turned back to Conover.

"So what am I looking at, besides tiny grooves?"

"Are they tool marks, maybe?" Wei-Ping said.

Harolyn stepped forward. "Wait a second, I think I recognize this."

Everyone stared at her. Dash cocked his head. "You do?"

"Yeah. Custodian, can you put up an image of scratches by an animal next to this?"

"There are more than sixty thousand such images available, varying by species, medium in which the scratches are made—"

"Let's say the terrestrial creature called a cat. And scratches in something relatively hard, like—I don't know. Whatever the hardest thing a cat could possibly scratch would be."

"That has got to be the weirdest, most specific database search I've heard of," Amy muttered.

An image opened next to the depiction of the stealth coating. It showed a series of parallel grooves, very similar to the ones in the stealth coating.

Dash made a *huh* sound. "Well, I'll be damned."

"What is a—what did you call it? A cat?" Conover asked.

"A small, furry creature, full of attitude. They've been kept as pets for humans since the days of Old Earth."

"Not on Penumbra, they're not," Conover said, but he gave a nod nonetheless. "Still, it looks like almost an exact match."

"Wait—this armor was scratched by a *cat*?" Leira asked, her face a mask of skepticism. "Where the hell did the Golden get a *cat*?"

"Hell of a cat," Benzel said. "If it can scratch something that we just called more or less impervious to damage."

"I doubt that it's literally a cat," Dash said. "Uh, right, Custodian?"

"That is, indeed, unlikely. However, Harolyn's observation that these appear to be scratch marks from some sort of organism would seem to hold."

"I suppose the marks could have been made while this stuff was wet, or whatever," Viktor said. "Assuming it goes through such a step, anyway."

"Well, right now we've got more questions than answers," Dash said. "Let's give Custodian and the other AIs a chance to thoroughly strip all this stuff down, do a thorough study of it, and then we'll meet to talk about it. Let's say two hours, in the Command Center." He scratched sweaty hair. "Meantime, I'm going for a shower."

DASH GAVE himself a moment to luxuriate in the fresh feeling of clean clothes and the smell of soap still wafting from his skin. The others had gathered into little groups in the Command Center, leaving him alone with a moment of doing nothing at all.

"Dash?"

And, so much for that.

He looked up at Al'Bijea. The elegant head of the Aquarian Collective approached him, Aliya at his side, ready as always to provide him with whatever assistance he needed. The woman, who rarely spoke to anyone but her boss, somehow seemed to always have the exact piece of information, bit of data, or particular statistic Al'Bijea needed. Dash wondered if she was somehow technologically enhanced, like Conover had eye implants. Or maybe she was just that damned good.

I need an Aliya, Dash thought, and for a brief moment, he imagined Leira in that role, at his side, always ready to serve his needs.

Al'Bijea stopped as Dash burst out laughing. "I'm sorry, Dash, did I interrupt—?"

"What? Oh, no. I was just thinking of something that would get my ass beaten *so* badly if I ever mentioned it. Anyway, you needed something?"

"Yes. I have gone over the data provided by Custodian regarding the resource needs of the—"

Aliya leaned in and whispered something.

"—the construction hub, for the new station. The Anchor. He has provided an overview of the amount and types of cometary and asteroid material needed."

Dash's good humor faded. Here came the bad news. This wasn't going to be possible—it required too much time and effort from the Aquarians, they didn't have the capacity—

He braced himself for yet another difficulty to deal with, on top of all the others already in the pile. "So what's the verdict? Is it going to be a problem?"

"Actually, it will be very easy—barely an inconvenience, in fact."

Dash blinked. "Oh, really?"

"Yes. The amount of material is considerable, but we have sufficient expertise in mass driving to facilitate it."

"Sorry, mass driving? Aren't mass drivers big railgun things used to shoot payloads off of planetary surfaces?"

"They are, and the principle is the same. We use magnetic drive modules attached to masses like comets and asteroids to accelerate them as needed. Now, ordinarily this would take a long time. For instance, in our home system, we have a constant succession of these objects arriving at regularly spaced intervals. Some of them were accelerated months ago, and a few up to several years previously. It's a complex operation, arranging it so that objects are accelerated such that they arrive when, where, and in the order you want them to."

"So this is going to take months? Years? Which means building the Anchor will take that long?"

"That is the beauty of it. Custodian has suggested a means of translating these objects, through—"

Aliya whispered again.

"Ah, yes. Through the Darkness Between, which is a sort of boundary region between normal space and unSpace, I gather. In any case, this would reduce the transit time to days or weeks."

Dash blinked again. *More* good news? What the hell was going on?

"Well, that's great!"

"Yes. I do have a request, however. We would like to license the technology involved from you."

Dash sat up. "No."

Al'Bijea frowned. So did Aliya, which was especially striking, because she was normally as expressive as one of the dummies used to study the effects of spacecraft accidents. But Dash held up his hand to head off any anger.

"No, you can't license the tech—and I cannot believe I'm saying this, considering how I've spent most of my life grubbing for credits —because you can *have* it."

Now it was Al'Bijea's turn to blink in surprise. "Have it? For nothing?"

"A thank you would be nice."

Al'Bijea grinned, but Dash just shook his head.

"We've already got mercenaries in this war. Clan Shirna was helping the Golden for basically cash and tech. The Bright and the Verity are doing it for the tech and because the Golden are helping them further their own vile, shitty ends. Let's keep all that on the bad guys' side of things. Over on this side, we do what's necessary and right to win this thing."

Al'Bijea nodded. "Very good. And allow me to offer that thank you." They shook hands, and Al'Bijea started to turn away, but he stopped. "You do realize that once this is over, and assuming we've won—"

"We'll win."

Al'Bijea gave Dash a searching look. "You truly believe that. In that case, so do I." He smiled. "Anyway, once this is done, you will face the question of what to do with all of this tech." He gestured expansively around. "There are so many technological accomplishments embodied by this station, those mechs of yours, the ships— too many to count, in fact—that we would not discover and develop for decades. In some cases, centuries. And in some, we may never develop them at all." Al'Bijea's eyes narrowed. "Which might explain why you are called the Messenger."

Dash cocked his head, genuinely intrigued by what Al'Bijea meant. "How so?"

"It is not that you are the Messenger, on behalf of the Unseen, regarding this war. Or, rather, you are not just that. You may also be the Messenger for the Unseen on behalf of the peace that comes after. You are their emissary. Their ambassador. That could end up being as important as leading this great effort against the Golden. And perhaps, in the long run, even more important." He nodded. "Yes, there is a reason you were chosen for this role, I think, Dash."

"I wasn't chosen for it, though. I just stumbled into it."

Al'Bijea glanced at Aliya, and they exchanged a smile.

"Now that is, I think, not something even *you* truly believe."

Dash watched as Al'Bijea and Aliya walked off, now in a hushed discussion. He had nothing but admiration for the dapper little Aquarian leader, but the man was so formal, almost bureaucratic; Dash had no doubt that he'd still be asked to sign some sort of agreement over the use of the Unseen tech.

"Messenger, I have the final results on my analysis of the Harbinger components you brought back to the Forge," Custodian said. Everyone fell silent to listen.

"Okay, go ahead, we're all ears here."

"The materials used in the armor itself are the same alloy and ceramic composites with which we're already familiar. The stealth coating is a graphite-like carbon matrix, which acts as a framework for complex molecules that are, in effect, nano-scale machines specifically designed to be able to change their properties along the electro-magnetic spectrum."

Dash frowned. "Pretend I'm not an expert in this stuff, because I'm not."

"Your eye is basically an antenna, Dash," Conover said. "Set up to absorb visible light. Its size and shape allows it to do that. But you can't see, say, radio waves, because their wavelength is too long, and you can't see gamma rays, because it's too short. If you were to make your eye much bigger, you'd be able to *see* radio waves, the way a big radio antenna does. But then you wouldn't be able to see visible light."

"Okay, got it. So these nano-machine molecules can, what, adjust themselves to absorb whatever energy is hitting them." Dash narrowed his eyes at the deck. "Which means I guess they have to work together, a whole bunch of them making whatever antenna is needed."

"That is exactly correct," Custodian said. "It is a complex process, the material being difficult and time-consuming to manufacture. If it were to be perfected, however, it would result in spacecraft that are essentially invisible throughout the entire EM spectrum."

"That would be a huge advantage," Benzel said.

"Huge doesn't begin to describe it," Dash replied. "It would be game-changing. Imagine trying to fight invisible ships. Hell, those three Harbingers were far from having this stuff perfected, and they were right on the edge of us being able to even find them, much less shoot at them." Any trace of his good humor from his conversation with Al'Bijea was now long gone. The prospect of the Golden gaining such an advantage was chilling.

Dash crossed his arms. "We need to know more. We need to know where this is being made, and how it's being made."

"So we can steal it, right?" Amy said.

"Damned right," Dash replied. "But even if we can't do that, we can't let the Golden get this stuff widely deployed, or else we are *screwed*."

"I do have another piece of information that you would no doubt consider interesting," Custodian went on. "I have determined that these armor pieces, and the stealth coating on them, exhibit widely varying ages."

"How wide a variation?" Dash asked.

"Some are, based on isotopic analysis, thousands of years old. Others appear to have only been recently fabricated."

"How is that possible?" Leira asked. "Were those Harbingers cobbled together out of mismatched pieces?"

Conover spoke up. "Did you guys actually keep track of which piece came from which Harbinger?"

Dash shook his head. "I sure didn't. It never occurred to me. Sentinel, did you?"

"Of course I did."

Dash had to smile. "Of course you did."

"The pieces retrieved from a single Harbinger exhibited this age disparity," Custodian said.

"So these things *were* cobbled together from different components," Dash replied. "And how about those claw marks? Were they actually claw marks, or were they something else that, you know, makes more sense?"

"I was able to discriminate between conventional tool marks, impressions resulting from minor damage, and what are, indeed, claw marks," Custodian said.

Dash looked at the rest of them. "So do you know what this means?"

They all waited.

Dash shook his head. "No, I'm actually asking the question. Does anyone know what this means?"

It was Ragsdale who eventually spoke up. "How about this?

Someone out there is using Golden tech that they've either found or have been given. Things like surplus Harbinger components. And they're adding stuff to it, like this stealth coating. And, whoever they are, they've got…claws?" He shook his head. "Okay, that sounded a lot less dumb in my head."

But Dash shook his head. "No, that's not dumb at all. I think that fits perfectly. And *that* means we have a new priority."

"Finding out who that is and what else they're up to," Leira said.

"Exactly. It looks like we have a new player in the game," Dash said. "We need to know who, and everything about them. And I can think of only one place to start."

"Looks like we're going back to that transfer station," Leira said.

Dash gave a firm nod. "Yup. And we're going in force this time. So let's saddle up, folks. We leave in four hours."

DASH STUDIED the Archetype's heads-up as he waited. Sentinel, Tybalt, Kristin, and the onboard AI for Conover's Pulsar, Hathaway, were conferring over the data collected during Dash and Leira's visit to this remote, probably rogue star system. They were also gathering more data, all with the goal of trying to determine what points in real space the transfer station connected. Despite the damage done when Dash and Leira had disabled it, it had been repaired and made operational again. There were, however, no indications of any other enemy forces nearby.

Still—mindful of the potential for stealthed-up, invisible ships, Dash had the fleet more dispersed, their fire control systems linked and slaved to either the *Herald* or the *Retribution*. Hopefully, coordinated fire would be enough to drive off any attackers that they might have trouble actually seeing. And, if things got too hairy, they could just run away.

"We have a solution," Sentinel said. "By analyzing the geometry of the transfer gates, and other readings from them, we have been able to discern the two regions of space it connects. There is only one viable candidate star system in one of those locations; the other has six possible terminal points."

Dash looked at the data that had scrolled onto the heads-up while Sentinel had been speaking. Not only was the system closer, it was a single system, meaning they didn't have to start hunting around among a bunch of them. "The flight time to that system from here is—I make it just over a day, right?"

"That is correct."

"Unless we can figure out how to use the transfer station ourselves," Leira said. "Wouldn't *that* be a surprise for whoever's at the other end of it."

"Sure, if we can get it working, and if it doesn't have some sort of security system that dumps us into unSpace with no reference points, and—"

Leira cut Dash off. "I was just thinking out loud, Dash, not really being serious."

"Fair enough. And you're right, it would be sweet to be able to do it. Sentinel, transfer all of the nav info to the fleet, and let's get moving once everyone checks in."

"Understood."

DASH GAZED in wonder at the system they'd found. He'd seen busy systems before, but this one was *crowded*.

"There's—what, eleven planets? Dozens of moons? And all those ships—" He whistled.

All of the activity seemed to be centered on a single station, a relatively small one orbiting the fifth planet, a rocky world with a thick, soupy atmosphere. A second station swung through a highly eccentric orbit that was inclined at a steep angle to the system's ecliptic, and that was where this end of the transfer station was. Currently, the two stations were about four hundred million klicks apart.

A steady procession of small, drone-like ships, similar to the ones they'd seen loading cargo at the remote transfer point orbiting the rogue blue star, streamed between them. A single large ship was making the transit, too, closing on the first station. Cargo pods were clustered on its hull, and it returned characteristic signatures of Dark Metal. They could detect nothing about it, otherwise. However, since it seemed to be coming into the system rather than leaving, they'd have the opportunity to investigate it later.

"Okay, Benzel, let's proceed with the plan," Dash said. "The Golden have to know their transfer network thing has been compromised, so if they don't already have forces here, they soon will."

"Got it. The *Horse Nebula's* just getting underway."

The plan was simple. They'd stealthed-up the *Horse Nebula*—although not as effectively as the Golden stealth coating would allow, which is why Dash really wanted to get his hands on that tech. Now, the minelayer would surreptitiously seed flash mines around the transfer point, as well as on approaches to the other station, while the rest of the fleet lay in wait. Ideally, if and when any new forces arrived, they'd be disabled by the mines and easy prey for the lurking Cygnus force. It was a risky plan, especially if the Golden were deploying Harbingers or other ships with the new stealth coating. The flash mines had been fitted with gravitational detonators, though, which would sense the presence of mass, rather than relying on other means of detecting their targets. As far as they knew, gravitational effects were the one thing that simply couldn't be concealed, at least not by any physics that even the Unseen understood.

Dash watched as the *Horse Nebula* went about its silent task. The ship was moving slowly, using only her magnetic drive, so she was producing no exhaust. Custodian was confident that the active measures installed on her would conceal any other signature she might produce, although if she *was* detected, the stealth measures wouldn't protect her. So, to some extent, this was also based on sheer luck.

"Dash, several ships have just translated into the system," Sentinel said, as the threat indicator lit up. Dash turned to the tactical display.

"Two fighter-sized craft, and—I don't recognize that other ship," he said.

"It is an unfamiliar design. It is relatively small but heavily armed. A fast-attack frigate, I would suggest, but it otherwise matches nothing in the available data."

"So the Golden must be building new ships on top of everything else."

"I am not so certain," Sentinel replied. "There are marked differences between this vessel and others of more typical Golden design."

Dash shrugged. "Well, once this fight is done, we'll take a look at it." He switched the fleet's general comm channel. "Okay, all forces, stand by to engage. I make contact in—twenty minutes."

"Dash, there are only two Harbingers and one other ship,"

Benzel said. "That's not much of a force. Could it just be a feint? There's a bigger force somewhere else?"

"Possibly." Dash frowned. Benzel had a point. "Change of plan. Let's just keep waiting. We'll make them come to us, just in case their idea is that we stumble into a trap." Which was odd in itself, Dash thought. Smart commanders didn't base their plans on their opponents screwing up. Taking the whole Cygnus fleet and racing off to attack the new ship and its companion mechs would be just that—a screw-up. So would splitting the fleet and only engaging with a part of it. That would be a bigger screw-up, in fact.

So, they would wait.

"Dash, the trajectory of the new arrivals is unusual," Sentinel said.

"Oh? In what way?"

Sentinel projected their current trajectory on the tactical display. Barring any major course changes, the delta-shaped fighters and their enigmatic companion wouldn't come anywhere near the Cygnus fleet. Rather, they were inbound on the station orbiting the fifth planet and would arrive at about the same time the large cargo ship did.

"So I guess they haven't detected us," Dash said. "For them, this is just a routine trip—"

But he trailed off. The threat indicator showed that the new arrivals were racing into the system at combat speed, with their weapons charged and all combat sensors—both search and target acquisition—radiating at full power.

"Okay, hang on. Those are ships on an attack run," Dash said.

"They do conform to the expected profile of ships intent on engaging in combat, yes," Sentinel replied.

Queries started to filter in from the other Cygnus leaders—

Benzel, Leira, Amy, Conover, all in rapid succession. Dash finally overrode the comm channel, cutting them all off.

"Guys, you're seeing the same thing I'm seeing here. We might be looking at another skirmish in the Golden civil war we keep speculating about. Regardless, let's just stay alert and see what happens."

Time passed as the two sleek craft and their accompanying fast-attack frigate charged on, drawing ever closer to the innermost of the two stations and the big cargo ship now in the process of docking with it. Dash now fully expected violence, but when it came, it was shocking in its ferocity.

As soon as they were within range, the fighters loosed a salvo of missiles. The frigate opened up a few seconds later with a plasma weapon of unfamiliar design—similar to missiles, but rather than a conventional warhead, they held superhot, highly compressed plasma contained in powerful magnetic bubbles. The station and freighter both responded with point defenses that swatted aside a few of the fighter's missiles, but they were hopelessly outgunned and most of the ordnance slammed home. Both the station and the freighter were shredded by a succession of colossal explosions. But the attackers weren't done; they closed in on the wreckage, smashing anything not already wrecked with chest-cannon attacks from the fighters and a potent, short-ranged x-ray laser from the frigate.

In less than a minute, it was over. All that was left of the station and the freighter were fragments whirling and tumbling amid a glowing cloud of vapor.

"Well, shit," Benzel said. "That was overkill if I've ever seen it."

"Yeah, somebody was definitely in a bad mood today," Amy replied.

"Dash, the attacking vessels are changing course," Sentinel said, projecting a new trajectory for them.

"They're going after the transfer station next," Dash replied. "Yeah, I'd really rather not have that destroyed, not until we know more about it. Benzel, it looks like they're going to pass close to some of our mines."

"Roger that. With their current course and velocity, they'll be in threat range in...looks like about five minutes."

"Good. As soon as they are, command-detonate all the mines you can. Let's see if we can flash these guys, disable their ships, and then finally get some answers."

"Roger that."

The moments ticked by. Dash couldn't help tensing up; if they detected the mines, they'd probably have little trouble avoiding them, destroying them, or both. Then he'd face a tough decision—try talking to them and give themselves away; or engage the enemy in combat and risk destroying them. Or, in either case, they might just flee, and the chance of the Cygnus force being able to catch them from a standing start was pretty small.

But the three attackers just drove relentlessly on, apparently fixated on the transfer station.

"Okay, *Horse Nebula*, over to you," Benzel said. "As soon as they're in range of at least nine of the mines—three per, should be enough—you're free to fire at your discretion."

A gruff voice replied. "Got it. Stand by."

Seconds passed. Dash gritted his teeth and waited.

The mines detonated, nine of them, almost simultaneously. The attacking ships immediately stopped accelerating and coasted along, their power emissions zeroed out.

Even as the mines detonated, Dash was powering up the Archetype and engaging the drive, aiming the mech to intersect his suddenly dormant quarry. The rest of the Cygnus task force did the same, the *Herald* and her consorts hanging back, letting the four mechs take the lead, a disengaged reserve to hedge against anything unexpected happening.

Dash watched the tactical display, and especially the power signatures of the fighters and the frigate. They needed them to stay dead for at least the ten minutes it would take them to get into weapons range.

"Okay, gang," he said to his fellow mech pilots. "We want to disable these guys, not destroy them. So power back your weapons and stick with precision shots."

Leira and the others acknowledged, and they drove on. Again, Dash found himself tensing, hoping that they didn't manage to get their ships back online before he and the others could intervene.

And, again, they didn't. Amy and Conover each engaged a fighter, while Dash targeted the frigate. Leira didn't engage; instead, she kept ready to get involved if and where she might be needed.

Dark-lance shots punched through the fighters, blasting drives and weapons into scrap, crippling them. Dash likewise put a shot through the frigate's engineering section. Just like that, all three of them were suddenly, and without extensive repairs, permanently disabled.

"I wish it was always that easy," Leira said.

"Yeah, same," Dash replied. "Okay, so we should be able to just snag those fighters—they're crewless, if I'm guessing-- and tow them back to the Forge. This frigate though—" He curled his lip in irritation. "We're going to have to board it, I think."

He didn't relish the prospect. Boarding actions— notwithstanding the Gentle Friends' apparent infatuation with them

—were dirty, dangerous affairs. Aboard the Archetype, Dash could afford to make a mistake or two, and the powerful mech would just absorb the result and carry on. When clad only in a vac suit and body armor, a single mistake could be the difference between having an intact limb or torso or head, and—well, not.

"Do you want us to do the boarding thing, Dash?" Benzel said. "It's been a while since we've done one, and I'd like to keep our people on top of their game."

Dash rolled his eyes at the anticipation in Benzel's voice. What the hell was it with the Gentle Friends' and their love affair with fighting in tight corridors and cramped compartments, at point-blank range?

"Actually, I want to do this differently," Dash said. "Let's flash another couple of mines, to make sure this frigate is really dead. In fact, I'm going to put a shot through its bridge to make sure it's really *really* dead. Then, let's tow it back home along with the AI fighters and deal with it there. Maybe its crew will be more inclined to negotiate, even surrender, when half the star-field is covered by the Forge."

"Your call," Benzel said. Dash couldn't help noting the disappointment in the man's voice.

"Sentinel, can you open a general broadcast channel on the comm. Let's see if we can get a message through to whoever these guys are."

"Channel open."

"Unknown ship, this is the Messenger. You're now prisoners of the Cygnus Realm. Don't do anything dumb, and no one'll get hurt. To prove it, and to encourage your cooperation, I'm going to destroy the bridge of your ship in one minute. I'd suggest you evacuate it."

"Wish I could see what's going on inside that ship right now," Leira said.

"I'm thinking a lot of, *holy shit, let's get out of here*!" Amy laughed.

"I hope so," Dash said, as the mechs backed away, outside the range of the flash mines. Those detonated at the fifty-second mark; ten seconds later, Dash held good to his promise and smashed a dark-lance shot through the bridge, turning it, and the structure immediately around it, to glowing scrap.

"Okay, everyone, let's get these guys trussed up and head back to the Forge before anyone else shows up to join the party," Dash said.

As the task force got to work putting the derelict frigate and fighters under tow, Dash reflected that it was nice to have come through an action with no casualties, no damage, and not even a shot sent their way.

Unfortunately, he thought, it probably wasn't something they should get used to.

10

Dash watched closely as the captured frigate was eased into the largest of the Forge's available docking bays. As the *Herald's* massive bulk backed away from the station, a tractor beam took over guiding duties on the disabled frigate. He and Leira had already brought the Archetype and the Swift into the bay so the mechs could, if necessary, intervene if anything went wrong. It was a risk for sure; Custodian was *almost* certain the frigate's reactor was entirely dormant and beyond repair, but *almost* certain wasn't *certain*.

As the frigate settled slowly onto the deck, Dash reflected on the fact there'd been little choice. The ship was small, only one hundred and sixty meters long, and about twenty-two meters across its beam. But scans had revealed that the compartments and corridors inside were also very small; any one of the humans who entered would have to crouch, or even crawl on hands and knees—not the best way to take on a probably hostile crew aboard their own ship, especially since they were, presumably, small beings themselves. That hinted at them not being Golden, or Verity, who were all human-sized—or had been so far.

As soon as the ship settled, a squad of Gentle Friends ran forward with a breaching charge. It was a rectangular contraption, two meters by one, that could be clamped onto a hull and detonated; the shaped charge system inside it would direct the explosive blast inward, slicing through a ship's hull in a similar-sized rectangle, but with minimal back-blast. They attached about a meter to one side of the nearest of the visible airlocks. Like the rest of the ship, the lock was a diminutive thing, more suited for a toddler than a grown human.

Leira crouched beside Dash behind a cargo container, one of a line of the tough crates that had been arranged to give the Gentle Friends a secure firing line if they needed it. "This is weird," she said. "Everything about this ship is so small." She raised her pulse gun to a ready position as the Gentle Friends retreated from their breaching charge. "Maybe it's automated and the interior's only meant for maintenance bots, or something."

"It's possible," Dash said, eyeing the frigate from stem to stern, watching for even a hint that it might have a nasty surprise in store. "Guess we'll know in a moment."

His eyes caught on the two scorched holes he'd blasted into the frigate with the Archetype's dark-lance, one through engineering, the other through the bridge. Those could have made good ingress points as well, but Benzel declared them too obvious. Ever a pirate, he wanted to perform another breach and enter while the crew was still recovering from the effects of the explosive charge. Dash just acceded; again, boarding actions were Benzel's thing, and Dash was quite happy to let him and his people do what they were so good at.

As soon as the breaching party was back under cover, Benzel turned to Dash, who nodded back at him.

"Firing in three, two, one—" Benzel shouted.

A flash and a dull thud erupted from the breaching charge. The spent charge casing toppled away from the hull, pulling a perfectly rectangular chunk of hull plating with it. Two squads of Gentle Friends immediately leapt from cover and charged at the opening, some with pulse- and snap-guns raised, others with boarding axes, heavy cutlasses, and even a few long pikes.

At the same time, small figures clad in hardened fighting suits tumbled out of the breach and began shooting. Custodian had applied a suppression field to the bay, which should have shut down any tech not specifically identified as friendly. Unfortunately, either dumb luck or clever planning came into play, as the attackers were firing slug-guns, whose chemical propellants were unaffected by Custodian's measures. One of the Gentle Friends went down, then the return fire began, pulse-gun shots flashing through the docking bay, snap-guns tearing through targets where their pairs of otherwise harmless beams converged.

Dash raised his weapon, as did Leira, but neither fired. There was just too much risk of hitting the Gentle Friends. Instead, Dash said, "Sentinel, Tybalt, move now!"

The two mechs came to life, warnings booming from their external speakers. The Gentle Friends, who'd been briefed on this contingency, immediately scattered. The Archetype and Swift each reached down and grabbed one of the small, suited figures, then they lifted them helplessly out of the battle. The remaining half-dozen fought on, braving a suicidal charge at the line of cargo containers, and were quickly gunned down for it.

"Benzel," Dash said. "Let's use the gas!"

Benzel nodded, then he shouted a command and another team of Gentle Friends ran forward. Desultory shots still snapped out of the breach, but suppressive fire from their fellow squads kept any of the crew from taking aimed shots at the gas team. Once against the hull, they clamped on another, smaller breaching charge, this one circular. It blew out a disk of hull plating, which was promptly stuffed with a flexible hose leading to a set of tanks.

An instant later, a shrill hiss echoed through the docking bay as the same incapacitating agent mounted on the Archetype rushed into the frigate under high pressure. It quickly flooded the interior of the frigate, wisps of it soon wafting out of the hull breach and the dark-lance holes.

Benzel gave the order to cut the gas off. Then they waited.

As they did, Sentinel and Tybalt handed their prisoners over to the Gentle Friends—literally handed them over to be trussed up and restrained. To their credit, the small figures seemed to have accepted their fate, at least for the moment, and didn't struggle. Even from twenty meters away, though, Dash thought he could feel hostility radiating from them, meaning they were probably biding their time, waiting for any lapse by their captors. But these were the Gentle Friends; they simply didn't lapse when it came to prisoners or loot.

"The ship is yours, Dash," Benzel finally said with a grand wave. "Still not sure what's inside it, or who's inside it, but they're all asleep. We can enter any time you want."

"Nope. Just open it up, end to end. The whole damned ship. I'm done screwing around," Dash said, his tone flat and cold. These would either be allies against the Golden, or they wouldn't, and Dash wanted to make it abundantly clear to whoever this was that there were no other choices.

"Got it, boss," Benzel said, then he turned to the rest of the Gentle Friends. "Okay, folks, we're going to scrap this ship right in place and drag out anyone or anything still alive in the process. Custodian, we'd appreciate a hand."

"I am dispatching maintenance remotes to the docking bay to assist right now," Custodian replied.

Benzel nodded. "Thank you, sir." He turned to the two conscious figures they'd taken prisoner, still clad in their armored suits, their faces concealed by smooth, elongated helmets that completely enclosed their heads.

"Let's see what we've got," Dash said, but the Gentle Friends squad leader securing the prisoners shrugged.

"Sorry, Dash, but we haven't figured out how to get these little guys out of their suits."

"We're not even sure if they can breathe our air," another added.

Dash sniffed. "Fine. Only one thing left to do, then."

Leira gave the two figures a cold look. "Space 'em?"

Dash raised an eyebrow at her, but he knew—or at least hoped—that her words were just for effect, so he gave a grim smile. "Savage. But, no. Not yet, anyway. Let's make our guests more comfortable, and then we'll all get to know one another, shall we?"

DASH ENTERED the room they'd chosen to interrogate their captives, an otherwise empty compartment in a part of the Forge that was powered up, but not actually yet in use. The two captives, still clad in their heavy suits and blank helmets, sat motionless, cuffed, and bound into chairs. Each was guarded by a pair of Gentle Friends holding pulse-guns at the ready, fingers resting lightly on the triggers. Two more Gentle Friends stood on either side of the door, and another squad waited in the corridor outside. Moreover, he was armed, as were Leira, Viktor, Benzel, and Ragsdale.

It suddenly struck Dash as totally incongruous. The two figures' feet didn't even touch the floor. It was as though they had two little kids in armored suits tied into their seats; they actually looked a little silly, especially given the raw firepower arrayed against them.

But there was nothing silly about this. In the next few moments, Dash would learn if he was about to speak to a potential new ally, or another enemy he'd have to confront and ultimately destroy.

"Custodian, do we know if our guests here can breathe our air?" he asked.

"I am almost certain they can, based on the small quantities of respiratory gas leaking from their suits."

"There's that *almost certain* again," Dash muttered. "Screw it. I've got too much to do to be a particularly gracious host." He pulled out a heavy utility knife and advanced on one of the figures. It cringed back, but he raised a hand he hoped seemed conciliatory then grabbed the shoulder of the suit and cut the fabric. Gases hissed briefly, giving Dash a momentary bad feeling; wouldn't it suck if it turned out Custodian was wrong, and these creatures actually breathed chlorine or nerve gas or something? But all he caught was a whiff of a musky, somewhat dank smell. Finally, he was able to pull the helmet free, revealing—

"What the hell is *that?*" Leira asked.

"Not human, that's for sure," Viktor said.

Dash stepped back from an elongated, furry face, dark eyes blinking furiously, a mouth full of sharp teeth hissing and spitting with anger.

"Mean little bastard, isn't it?" Dash said, staring. He wasn't sure what he'd expected, but it hadn't been *this*.

"It looks like a…oh, whatever those things are from Old Earth. We were taught about them in school, in terrestrial biology. The— you know, the ones that ate snakes or something?" Viktor said.

"The designation you are looking for is *weasel*, I believe," Custodian said. "That is the closest match in the available human databases, anyway. Although, this being is much larger, obviously sentient, and is in the process of cursing you and your entire familial line in a particularly colorful, albeit anatomically improbable way."

"You can understand them?" Dash asked.

"Yes. Their language is a dialect of the Verity, although with far more hissing," Custodian said.

"Okay, let's hear the translation, then," Dash said, turning his knife to the second creature. With two efficient cuts, he had the second alien exposed. It too was angry—in fact, angrier. It curled a small, pink tongue as if to spit, but Dash stuck warning a finger in its face. "Enough!"

"Enough?" the creature hissed, its translated voice rattling from the comm. "Enough will be when your line is at last extinguished, when your—"

Dash grabbed the alien by its small ear and twisted its head to face him squarely. "I. Said. *Enough.*"

The alien opened its mouth, flashing small teeth gleaming with malice and saliva. But its mouth closed as it assessed the situation. Apparently, despite resembling nothing more than an oversized and very angry weasel, there was some discipline under that sleek pelt of fur.

"I am Vynix, Burrow Commander, First Rank," it—actually, he —snapped through the translator. His voice sounded utterly natural, which meant their language was in the system's databanks. Without a sound, Viktor hung small translators around each prisoner's neck.

Dash nodded at that. Talking was good. "And I'm Dash. I'm the Messenger, leader of the Cygnus Realm, in command of—well, everything you see here. Including you. Is that clear?"

"Clear."

"Excellent. Moving on, then. We'll certainly be getting to know one another better, but I have some urgent questions in the meantime. What's the purpose of that transfer point you were about to attack, and where is it sending Dark Metal, or whatever else is being sent through it?"

Vynix was silent for a long moment, his small ears twitching, seemingly in annoyance. "I will not answer that." He looked askance at the other alien, who blinked back at him, but said nothing.

"Good. That means you know," Dash said, smiling broadly. "My worry was that you didn't have the information at hand—or paw. Or whatever. Regardless, you'll tell us—or me, specifically, because the option is something I don't think you've considered."

Vynix pulled his lips back, hissing. It was laughter, but it sounded like a bad comms channel. When he finally spoke, his voice dripped with bemused contempt. "Please share your tales of horror and pain and punishment, Mess-inn-jurrrr." His partner remained silent and still, just staring.

"Well done on my proper title. Anyone who knows me understands how important I hold ceremony," Dash said, managing to make his voice sound gravely sincere.

There were several stifled coughs in the room. Leira turned away, covering her mouth and what was probably a goofy smile.

"Custodian, a star map, if you please. From here to the core, in detail," Dash said.

A holo image appeared, dominating an entire wall with the requested star chart. Vynix and his cohort did their best to look entirely uninterested in it, in a way that Dash found strikingly human—which meant weirdly incongruous when done by anthropomorphic weasels.

"You'll note that—I'm sorry, may I have your name as well?" Dash asked the silent alien. It simply stared at him with large, brown eyes. "Oh, I understand you might not want to, but in case anything happens to Vynix—not that anything will, of course, but—"

"Tikka," the alien said. "I am littermate to Vynix, and second in command of the burrow."

"Your brother, I take it?" Dash asked Tikka.

"Yes." She glanced at Vynix, who started to hiss, but cut it abruptly off.

"Good. Now that we're all introduced, more or less, let me continue with—what would you say I'm explaining, Leira?"

She gave the aliens a smile that was outright pleasant but still somehow managed to throw in a touch of menace. "Well, I'd say a plan for killing every single one of them from here to the galactic core, if I'm guessing." She sighed and shook her head. "Which means exterminating *another* race."

Viktor crossed his arms. "Yeah, that's getting old. I want to do something different, maybe conquer some territory or something, just for a change."

"Well, once these little critters are gone, we'll have all of their territory to choose from."

"That's a good point," Viktor said, scratching an ear. "Do you think they have beaches? I like beaches."

"Me too," Dash said with a grin.

Vynix and Tikka recoiled at the casual discussion of their race's obliteration. Dash spread his hands helplessly. "What can I say? They *get* me. See, I'm not going to torture you—no one here will harm you, in fact. But our policy is not one of peaceful coexistence with those who aren't our declared allies. We don't have that luxury, you see—not with the way the Golden have made it clear—"

"Who are the Golden?" Tikka interrupted.

Dash stopped and tilted his head in genuine surprise. Tikka's question had actually sounded sincere. "The Golden. What, you don't recognize the word?"

The aliens both opened their jaws then slowly closed them again. Dash figured that was—how they shrugged?

"The word, yes," Tikka said. "But not how you used it."

Dash narrowed his eyes. "Maybe we better start at the beginning. Who are you? Your people? What are you called?"

"We are Rin-ti," Vynix answered.

"And who do you serve?" Leira asked, now obviously as intrigued as Dash.

Tikka's brown eyes narrowed, her face pinching up in what was apparently a frown. "We serve the Rin-ti, of course. What of you? Who do you serve? The Metalworkers?"

Now it was Dash's turn to frown. "The Metalworkers? Who are they?"

"They are the...the ones who make," Vynix tried to wave his arms, but then he turned to Tikka, who gave another shrug.

"The chains," she said. "They make the chains."

"Is your race enslaved?" Dash asked.

"Slaves? No. We refer to the—" Tikka went on, but the translator couldn't parse it. Finally, the comm emitted a single, under-standable word.

"—Designers."

Dash glanced at Leira, catching her eye. Like him, she knew that this was important, even crucial to understanding these Rin-ti. "What do your Designers look like?" he asked.

"That's complicated," Tikka replied.

"Try me."

Tikka spoke, but again, the translator couldn't convert it to anything they could understand.

"I said they speak a language similar to that of the Verity, but not identical," Custodian explained when Dash asked him about it. "There are obviously concepts regarding which their language diverges from the translation matrix. Over time, I can accommodate that, determining common word roots and—"

"That's fine," Dash said. "We don't have time for that right now." He was about to ask Custodian to put up an image of one of the Golden corpses they'd been keeping in storage, but he had a better idea.

"Ragsdale, have them released, but keep their—er, paws bound." He looked back at the Rin-ti. "How about we go for a little walk?"

———

THEY'D KEPT the Golden corpses they'd retrieved in storage in widely separated parts of the Forge, thoroughly isolated from one another physically *and* electronically, just in case their embodied tech had some way of communicating. Dash had Ragsdale and the Gentle Friends bring the Rin-ti to a compartment opening off one of the fabrication bays, where one corpse was housed in cryogenic stasis.

They stopped in front of the cryo-storage unit, the humans moving aside to give the Rin-ti an unobstructed view.

"Okay, Custodian, open it up," Dash said.

The unit unsealed with a soft hiss, then a plume of white vapor sank to the deck and rolled around their feet like an icy fluid. The heavy door slid aside, revealing the partial Golden corpse frozen inside.

Dash watched the Rin-ti carefully, waiting for their reaction—

Which was a blank stare.

Tikka turned away and looked up at Dash. "That is not a Designer."

He searched her face for a hint of deception. Had she been human, Dash was confident he could tell if someone was trying to dissemble or pull one over on him. Tikka wasn't, so he couldn't be *sure*—but instinct told him that these creatures genuinely had never seen a Golden before.

"Well, this is a Golden," Dash said.

Tikka looked at Vinix, who opened and closed his mouth in that apparent shrug. She turned back to Dash.

"We believe you. However, this means nothing to us. The Designers are—" She paused, and Dash waited for her to go on with something the translator couldn't unravel. But she'd apparently just been searching for an apt description. "They are more like us, and include less—"

The word didn't translate. Tikka narrowed her eyes and pointed at a mechanical bit of tech embedded in the frozen corpse. "Less of that."

"Less tech."

"Yes."

Dash nodded. "Okay, just wait here for a moment while I confer with my colleagues."

While the Gentle Friends kept watch, Dash gestured for Leira, Viktor, and Ragsdale to join him.

"Do you believe them?" Viktor asked.

Dash nodded. "Yeah, I do. Which is weird—I mean, how could they possibly not have heard of the Golden? Who they hell do they think they're fighting?"

"That's a good question," Ragsdale said. "Maybe they're just xenophobic, like the Golden, and attack whoever they happen across."

"Do they seem especially xenophobic to you?" Dash asked.

Ragsdale turned and looked back at the two Rin-ti, who were examining the Golden corpse with open curiosity. "No, not especially."

"Dash, I think we should give them the benefit of the doubt for now and try talking to them," Leira said.

Dash grinned. "Says the woman who talked about spacing them."

Leira shrugged. "A girl can change her mind."

Dash nodded. "Anyway, I agree with you. We do need to try talking to them. They might be powerful allies."

"Or they might be these two, and a handful more, and that's it," Ragsdale said.

"Only one way to find out." Dash turned back to the Rin-ti.

"Okay, Tikka, Vynix—and I apologize if I should have addressed you the other way around, but I don't know your protocols—how about we take off those cuffs and treat you more like guests and less like prisoners. That's as long as you promise to, well, not try to kill us or anything like that." Dash smiled, hoping that the Rin-ti didn't interpret human smiles as a challenge or an insult.

Vynix nodded. "We have been discussing the same thing. We would prefer to not consider you enemies, at least for now. Instead, perhaps we can find common ground—perhaps even assist one another."

"What sort of assistance are you looking for?" Dash asked.

Vynix stared for a moment. "We are not diplomats. We would prefer that you discuss such things with those who are. If you can give us access to a long-distance communications system, we can arrange such a meeting."

"Oh, I think we've got some long-range comms kicking around here somewhere," Dash said, smiling. Again, the Rin-ti didn't react, or at least didn't react badly, so he assumed that smiling and friendly tones were at least okay.

DASH WATCHED, genuinely curious, as the two Rin-ti carried out an animated discussion with a holo-image of another Rin-ti located—somewhere, he wasn't sure where. And neither would Custodian be able to tell him afterward. The Rin-ti had asked that their communications remain private, so not only did they stay out of earshot, Dash had explicitly instructed Custodian to not translate, record, or otherwise involve himself with their comms.

Ragsdale, who'd originally suggested bringing them here to the War Room, rather than to the Forge's Command Center, had bristled at that. "It's an opportunity for some valuable intelligence, Dash."

"It is, sure, but this is also a gesture of good faith—at least on the exterior. I'll have Custodian monitor everything, and leave the deception to me. You're a spy at heart, but you smile too much. You'll give it away."

"I don't smile," Ragsdale said, not smiling.

"Maybe not with your mouth, but your eyes dance. You're too damned cheerful. Let me handle the story," Dash said, smiling.

Ragsdale had scowled, muttered something about hating it when Dash was right, and just settled for throwing darkly suspicious looks at the Rin-ti as they chattered away in their own language.

Eventually, they signed off the comm then turned back to Dash and the others.

"We have arranged for you to meet with an envoy of our people," Vynix said. "The location proposed is called The Three Fangs."

"Custodian? You got that on a star chart?" Dash asked.

"I have no records regarding a star system with that designation. Perhaps the Rin-ti could point it out on a map."

The holo image of the galactic arm—an image Dash was pretty sure was now etched into the back of his eyes—appeared. Vynix studied it for a moment then used his paws to zoom in the spinward edge of the arm, about two thirds of the way back toward the core. He peered at the image then pointed at a particular system. "There. That is the Three Fangs."

"Vynix has indicated a system which, in our charts, has only an alphanumeric designation. It is a remote trinary system, considered a navigation hazard because of powerful stellar emanations resulting from interaction among the three stars."

"Okay, well, update our chart to call it the Three Fangs," Dash said, then he turned to Vynix. "Why there? Seems like a pretty unfriendly place."

"It is. It's quite dangerous, in fact. But it is also a neutral location, and one not likely to be visited by others," Vynix replied.

"There is also a long-abandoned stellar observatory located on the margin of the system," Tikka said. "It is no longer operational, but its life-support systems have been reactivated."

"Whose observatory is it?" Leira asked.

"From the nature of the compartments and corridors, it was clearly built by humanoids of your size. Otherwise, however, we don't know," Vynix said.

"The location is known to us as Mark: Deep," Tikka said.

Dash looked at the others. Leira and Viktor just shrugged; Ragsdale continued to look suspicious, but he gave a curt nod.

"Okay, then. Vynix, Tikka, you are now official guests of the Cygnus Realm. You won't have complete run of the Forge, and we will assign you escorts, but you're no longer prisoners. And neither are the rest of your crew—well, those who survived, anyway."

Vynix waved a paw. "An unfortunate circumstance. Such tragic episodes are, unfortunately, a part of every war."

"Okay," Dash said. "We'll take a day to get ready, and then we'll all head to Mark: Deep."

"Yeah, it'll be good to get out for a change," Leira muttered, rolling her eyes.

11

MARK: Deep proved to be as enigmatic as the Rin-ti had hinted at. A disc-like design, it revolved around the trinary star system called The Three Fangs in such a remote orbit that a single turn would take a little over thirty-five years. One look at the data sluicing in from the three stars—a red giant, a white main-sequence star, and a white dwarf—made it clear why. The interaction between the three stars was an intricate gravitational ballet that was impossible to predict more than a few revolutions in advance. The trio also spawned colossal blasts of energetic particles and radiation. Dash could only compare them to the blue giant called Typhoon he'd once visited while hunting down Golden skyhooks. Its stellar weather had been just that, a typhoon of deadly radiation; this was far, far worse.

"I wonder who built this place," Dash said, as the *Herald's* shuttle eased its way into the open hangar. "It kind of looks human in some ways, but alien in others."

"Maybe it was a joint effort by someone working with someone else, sometime in the past," Viktor said.

Harolyn chuckled. "Could you possibly be any less specific?"

Besides the *Herald*, which had carried all the Rin-ti survivors from the frigate they'd captured, they'd brought the four mechs and four more ships, which kept station some distance away from Mark: Deep. Dash and Leira were part of the delegation meeting with the Rin-ti, while Amy and Conover also stayed with their mechs, a hedge against any interference by outside parties—or duplicity by the Rin-ti.

"Okay, we're docked," Dash said into his comm. "Benzel, you, Conover, and Amy have overwatch on this. We'll keep you posted about what's going on."

Dash said it loud enough to make sure Vynix and Tikka heard him loud and clear—another hedge against any Rin-ti scheming. Tikka actually gave Dash a look that suggested she knew it. He smiled back.

"Okay, Dash," Benzel replied. "We have the rest of the Rin-ti over here ready to go once the shuttle gets back. It'll take two trips to transport them all. We *are* transporting them all, right?"

Dash curled his lip. Benzel was among those who thought they should keep some of the Rin-ti aboard the *Herald* as guests, which really meant hostages. But Dash had no desire to start what he hoped would be a mutually beneficial alliance on such a note. "We are, Benzel, as soon as you can. Oh, and that other matter we discussed? Keep an eye on that."

"Will do."

They exited the shuttle to find a group of Rin-ti waiting for them. Vynix and Tikka greeted them in their own language; Dash's comm, set to real-time translation based on Custodian's language database, allowed him to confirm it was just what it seemed to be: a greeting. They were then led deeper into the station along a set of stairs that seemed just a *little* too narrow for Dash's liking. Similarly, Dash had gone up and down thousands of steps in his life without even a flicker of thinking about it, but a set of stairs were somehow proportioned *just* a little wrong, making him catch his toe a couple of times as he lifted his foot. He saw Harolyn and Leira do the same.

Leira caught his eye. "Whoever built this place, they definitely were not human."

Dash nodded. "Funny how even making things a little off like this catches you so much, huh?"

"Yeah. I'm glad the Forge wasn't built like this. There was enough to get used to there without tripping over the stairs."

They reached the top of the stairs and another compartment—this one with a group of Rin-ti waiting. Vynix and Tikka launched immediately into an animated discussion with the waiting Rin-ti as soon as they entered the compartment. Dash ordered their translators deactivated, again to allow the Rin-ti to speak privately. Dash took the moment to take in their surroundings, while hoping the aliens weren't discussing the best way to prepare the humans for dinner.

"This looks like it was a control room of some sort," Viktor said. "Most of the tech is gone, though, probably scavenged."

Dash nodded. There were consoles and displays around the room and a large viewscreen filling one wall. But most of the consoles were now just empty cases, their components gone, optical cables and other conduits left hanging, no longer connected to anything.

Vynix turned back to them and gestured for Dash to restart their translators. "We've removed much of the tech from this station but have kept it intact, its life support and environmental systems still running, as a neutral meeting place."

"I'm willing to bet you've installed some tech of your own, too," Dash replied, smiling. "Some early-warning scanners to keep watch over this region of space, maybe? Possibly some security systems, too, in case one of your, um, *neutral* meetings goes wrong, so you have an edge?"

"You are correct," one of the new Rin-ti, apparently a female, said to Vynix. "They are quite cunning, aren't they?"

"At least, that one is," a male put in, pointing a claw at Dash.

Another female Rin-ti raised a paw. She seemed older than the others, a little more bent and more grey. "Do not speak of our visitors as though they aren't here," she said, then turned keen eyes on Dash. "My apologies. You are the Messenger, correct? The leader of your people?"

"I am. I'm called Dash."

The older Rin-ti bowed her head and raised both paws. "This one is Sonus, High Seer of the Expansive Burrow. We meet you in the spirit of peace."

Dash glanced at Harolyn, who just returned a blank look. It had obviously been a formal, ritualized greeting, but if there was a correct response, it hadn't been explained to them.

He turned back to Sonus. "Ah. Of course. Well, let's begin with my name and job description. I'm Dash, I'm the Messenger, we're from the Cygnus Realm, and I have a plan to kill every Golden in the galaxy. Quickly, I might add."

Sonus's eyes glittered back at Dash—a smile, he thought, but one that didn't actually involve the mouth. "Vynix said you and your people are very casual in your dealings. So are we. The Great Greeting is the only formality we'll make you endure."

"We appreciate that. I'd hate to insult you guys without meaning to."

The first female who'd spoken, the one who'd labelled Dash *cunning*, darkly muttered something their translators didn't catch. Sonus turned to her and said something back.

"We didn't just do that, did we?" Dash asked. "Insult you? Because, if so, I'm——"

"It is not a matter of insult," the younger female said, raising her voice. "It is a matter of truthfulness. We're well aware of how you attacked our forces led by Vynix and Tikka, then you captured them and seized our ships. Yet you claim to come to us in the spirit of *peace?*"

Sonus once more raised a paw. "Crollock gives voice to the warrior spirit of her litter. It is not necessarily a sentiment shared by all Rin-ti."

Dash took note of that *necessarily* she'd used to qualify her words. He tried to look as open, honest, and friendly as he could.

"We're very sorry that happened," he said, and he saw Harolyn nod her approval. At her heart, she was a diplomat. Dash was not. That didn't mean he couldn't be diplomatic, when it suited.

"However, you were using tech that, until now, we've only seen deployed by our enemies, the Golden," Dash said. "Those two AI fighters you used to attack that Golden outpost are what we call Red Barons. Sort of. To us, they're something to fight, and you *were* just engaged in battle. Call me. . .curious. I'd like to know more."

Sonus nodded. "I understand. That technology is not ours. Rather, we have obtained and repurposed it for our own use." She shrugged in that peculiar Rin-ti way, opening and closing her mouth. "It is unfortunate that such things happen, but they are an all-too common, not to mention tragic, consequence of war."

Crollock looked like she wanted to mutter something more, but she satisfied herself with a hard stare at Dash and his companions.

A third Rin-ti from their delegation stepped forward. "I have a question."

Sonus glanced at him, then back to Dash. "This is Wyxol. He is of the litter of learners, those who seek and store information. You may ask your question, Wyxol."

"Messenger, we have amassed considerable information regarding your species, over a long period of time. Frankly, we find you not particularly interesting." He shrugged with his mouth. "My apologies for such a blunt statement, but aside from being prolific in numbers, we have only watched you through the lens of the threats or opportunities you pose to our people."

Dash smiled. "Hey, I don't disagree. I think a lot of humans, and what we all do, is pretty boring and pointless, too."

Wyxol hesitated a moment, seemingly taken aback by Dash's casual willingness to throw a slur on his own people. But he recovered and went on.

"How, then, is it possible that you possess such tech as that described by Tikka and Vynix? I have reviewed our archives and can find nothing to suggest that you are capable of building and employing such things as—" He looked at Tikka. "What did you call it?"

"The Forge."

"Yes," Wyxol went on. "This Forge of yours. How could we have been so wrong about your people?"

"That's because it's not our tech," Dash said. "Like you, with those Harbingers, we just kind of came into possession of it. It was created by a race known as the Unseen."

"The Unseen." Wyxol nodded. "We have heard of them but have long considered them just a legend."

"Same with us," Harolyn said. "They were nothing but legends for me, too. That was until Dash showed up in that mech, the Archetype, and brought me to the Forge." She gave a thin smile. "Turns out they're *quite* real."

"This does not surprise us," Sonus replied, and Wyxol nodded again. "This station is evidence of races that have preceded us."

"There's also the fact that you're using Golden tech," Leira said. "Again, those Harbingers come to mind. We'd love to know how you came to possess those, by the way."

"All in good time," Sonus said. "We are still in the very early stages of getting to know one another."

"We keep our secrets safe," Crollock put in, her eyes narrowed. "Until we know we can absolutely trust those seeking for us to reveal them."

"And that's perfectly fair," Dash said. "For now, you just have to understand that the Unseen and the Golden were bitter enemies— mainly because the Golden are determined to wipe out all sentient life in the galaxy. The Unseen fought hard to prevent that. Now, as you'll appreciate, so are we."

"You keep mentioning these Golden," Wyxol said. "Tikka and Vynix have described what they were able to learn about them, thanks to your descriptions," The Rin-ti was obviously intrigued, but Sonus had already introduced him as a *Learner*, so that didn't surprise Dash. "What more can you tell us about them?"

Dash nodded to Leira, who unclipped a data-pad from her belt and activated it, projecting a holo image of a Golden. It was a composite assembled by Custodian, based on images of the corpses they'd retrieved and archival records.

Just as Tikka and Vynix had, Sonus, Wyxol, and Crollock gave the image a curious look.

"So these are the creatures that you believe built the mecha constructs we employ?" Wyxol said.

"That's right," Dash said. "The Harbingers, as they're called, are one of their foremost weapons. We've encountered them quite a bit, both piloted versions and ones controlled by AIs."

Crollock, her eyes still narrowed, walked around the image as Wyxol and Dash spoke. She finally stopped and turned to Dash, her teeth bared.

"You show us a picture of something. You claim that it is a great enemy of all living things." She turned to Sonus. "But we have no proof, nothing to say that *they* are not the enemy, and that they seek to confound and co-opt us as their pawns."

"We saw the Forge," Tikka said. "We were there. And we saw the corpse that they claim to be one of the Golden—"

"I am not saying these things are not real," Crollock snapped back. "I am saying that we know nothing about the motives of these creatures. They attack us, they take our ships, they kill our warriors, and now they claim to seek our friendship?" She glared at Dash. "I do not trust them," she hissed.

Dash held up a conciliatory hand. "I realize that we got off on the wrong foot, but my policy is quite simple. I give everyone a chance to deal with us in a fair manner. When that chance is wasted, then my temperament changes."

"You'll also notice that we didn't just destroy your ships," Viktor said. "We did capture them, yes. But we brought them back to the Forge and only defended ourselves when your people attacked us."

"And as soon as it became clear we'd become enmeshed in a big misunderstanding, we stood down immediately," Harolyn added. Tikka and Vynix here went from prisoners to guests. And here we are, ready and willing to talk."

Dash had been watching Sonus as the tense conversation bounced back and forth. She had followed it, but she also tossed glances back at Dash, making it clear that she was also watching *him*. Dash gave her a wintry smile of his own, dispelling the youthful nature of his face. At that, Sonus twitched, seeing him in his true state.

As a warlord. A friendly warlord, to be sure, but a man who had goals that he would not abandon. Sonus gave a tiny nod as that knowledge settled in her mind.

Crollock spun toward Sonus. "We should take nothing they say at face value. There is too much at stake."

Sonus finally spoke. "You must understand, Messenger——"

"I prefer Dash."

"Very well. You must understand, Dash, that we are beset with enemies all around us. We have fought costly wars with the Cserrine Bridge, the Waunsik, and even our own kind, the Inner Brood. We have what could be best described as an uneasy peace with those around us. Crollock, as a warrior, sees all strangers as potential enemies—at least until they can prove that they are friends."

"Which is something we wish to become," Dash said, "but not at the cost of a single one of my people, and I might point out that you fired first, even if it was in a different direction."

"I understand, and you have the upper paw. But first, we must understand you. We do not even have a clear idea as to what territory your—Cygnus Realm, you called it, correct? We do not know what space or star systems your Cygnus Realm claims."

"Well, right now, anything that's claimed by the Golden is automatically claimed by us," Dash said. "Beyond that, though, we haven't really claimed anything, except maybe the immediate volume of space around the Forge. And even that's not fixed, because the Forge is mobile. It's very good at dominating anything up to, say, a single, typical star system. And someday, we intend to have more permanent boundaries. But right now, we're pretty much focused on finding and defeating the Golden, as stability and peace are impossible while they exist."

"You say you are very powerful, that your Forge is very strong," Crollock shot back. "But the only proof we have of that is your attack on Vynix's ships, and that was an *ambush*." She said *ambush* in a way that made it sound like a curse. "How do we know that you are even capable of the things you claim?"

"Well, Vynix and Tikka here have seen what we can do first-hand, and they've seen the Forge—" Dash said, but Sonus cut him off.

"Yes, we know. However, even you, Dash, must admit that your claims currently have no clear substance. They are just that, claims," she said. "Before we proceed, we need to know more about you and what you are truly capable of."

In answer, Dash activated his comm. "Benzel, are the Rin-ti still broadcasting?"

"They are. Wide-spectrum, high-power, no attempts at stealth or concealment at all," Benzel replied.

Dash looked at Sonus with a hard smile. "We noticed that you guys are making an awful lot of noise. Put that together with the fact you've recently been at war and have settled into—what did you call it? An uneasy peace?" His smile widened but stayed hard. "You let yourself be followed, didn't you? Who's the enemy?"

Sonus's lips drew back in a toothy smile. "You're quick. I do like that, at least. Indeed, we should have guests in moments. We've been harried by a militant cadre of Waunsik who reject the peace agreement we have with their people and want nothing less than to control all of our systems. They even have designs on this one."

"Sentinel, what do we have on these Waunsik?" Dash asked.

"Not a great deal. Anecdotal references only. In summary, the Waunsik are a reptiloid race, feathered, with a reputation for cunning aggression," Sentinel replied.

"Aggression is their particular hallmark," Sonus said. "The hunting rituals of the Waunsik require that their enemies be taken alive so that they can be eaten in front of a high council to assure—"

"Honor or something like that, I bet," Dash said. "Feathered lizards. Guns. Wanting to eat us. Okay, I've got it. Sentinel, scans please."

"Targets inbound from the direction implied by Sonus's description. There are six vessels in total, including one of heavy cruiser size, the rest similar to frigates, except for one small craft, which is corvette-sized."

"Any Dark Metal?"

"There are no Dark Metal signals from the approaching vessels—which, incidentally, have completed their translation and are now inbound toward your location at high acceleration."

"Alright, let's go greet them." He looked at the elder Rin-ti. "Sonus, please pay attention." Dash maintained a pleasant expression but put iron in his voice. "I won't repeat this performance. Not for you, anyway."

"I understand," Sonus replied evenly.

Dash gave a brief nod, then turned away and led the others back to board the shuttle.

DASH STUDIED the Archetype's tactical display. Not that there was much to study—the Waunsik were simply charging straight into the system.

"Dash, are you sure we should fight these guys, these Waunsik?" Leira asked over a private comm channel. "Seems like we're doing the Rin-ti's dirty work for them. For all we know, the Waunsik might be better allies for us."

"Am I sure? No, of course not. But we have to assume some risk, make some decisions," Dash replied. "And since we know the Rin-ti are using Harbingers they got from somewhere—and might also be the ones that developed the stealth coating on them, because, remember the claw marks?"

"They do have claws. Lots of them," Leira agreed.

"And these Waunsik aren't using any Dark Metal at all, which begs the question-- who's the better potential ally?" Dash asked.

"But if that's the case, then remember those stealthed-up Harbingers attacked *us* without warning."

"Oh, I haven't forgotten. And I think we'll eventually be having that discussion with Sonus. For now, let's see these Waunsik off, show Sonus and Crollock and the rest of them just how good we are at kicking ass, and then get down to details with the Rin-ti."

"You're the boss."

Dash looked at the tactical display again. Still no change by the Waunsik; they just bored straight in, apparently determined to engage in battle as quickly as possible. Dash deployed the four mechs ahead of the *Herald*. The big ship's four consorts would act as his reserve—just in case there was more going on here than met the eye, on the part of the Waunsik *or* the Rin-ti.

"Okay, folks, I make it five minutes until we're in weapons range. I'll take on the heavy cruiser. You guys divide the other five ships among yourselves. Let's get this done and over with as quickly as possible."

"Dash, do we really want to fight and kill these Waunsik?" Leira asked. "We really don't know much about these Rin-ti or their history with this race."

"That's a good point. For all we know, the Rin-ti might be oppressing and brutalizing the Waunsik, and we'd be helping them with that," Conover said.

"We do seem to be kind of doing their dirty work for them here," Amy put in.

"Way ahead of you, guys," Dash said. "Yes, I'd like to minimize the losses we inflict on these Waunsik because we really don't know much about their conflict with the Rin-ti. We don't know who started it, how long it's been going—and let's face it, this is mostly a tech demonstration for the Rin-ti. So, let's fight to *disable* these Waunsik only. That means the usual—low power yields on the weapons, and firing solutions to target weapons and drives. But leave their ships *intact*. Understood?"

The others acknowledged, and Dash watched the range diminish. A few seconds after the threat indicator showed the Waunsik sensors switch from surveillance to target acquisition mode, the largest of the approaching ships fired a quartet of missiles, one locking onto each mech.

"That makes me nervous," Leira said. "Why do they think one missile will be enough for each of us?"

"Not sure," Dash said. "Sentinel, can you scan those missiles, get some sense of what they're about?"

"They appear to be designed to generate a powerful electromagnetic pulse effect, similar to our own flash mines. I would suggest that, like us, the Waunsik are interested more in disabling our vessels than destroying them."

"Huh. Okay, that fits with the Rin-ti's claim that the Waunsik are all about capturing and eating their enemies. And since I don't particularly want to be eaten, I guess I have to ask, would it work? Are we actually vulnerable to it?

"It is unlikely; these mechs are hardened against even extreme EMP yields. However, without further data, it is impossible to say for sure."

"Yeah, let's not take the chance. Okay, folks, weapons free. Let's take out those incoming missiles."

Almost as one, the mechs opened fire with dark-lances.

Every shot missed.

Dash frowned and reacquired the target, generating a new firing solution. He triggered the dark-lance and missed again.

"Sentinel, talk to me. What's going on?"

"I am working with the other AIs to analyze. One moment please."

"You've got about forty-five moments, as in that many seconds, before these things impact," Dash said, keenly aware that, as tech demonstrations went, this one wasn't going well.

A pause made Dash press his lips into a thin, hard line and he watched the tactical display, the incoming missiles crawling across it, closing. He was about to speak up, but Sentinel pre-empted him.

"It would appear that these missiles are each generating a complex displacement field. The effect is to paint the missile on our sensors as being other than where it is. Accordingly, our firing solutions are invalid. It is quite a sophisticated technology."

"Praise it later. What can we do about it?" Dash tried to imagine manually targeting something as small as a missile, boring straight in at them—

"Dash, I have an idea," Conover said. "Kristin thinks we can use the Pulsar's ECM to turn the tables on them, make these missiles think that this mech is, well, all four of them."

"What, and have all four missiles attack you? Losing the Pulsar isn't my idea of success here."

"That's no problem, Dash," Kristin said. "We'll run off and lead them into the storm cloud of charged particles being emitted by those three suns. That'll fry those missiles for sure!"

Despite the tense uncertainty of their situation, Dash couldn't help smiling at the bouncy, fluffy demeanor of the Pulsar's AI. It was only a personality overlay, of course; beneath the flighty surface, Kristin was essentially the same complex and powerful AI as Sentinel, Custodian, and the others.

She'd drive me crazy, though, Dash thought, and took a second to appreciate Sentinel's calm, grounded attitude.

"Twenty-five seconds to detonation, assuming the warhead yield we've estimated," Sentinel said.

"Okay, Conover, do it," Dash called out.

At first, nothing seemed to happen, and Dash found his gut clenching up. But then the three missiles not targeting the Pulsar began to deflect—and the deflection increased as they accelerated toward Conover's mech. The Pulsar, in turn, accelerated through a wide, sweeping turn, one that let the missiles get close to, but just short of separation distance. The mech had to keep that separation, though, and this was where one of the lighter mechs, the Swift or the Talon, would have an advantage.

"Sentinel, extrapolate this," Dash said. "Is he going to make it?"

"Assuming the Pulsar and the missiles maintain their maximum possible acceleration—or, at least, what we believe that to be, for the missiles—then he likely will, yes. However, the Pulsar will be subjected to an extreme radiation environment. That in itself will likely cause significant damage to it."

Dash said nothing. Conover knew what he was doing, and he knew the risks. Dash had to cut the last of the protective strings that still stretched between him and the kid, who was no longer a kid at all. It might be hazardous for Conover and the Pulsar, but it was also their best prospect for success.

"Okay. Leira, Amy, let's go take care of these Waunsik, shall we?"

"We've got your flanks, Dash," Amy said. "Let's do it."

Pulling his eyes away from the icons representing the Pulsar and the missiles chasing it, Dash focused his attention on the Waunsik ships and kicked up the Archetype's drive.

THE ACTUAL BATTLE with the Waunsik proved to be anticlimactic. They fired no more of the EMP missiles; Sentinel speculated that their own ships weren't immune to the effects, so the weapons had a minimum safe range, and the mechs were now inside it. Instead, they opened up on the Archetype and its consorts with a mixed array of particle-beam projectors, gigawatt-lasers, plasma-cannons, and short-range missiles.

The mechs blithely sailed through the storm of incoming fire, closing to short range, then slamming low-yield shots from their dark-lances through exhaust arrays and weapon mounts. Dash even got in close enough to deploy the power-sword and carve components away from the Waunsik cruiser—sensor clusters to blind it, weapons to render it impotent and, finally, its drive assemble to fully disable it. He was careful to keep his blows away from the bulk of the ship, including its bridge and parts that were probably just hab.

The Waunsik did manage one surprise, though—several of their ships mounted short-range projectors that fired expanding clouds of monofilament fiber, through which small-but-powerful, one-shot capacitors passed tremendous jolts of electrical current. It was, it seemed, a discount version of their EMP missiles that could be used at shorter ranges.

"This weapon would incapacitate many conventional ships," Sentinel said, as Dash flexed his arms and legs, the limbs of the Archetype responding in-kind, their prodigious strength simply shredding the cloud of monofilament that briefly engulfed it. "The *Slipwing* and *Snow Leopard* would certainly be disabled; even the *Herald* may suffer deleterious effects from it."

"Yeah. These guys definitely seem to be all about taking their opponents alive. Guess they're tastier that way. Still, good to know, in case we ever end up on the other side of a battle with the Waunsik again."

Less than five minutes later, the entire Waunsik flotilla was dead in space, except for the single, small ship that had accompanied them. It had suddenly loosed a tremendous burst of acceleration and attacked the Talon. Amy damaged it with her dark-lance, but not enough to stop it from closing and detonating with a powerful directional EMP that briefly knocked most of the Talon's systems offline.

Dash scowled. "Was there any crew on board that thing?" he asked Sentinel.

"I detected a bio signal, yes."

"Suicide attack, then."

"Perhaps a ritualistic one, a disgraced Waunsik being given an opportunity to cleanse its name. That would fit with the scant information available on this race."

As the battle wound down, the three mechs withdrew, and Dash finally let himself check on Conover. He found the Pulsar on its way back, with no sign of the missiles that had been pursuing it.

"As Kristin predicted, the Waunsik missiles didn't last long once we were deep enough inside that rad storm," Conover said. "Unfortunately, it wasn't very good for the Pulsar, either."

"No, it sure wasn't." Kristin said. "We're actually radioactive now! Neutron bombardment created a whole slew of short-lived radioisotopes in our armor and hull. You're definitely going to want to park us somewhere safely away from everyone else—for the next week or so, anyway."

"Uh, Conover, you're radioactive?" Amy said, her voice taut with concern.

"The Pulsar is. I'm not. I'm pretty well shielded in the cockpit. Getting out of this mech is going to be interesting, though, because Kristin's right—these neutron-activated radioisotopes have half-lives from a few hours to a few days, so it'll be a week or so before it's safe to come near the Pulsar."

"Holy crap, that must have been some intense radiation, then," Amy said. The relief was evident in her voice.

"Right?" Kristin replied. "I mean, if we'd gone much further into that rad storm, things could be a lot more interesting!"

"Dash," Benzel cut in. "Sorry to interrupt, but there are three Rin-ti ships underway, heading toward the Waunsik."

"Yeah, I thought that might happen," Dash said. "They figure that, now that we've disabled them, they can just pick them off at leisure."

"Can't say I really blame them," Leira said. "If someone had a tendency to eat my people, I'd probably have a hate-on for them, too."

"I suppose, but we didn't go through this just to turn things around and serve up the Waunsik to the Rin-ti on a platter. So it's time for another demonstration. Benzel, put yourself between the Rin-ti and the Waunsik. And if that doesn't deter them, feel free to fire a warning shot or two."

"Got it."

Dash led the mechs back toward the Mark: Deep station. The Rin-ti ships continued their course toward the disabled Waunsik, while Benzel moved the *Herald* and her companions to a point between them.

Time passed, all the various ships keeping to their trajectories. Once more, Dash found himself in a state of mild unease. He really hoped the Rin-ti would get the message and back off. Sonus had said they were at peace with the Waunsik, which meant these might be a rogue element, but either way, Dash knew that blood would likely be spilled merely to prove a point.

"There is an incoming transmission from Sonus," Sentinel said.

Here we go. "Put her on."

A window popped open on the heads-up, framing Sonus. "Messenger—Dash—can we assume that your ships are deliberately interposing themselves between ours and the Waunsik?"

"Yes, you can. Look, I know you've fought a while with these—"

"You do not need to explain," she said. "In fact, I am quite pleased with this outcome. Our ships will be ordered to stand down immediately. Please inform your people to that effect, so we have no further *unfortunate incidents*."

"Wait—that was another test, wasn't it?" Dash asked. "To see what we would do once the Waunsik were defenseless."

"We have no love for the Waunsik, but we do not irrationally hate them, either. The fact that you defeated them while sparing as many as possible, and then protecting them from us once they were helpless, tells me much about your character, and that of your people."

"To borrow a phrase from you, you're quick and smart. I like that."

"I appreciate the compliment. We will, nonetheless, take the Waunsik captive and intern them, in order to return them to their own ruling council for judgment. They will likely all be declared disgraced, which means the officers will be allowed to man the suicide craft you saw."

"Do I need to ask what happens to the rest of them?"

"As a matter of ritual, they will be killed and eaten."

Dash gave a grim nod. "So I didn't need to ask. That's harsh—but it's also their own affair." He narrowed his eyes at Sonus. "Just one thing—"

"We will not harm them," Sonus said. "You have my word."

"Okay, then. I guess we both need to start trusting one another. Benzel, stand down and let the Rin-ti pass."

"Will do, but one thing, first. I have a pretty pissed off Waunsik on the comm who wants to let us know that we are now their mortal enemies, that they will hunt down and consume us, our families, our pets—"

"Our pets? Really?"

"Nah. I just thought it sounded good," Benzel said, laughing.

Dash thought about the fate that Sonus had described as awaiting these Waunsik. He actually felt a little sorry for them.

A little.

"Tell the Waunsik that we're suitably terrified by their threats and then sign off."

"Tell them we're terrified? Really?"

"Yeah. If it makes them feel better, more power to 'em."

Dash switched back to Sonus.

"Okay, we've demonstrated our power, passed your tests—so are you convinced we are what we say we are?"

"I am. Very much so, in fact."

"Good. Now, tell me about your angry cousins toward the core."

12

"Wait, the Waunsik did *what?*" Dash asked.

"They have declared war on you," Sonus repeated. "We just received notification from them."

Dash gave Sonus's image on the heads-up a hard look. Before he could speak, though, Sonus went on.

"I know. We are the ones that essentially put you in a position of conflict with the Waunsik. It would appear that, in our efforts to be clever, we were actually careless regarding the consequences."

Dash let his glare linger. His mind, though, was already turning over the implications. This gave them a major moral lever to push when it came to the Rin-ti, because Sonus was right. It really *was* their fault that the Waunsik had declared war on the Cygnus Realm. Of course, that might have been their intent all along, which led to the distasteful possibility that the Rin-ti were simply using them. After all, if they fought the Waunsik and defeated them, the Rin-ti only stood to benefit. It would work out even better for the Rin-ti if they destroyed the Waunsik altogether, and better still if it hurt the

Cygnus Realm forces in the process, if that was part of Sonus's intent.

But it struck Dash that forcing someone's hand was a game that he could play, too.

So he shrugged. "Oh, well. If they want to come after us, they can. We'll be more than ready for them. In the meantime, our fleet is ready to depart, so—"

"You're simply going to leave?"

"Well, yeah. I think we've concluded what we need to do here. We'll be in touch."

"The Waunsik have been roused to anger—"

"Yes, they have, haven't they?" Dash locked his eyes on Sonus's as he said it.

She pulled her lips back in a smile. "Ah. You suspect that we engineered this conflict for our own benefit."

"I never said that. And I'm sure you'd never do something like that, would you, Sonus?" Dash said, smiling back.

"Truthfully, we did not. We really only did want to see if your capabilities were really what you claimed them to be."

"And they are, which means we could go and take out the Waunsik if we wanted to. The question is, why would we want to?"

Sonus smiled again. "It would seem that we shall be formalizing our alliance with you sooner than either of us thought."

"It sure would. And to that end, if we're going to attack the Waunsik, then we'll happily have one of your squadrons accompany us."

"I think that can be arranged."

"Good, because we're ready now.'

Sonus blinked. "Now?"

"Might as well. We're already here, with a chunk of our combat power ready to go. And you've got a squadron of ships here. No point waiting."

"Very well. I will place command of our force under—"

"How about Tikka and Vynix?" Dash said. "We've gotten to know them, and them us, pretty well." He left it at that, not saying that he didn't want to have to deal with the cantankerous Crollock, despite the fact that she seemed to be a senior Rin-ti military leader.

Sonus nodded. "Very well. Tikka and Vynix will join you shortly."

"Sounds good. Dash out."

As soon as he signed off, the general comm channel came to life with Leira's voice.

"Okay, Dash, I have to admit, I was getting ready to start kicking some furry weasel butts, but—"

"But you handled that like a pro," Harolyn said. "You sure you weren't a diplomat in a former life?"

"No, but I seriously doubt it," Dash replied. "It's more like I've spent a lot of my life talking my way out of trouble."

Harolyn laughed. "The two aren't mutually exclusive, you know!"

THE JOINT CYGNUS and Rin-ti task force sidled up to the boundary of what the Waunsik apparently claimed as their own territory, but with their active scans shut down. Benzel had recommended they just spend some time listening to whatever comm traffic might leak out of Waunsik territory.

"You can learn a lot just by discretely hanging out and seeing what you can overhear," he said.

"Let me guess, that's a privateer thing," Leira said.

"Something like that," Benzel replied, the grin in his voice evident.

For a while, they heard nothing. Just as Dash was about to get the task force back into motion, Conover came on the comm.

"We've picked something up," he said. "It's encrypted, but Kristin's trying to break—oh, and she's done."

"It wasn't really a very sophisticated code," the Pulsar's AI chirped. "I mean, I'm sure they thought it was, but really—"

"Uh, Kristin? What did whatever you decrypted *say?*" Dash cut in.

"Oh, okay. It seems that the nearest system, six-point-seven light years core-ward of us, is calling urgently for reinforcements. It seems the Waunsik force we defeated back at Mark: Deep was based there, and with those ships out of the picture, they're worried about their defenses."

Dash nodded. "Perfect. Sentinel, any Dark Metal signals coming from Waunsik space?"

"There are none evident. It would appear that Waunsik technology does not make use of Dark Metal."

"Okay, that'll make things easier. We can still salvage their tech and scrap, though. The Rin-ti also say the Waunsik do a lot of asteroid mining and comet harvesting, so there's that, too." He switched to the general task force channel. "Okay, everyone, we're going to strike now, while that first system is only lightly defended. Maybe it'll be enough to convince the Waunsik to back off."

"And if it's not?" Viktor, aboard the *Herald*, asked.

"We send an ultimatum and follow it with a demonstration that's impossible to misread. If *that* doesn't convince them, then we'll take down their whole damned empire as fast as we can," Dash replied. "This sudden war we find ourselves in is either going to end because the Waunsik don't *want* to fight anymore, or because they *can't*."

As Dash was studying the tactical display, data being transmitted back to them by the stealth drone they'd deployed, Benzel came on the comm, on a private channel.

"Dash, something kind of occurred to me, here."

"What's that?"

"Well, if the Waunsik in this system are complaining that their defenses are weak because of the loss of that flotilla that attacked us at Mark: Deep, then that flotilla—"

"Probably wasn't actually a rogue force operating without authority from the Waunsik leadership?"

"Yeah, exactly."

"That sure seems pretty clear. The Waunsik were double-dealing, pretending to maintain a peace treaty with the Rin-ti while dispatching rogue forces to attack them."

"And the Rin-ti were trying to manipulate us into fighting them."

"Maybe. I actually believed Sonus when she said that they hadn't intended to drag us into an actual war, but here we are."

"I'm telling you, privateering is a lot simpler. All this scheming and politicking is making my head hurt."

"Tell me about it," Dash said. "I used to be a courier, remember? I kind of miss the days when my biggest problem was being broke."

"I have to be honest—I'm not really inclined to trust any of these assholes."

"Neither am I...yet. But conniving politicians are going to do what they do, so we're just going to have to—"

He broke off as new telemetry arrived from their stealthy reconnaissance drone. "Hello, what's this?" Dash said. "Sentinel, am I seeing data here that says that moon—the one orbiting the fourth planet—is artificial?"

"It is not artificial, but it has been extensively developed. The probe's scanners are limited, but the data suggests there are expansive sub-surface excavations, including a large opening that may be a hangar or launch bay. There are also numerous surface installations—comm and scanner arrays, and weapons clusters."

"So that seems to be where all the action is," Dash mused, narrowing his eyes at the heads-up.

"I would point out that there are still twenty-two Waunsik vessels in this system, as well as two freighters, and that two of the warships are heavy cruisers. That would also seem to constitute *action.*"

"Yeah, but that moon is important." Dash considered the tactical problem a bit longer then switched to the general comm. "Okay, Benzel, we'll keep this simple. Take the *Herald's* squadron and our Rin-ti allies straight in. Be kind of obvious about it. I want to see if we can pull the Waunsik away from that moon with all the tech in and on it. "

"We have a minelayer with us," Benzel replied. "If you really want to provoke them, we could start laying a minefield, put it across what seems to be their primary space lane in and out of the system. Nothing pisses someone off more than having their territory mined."

"That sounds like the voice of experience talking," Leira put in.

"I'll tell you the story over a drink some time," Benzel replied.

"Okay, sounds good. When this is done, though, we'll want to recover whatever mines don't get expended. I have a pretty strong hunch this isn't going to be our last battle against these guys."

"Got it."

"Sounds like you have a separate plan for the mechs, Dash," Leira said.

"I do. I'm going to leave Conover with Benzel's squadron, just in case anything comes up. I especially want him to be able to take care of our Rin-ti friends. You got that, Benzel?" Dash said with a hint of emphasis in his voice, hoping that Benzel got what he was saying, based on their earlier conversation about duplicitous aliens.

He wasn't sure if Tikka and Vynix, who were aboard the *Herald*, were within earshot and didn't want to make them suspicious, or waste the time getting Benzel on a private channel. Dash didn't *think* the Rin-ti would turn on them, but leaving one of the mechs watching over them might make them think twice, in case they were considering it. After all, this could all still be some convoluted Golden plot, and both the Rin-ti and the Waunsik were *their* allies.

"Yeah, got it, Dash. I'll talk to Conover, make sure he takes good care of our Rin-ti friends."

Dash smiled. Benzel had gotten it, as just as he'd expected. "Good. Now, as for me, Leira, and Amy, we're going to go for a little flight. We'll translate well away from the system, then back, onto a whole different trajectory, and make a run straight at that moon. By then, I'm hoping Benzel will have the Waunsik ships well tied up. Everyone good?"

The acknowledgements rolled in.

"Okay, everyone, we launch in five minutes. Oh, and remember that these Waunsik guys apparently like eating their enemies, so don't let that happen."

Amy laughed. "Yeah, not being eaten is good!"

DASH WATCHED the target moon closely as they approached it. Amy led the Archetype and the Swift by a few hundred thousand klicks, taking advantage of her mech's stealth, speed, and agility to scout ahead of them. Dash wasn't really too worried about the Waunsik tech, which was much closer to the level of the *Slipwing*—before she was upgraded—than the *Herald* or the mechs, but a fusion mine was still a fusion mine, and stumbling into one would still suck.

He switched his attention briefly back to the battle now raging between the Waunsik fleet and the Cygnus force under Benzel. The wily old pirate was playing a slow game, deliberately keeping his distance, poking and prodding the Waunsik with enough hit-and-run style attacks to make sure they stayed infuriated and focused on him. As long as he managed to avoid getting decisively engaged, he could probably keep this going for at least a couple of hours.

The Waunsik, they'd come to realize, had a hyper-developed sense of honor, meaning all challenges and insults in battle had to be met head-on and resolved. It actually put Benzel in the odd position of trying to not win his fight *too* quickly.

"Dash, we just got lit up by target-acquisition sensors from the moon. And, yup, incoming attacks."

After a pause, Dash saw the icon representing the Talon suddenly slew to one side.

"Whew!" Amy said. "They've got some petawatt lasers down there, so watch out for those. Hathaway says that their lateral tracking is slow, so jinking hard seems to keep them from getting a good firing solution."

"Got it," Dash said. "Let's hold off on using missiles. Hang onto those until we need to use them. So energy weapons only, guys. And weapons-free as soon as you're in range."

Leira and Amy both acknowledged, and Dash watched the distance close.

A targeting sensor painted the Archetype. Dash jinked hard, like Amy had suggested, and the petawatt laser beam blazed past, a miss. The sensor groped around for the mech, like a searching hand, and found it again. Dash jinked, and the laser missed again. So it went as they bored in. Details on the moon resolved, various installations lighting up with target analysis data.

"Leira, I want to get to that big hangar opening, or whatever it is, there on the moon's north pole. See that big canyon that stretches away south of it? I'll take on everything to the right of it. You take the left. Amy, targets of opportunity, and watch our backs."

They both spoke at the same time, saying, "Got it."

A petawatt laser beam struck the Archetype a glancing hit, making the mech's shield go briefly opaque, before Dash could dodge away from it. "It would appear that the Waunsik targeting scanners become more adaptive at shorter ranges," Sentinel said.

"You think—? Oh. Dammit to hell. They *do*."

Two—no, three lasers converged on the Archetype, forcing Dash to dodge through the full glare of one of them. The mech's shield held, but now it had to disperse stored energy, diminishing its efficiency. "Looks like they're learning, too," Dash muttered. "Time to shut these stupid lasers down."

He selected a laser array, targeted the dark-lance, and fired. The squat installation, perched on the edge of a crater, exploded. More blasts flickered and rippled across the moon's surface as Leira and Amy opened up. In less than a minute, there was no more fire coming from the moon, leaving the route open to get to the intriguing set of massive hangar doors.

"Okay, guys," Dash said. "I want to find out what's inside this moon without entirely wrecking the place. A facility this big and complicated has got to be more than just a big hangar or something."

"A fortress?" Leira asked.

"Maybe a command center or something," Amy said.

"Only one way to find out," Dash replied, then accelerated the Archetype toward the surface and the massive doors at the north pole.

A barrage of point-defense fire immediately engulfed the Archetype. It splashed harmlessly against the mech's shield, but given enough time and fire, the shield would be saturated. Dash didn't want to degrade the Archetype's armor unnecessarily. "Guys, you want to take care of all that point-defense shooting for me?"

"We're on it," Leira said, and she opened up with her dark-lance. Amy joined her. In just a few seconds, the point-defense fire abated.

Dash landed on the edge of the big doors—four of them, which were sealed closed. "Sentinel, can the Archetype move one of these doors on its own?"

"The moon's gravity is relatively weak, so yes. But these are big doors, with a great deal of inertia, so it will be a slow process."

"Fine, screw that." Dash deployed the Archetype's power-sword, activated the thrusters, and moved to the middle of one of the four doors. He wound up and slammed the big sword into the alloy of the door. Crackling with power, it slid through the tough metal; he then pulled, dragging the sword through the door's substance, carving out an opening big enough to get the mechs through it. The glowing edges of the gash quickly cooled.

"Hey, Leira," he said. "Ladies first?"

"I'm good."

He chuckled then made to power up the thrusters again, but paused.

"Hey, Benzel, how about a sitrep?"

"So far, so good," Bezel replied. "Still, these guys of the Waunsik Spinward Fleet are pretty damned determined to get to grips with us."

"Spinward Fleet?"

"Apparently. Caught that in some decrypted comm traffic. That's apparently what they call themselves."

"Alrighty, then."

"Anyway, they did manage to flash one of the Rin-ti ships with one of those EMP missiles of theirs," Benzel said. "But Conover moved in to cover it while they got back online, and the Waunsik backed off. Looks like they're leery of our mechs."

"Good," Dash said, finally activating the thrusters and easing the Archetype into the gap. "Now let's see if we can change that from *leery* to *terrified*." He flashed forward at full power, coming to a stop close to the nearest structure on the barren moon.

Dash swung the power-sword, slashing through a gantry acting as a docking pier. The cavern that had been hollowed into the moon was truly vast, a cube ten klicks on a side. It looked to be a secure base for what seemed to be the entire Waunsik Spinward Fleet, a secure anchorage for the storage and maintenance of ships. Right now, though, it held only a dozen or so small merchant vessels.

Sporadic fire rippled against the Archetype's shield. There were no weapons arrays in here, just Waunsik ground forces, presumably deployed as a security force and firing heavy weapons. They made little impression on the mech, though, so Dash just ignored them.

He turned and swung the power-sword again, demolishing another docking tower, then surveyed his destructive handiwork. He'd decided to leave the merchant ships intact; he didn't want to leave the Waunsik here entirely cut off and facing starvation. Part of him still hoped that he could end this without entirely destroying them.

"Dash, Benzel here."

"Go ahead."

"We've pretty much got things wrapped up. Conover just took out a heavy cruiser and a couple of corvettes, and we've dealt with the rest. Kind of a one-sided battle, actually. These Waunsik ships are fast—hell, they had some fighters that were some of the hardest accelerating I've ever seen—but their tech just isn't up to what we've got."

"Yeah, we've got this moon neutralized, too," Dash said, nudging a drifting piece of debris from the Archetype with a wave of his hand. "Now, let's—"

"Messenger, there is an incoming transmission from the Waunsik."

"Huh. Either a surrender, or some last statement of defiance. Benzel, just hang on. Sentinel, put it through."

A window popped open, holding the image of—

A feathered dinosaur. There was no other way to describe it. He even remembered the type it resembled from a brief burst of interest in Old Earth dinosaurs he'd had as a kid—a velociraptor.

"Human you are Mess-in-jur."

The creature's actual voice was just an ear-grating string of snarls, growls, and hisses, thankfully muted by the translator's dubbed overlay. Dash nodded.

"I am. I lead the Cygnus Realm."

"You attack us why."

"Because you declared war on us?"

"You attack us first."

"Yeah, well, that squadron you sent to Mark: Deep wasn't exactly on a goodwill visit, now was it? And before you start making noise about this being between you and the Rin-ti, and claiming we're interlopers and all that—yeah, we are. And this interloper just doesn't have time or interest enough to play diplomat between warring factions."

"You want what."

"For you to stand down. All your forces, here on this moon, and out in space. Have them power down their weapons, turn off their target acquisition scanners—oh, and forget about trying to eat anyone, because that's just gross."

"It is our way—"

"Yeah, I don't care. I just want this fighting to stop so I can move on to taking care of more important problems, like the Golden."

The Waunsik stared back at Dash—literally stared, unmoving. Dash frowned. Had the comm frozen somehow?

"Very well we stand down."

The image flicked closed as the comm was cut.

"Benzel, are what's left of their mighty Spinward Fleet standing down?"

"You mean the three ships still able to move under their own power? Yeah, they are. Weapons and targeting scanners have gone offline. They're done."

"Dash, all the targeting scanners still radiating from this moon are shutting down, too," Amy said.

"Okay. Good. Sentinel, get someone from the Waunsik back on the comm so we can work out the details of their surrender."

DASH WATCHED AS, one-by-one, the merchant freighters emerged from the wrecked hangar and formed up a few thousand klicks away from the moon. They carried the entire Waunsik contingent that had been based there.

The Archetype, flanked by the Swift and the Talon, hung a few tens of thousands of klicks away, monitoring the Waunsik withdrawal. Once they were clear of the system, he intended to have a strategy discussion about what to do next. The idea of establishing their own base here appealed to him, but it was an awfully long way from the Forge.

"Okay, that's the last of these freighters," Leira said. "Fourteen of them, in total."

"Sentinel, are there any Waunsik life-signs let on the moon?" Dash asked.

"None that I can detect."

"Perfect. Okay, open a comm channel to the Waunsik ships."

A moment passed, and then the comm window popped open again, once more showing what absolutely was a feathered veloci-raptor. Whether it was the same one as before or a different one, Dash couldn't tell. The feathers might have a different pattern of colors, but he wasn't sure.

"Alright, you can get underway—" Dash began.

"No."

Dash frowned. "No? Is there a problem?"

"Yes honor demands retribution or sacrifice."

Dash did not like the sound of that. "Listen, I don't even know your name—"

"Honor demands," the Waunsik said, then the channel closed.

"Dash, the Waunsik flotilla is underway. It is on a closing trajectory with our fleet."

"They're attacking us? Seriously?"

"Dash, what the hell is going on?" Benzel asked over the comm. "Those Waunsik freighters are coming right at us."

"I know. Suicide charge. Seems that honor demands retribution, or sacrifice."

"Shit, "Benzel said in a conversational tone.

"Exactly. They're boneheads under all those feathers," Dash said, watching the tactical display. If they did nothing, the Waunsik freighters would begin colliding with their ships in about two minutes. They could probably outmaneuver them, but the Waunsik would probably just turn it into a chase.

The moment stretched, and Dash decided. "I told these assholes I don't have time for this, and I meant it. Cygnus ships, weapons free."

Dash waited for objections, but there were none—just a sudden barrage of dark-lance and nova-gun shots that tore through the lightly armored Waunsik freighters. They managed a few half-hearted shots back from gigawatt lasers, but they might as well have been tossing pebbles. Still, they kept coming, their drives ramped up to emergency overpower, trying desperately to close with the joint Cygnus and Rin-ti fleet.

None of them made it. But it wasn't a battle, not by any stretch of the imagination. It was a massacre. And it was over in about thirty seconds.

The firing stopped, leaving Dash and the rest confronting nothing but an expanding cloud of debris, vented atmosphere, and bodies. A long moment passed in silence.

Amy finally broke it. "Well, that was ugly."

"Yeah, it was," Dash said. "But if this is the Waunsik way, then they've got no one to blame but themselves."

He stared at the wreckage for a few moments then came to a decision. "Benzel, can you recover one of the more intact wrecks—a freighter, a warship, I really don't care. Then find an intact translation drive, strap it to the wreck, and we'll send it on its way to the Waunsik home world. Vynix and Tikka should be able to give you the coordinates."

"Uh, sure, we can do that, Dash," Benzel replied. "Have to ask, though—is there a point, besides making ourselves out to be badasses?"

"Yeah. We're going to include a—let's call it a diplomatic missive with it. One that gives them an option other than obliteration because of how their society works. I have no interest in scouring the systems of Waunsik—not when they can be useful."

"Kind of you," Benzel said, drily.

"I'm a softy. Part of my charm."

DASH CRANED HIS NECK, taking in the far side of the vast hangar, which was ten klicks away. It was a little vertigo-inducing, standing here on a platform attached to the ruins of a gantry, gazing up, down, left, and right to rock walls kilometers away. The Archetype kept station a few hundred meters away, flanked by the Swift, occasional bursts from their thrusters holding them in position against the weak gravity.

But it was still strong enough to give a sense of up and down, which is why he found himself a little disconcerted by the sheer size of this hangar. Granted, if he jumped off this platform and fell, it would take several hours for him to hit bottom—and even then, it would be about as violent an impact as jumping off a chair in standard G. Still, he couldn't convince his inner ear of that.

"This is one big ass room" Leira said, her voice crackling over the comm. There was no atmosphere in the vast cavern, and probably never had been. Pressurizing and depressurizing a volume this big simply wasn't practical. But there were numerous compartments and tunnels that burrowed off of the hangar that *were* pressure sealed. Most of them needed to be repaired, thanks to the damage he'd done in here with the Archetype, but they were still otherwise substantially intact.

"It is," he agreed. "But I think we can use this, set up a forward base here."

"Bit of a fixer-upper, don't you think?"

Dash smiled. "Eh, between the Gentle Friends, the Aquarians, Katerina Vensic's people, and the Local Group, we've got more than enough manpower *and* expertise. Besides, they'll enjoy the challenge."

"We're a long way from the Forge, Dash. Are you sure we're not overextending ourselves?" Leira asked.

"What makes you think I've ever been sure of anything?" Dash countered, grinning through his helmet's faceplate. "We'll keep it as an option until the experts have had a chance to look it over and let us know what they think about repairing and upgrading it." He looked around again. "Not sure what the Waunsik called this place, but we need a name for it. I'm thinking—" Dash paused and searched his memory for inspiration. The moon was only about a hundred klicks across, which actually made it a big asteroid...

"Sentinel, what was the name of the first Old Earth asteroid station? The one that was the first major human outpost in space?"

"From the *Slipwing's* database, it was called Mathilde."

"Right, yeah." He glanced at Leira. "Knew I learned that back in my school days."

She shrugged. "Okay. I was probably cutting class with my friend."

"Ooh, a bad girl. Tell me more."

"Later, not over the comm."

"Especially when I'm *right* here," Benzel said, coming up behind them. A crackle announced he'd joined their channel. "I'd tell you two to get a room, but they're all depressurized."

"So what do you think, Benzel?" Dash asked. "Can we get this place back up and running, put it to use?"

"Don't see why not. It'll take a lot of work, but we could probably make quite the fortified base out of it."

"Point: Mathilde. That's what we'll call it," Dash said.

"Point: Mathilde." Benzel pushed up his lower lip, then nodded. "Good name. First major Old Earth outpost."

Dash and Leira both gave Benzel a stare, and he smiled.

"What? Hey, I know stuff. Not just another pretty face, you know."

"That's for sure," Leira said.

Benzel stuck out his tongue at her, then he turned back to Dash, his dark eyes gleaming behind his faceplate. "So I'll send word back to the Forge, along with specs for this place. Meantime, what's next for us, boss?"

"We repair, get to know our new Rin-ti allies, launch that kludged diplomatic message to the Waunsik—and then we wait," Dash said.

"For an answer?" Benzel asked.

Dash shook his head. "No. An opportunity."

13

Dash rarely got aboard the *Greenbelt*, and when he did, it was always a serene and soul-satisfying experience. The park Freya had engineered in a disused part of the Forge was pleasant enough, but it wasn't very large, and it was well used enough by the Forge's growing complement to not really offer what you could call solitude. You could find alone time in many other parts of the Forge, but only if you were okay with trying to find your happy place among alloy decks and bulkheads and endless, snaking conduits.

The big farming ship now kept on permanent station a few tens of klicks away from the Forge was different, though. Its huge volume of what amounted to nothing but space to grow crops offered lots of opportunities to just get away from it. Dash loved walking along rows of corn that towered over his head, or sitting among Freya's orchard of hybrid apple-stabfruit trees. Dash especially liked these; the thorny stabfruit, native to Gulch, were sour to the point of being inedible, but when hybridized with terrestrial apples into stab-apples, they somehow produced the juiciest, sweetest fruit he'd ever tasted.

He stood among the stabfruit hybrids now, but not alone. Freya accompanied him, as did Tikka and Vynix, who had become the Rin-ti's *de facto* ambassadors to the Cygnus Realm. Tikka had expressed some frustration about the availability of food aboard Rin-ti vessels, which was apparently a perennial problem for reasons Dash didn't really get. It had something to do with the types of food they produced, and how they produced them. He'd turned to Freya for help.

"So, thanks to tech we've obtained from the Unseen and the Golden, we can blend together almost any types of produce," Freya said. "Mind you, some of them don't work out very well. I tried making a hybrid of terrestrial bananas and a sort of starchy, apple-like thing sampled from one of the jungle planets we visited. The result tasted fine, but it smelled like dirty socks."

Vynix and Tikka just stared. Dash caught Leira's eye and nodded down at their booted feet. "Don't think they wear socks. They've got all that fur, instead."

Freya chuckled. "Good point." She turned back to the Rin-ti and screwed up her face like she'd just smelled some dirty socks, then she pinched her hose and made a retching sound.

The two Rin-ti's lips pulled back from their teeth and they hissed, an alarming display to anyone who didn't know that this was their form of laughter. The fact that they seemed to reserve it for things that truly delighted them prompted Dash to give Freya a *well done* look.

Tikka cocked his head. "You have obtained tech from the Golden? I thought they were your most bitter enemy."

"Substitute captured, for obtained, and you've got it right,"

Dash replied. "In fact, this ship, the *Greenbelt*, belonged to the Verity, and it's mostly Golden tech." He shrugged. "Hey, I'm quite happy to steal their stuff and use it against them."

"Well, in any case, this really is very interesting," Vynix said. "You humans eat a great many more types of food than we do. We mostly eat——"

The translation ceased, giving Dash and Freya their chance to stare blankly.

"Custodian, can you work out what that means?" Dash asked.

"One moment." The AI then spoke in what Dash knew was a modified form of the same root language that was the foundation of the Verity tongue but didn't translate it. That had bothered Dash; why would the Rin-ti be speaking a language similar to one of the Cygnus Realm's most bitter enemies? Custodian had worked out, though, that it was the Verity who actually adopted it sometime after they'd split away from Kai's brotherhood, the Order of the Unseen, from a much older root language common closer to the galactic core.

Vynix and Tikka listened to Custodian, then Tikka said, "Yes. An aquatic source, that's correct."

"Many small creatures, if that helps," Vynix added.

A holo image appeared, showing a fish. "Are these creatures similar to this?" Custodian asked.

The two Rin-ti studied it for a moment. "Similar, yes. Quite different in detail, but the same idea," Tikka finally said.

Vynix turned to Freya. "Our most important food is *fish*, yes. The term is good enough."

Freya curled her lip in thought. "Huh. Fish. You see fish being an important foodstuff on a lot of planetary surfaces, but you're right, they don't tend to make it into space much." She looked at Dash.

"They're hard to cultivate in space. Water's heavy, and you need a lot of it to give a decent yield. And they don't tend to keep very well, at least not without a lot of extra tech to stop them from going off."

Dash frowned. "Going off?"

"Rotting."

"Oh. Yeah, I could see that being a problem on board a ship."

Freya nodded. "Even a small amount of spoiled fish—any aquatic creature, really—can make a whole ship reek like—" She made her stinky-socks face again. Again, the Rin-ti laughed.

Dash smiled. "You certainly seem to be charming our guests," he said. "Now, is there any way we can help them out with this food problem of theirs?"

Freya gave another thoughtful look. "Well, I'm assuming the Rin-ti physiology and metabolism is likely based around their fishy food supply, so all of the problems I just described have to be dealt with all the time." She narrowed her eyes and stared at nothing in particular for a moment, then she gave a sudden, emphatic nod. "Right. I know what we can do. There's a section of the *Greenbelt* two modules forward of here that's obviously meant for hydroponic crops—you know, plants that grow in water, basically. We haven't delved into that yet, but maybe now's a good time."

"You could cultivate fish here?" Vynix asked.

"Well, I have to do some research, but if we found a way of cultivating fish in the same water being used for hydroponic crops, we'd accomplish two things at once." She raised a finger in caution. "I do have to do my homework, though. Hydroponic plants are fussy about things like particulates and pH in the water and the like, so we'd have to come up with species that are okay living in the same water as these Rin-ti fish."

"But you can do it," Dash said, momentarily frowning as a pair of the *Greenbelt's* crew wandered conspicuously into view. He gave them a *look*, and they moved off among the trees.

"Sure. Don't see why not."

"Good. Let's make it a priority, in fact. We produce more than enough food for everyone as it is, so your other projects can wait."

The Rin-ti turned to Dash. "You are putting priority on working out a way to produce food for us?" Tikka asked.

"Yeah. If we can help you out, we will."

The two Rin-ti dropped to their knees in front of Dash. It left him nonplussed, his wide-eyed stare flicking from them, to a smiling Freya, then back to them. "Uh, guys, look, you really don't need to kneel—"

"Apologies," Vynix said. "This is how we show great respect, in a formal way. It is intended to convey submission, and therefore great trust."

"Yeah, you do not need to submit to me."

Tikka laughed that toothy, hissing laugh. "We're not *actually* submitting to you, Dash. This is just an ancient custom among our people."

"You humans insist on grabbing one another's hands and shaking them up and down," Vynix put in, as the two Rin-ti rose. "I read that it is an ancient custom of your people, warriors in particular, to show that your hand is empty of weapons. I doubt that that is what you think when you do it, though."

Dash nodded. "Good point."

"To put it another way, then, thank you," Tikka said.

"Glad we can help out."

"Uh, Dash?" Freya said. "There is one thing."

Crap. Had he just over promised? Damn, he should have talked this over with Freya first. "What's that?"

"Water. We need a *lot* of it to get the hydroponics up and running. But we don't have it, which is really why we haven't started doing this sooner." She shrugged. "Like I said, it's heavy and bulky. We have enough available aboard the *Greenbelt*, with recycling, for what we need, but definitely not enough for this."

Dash looked at her for a moment. "Custodian, can you get Al'Bijea on the comm?"

"One moment."

Dash readied himself to figure out what to do while they waited, but the Aquarian leader came online almost immediately.

"You caught me right at the end of a conference comm with a potential new client," Al'Bijea explained. "So I was already right here, at my terminal. How can I help you, Dash?"

"We need water. A lot of it, in fact. Can you help us out?"

"I'm sure we can. We've just begun harvesting ice from a new cometary field, so we've got ships full of the stuff inbound to the Ring every two or three days, for transhipment on to other customers. But we have a considerable surplus. Why?"

"I'm going to let you talk out the details with Freya. But the sooner we can arrange this, the better."

"You're suddenly very thirsty?" Al'Bijea asked, laughing.

"If I'm going to go to the trouble of drinking something, it's going to be stronger than water," Dash replied. "This is for a project we're going to start on the *Greenbelt*, one that we hope will help our new friends, the Rin-ti."

"Ah, very well. I shall have Aliya make arrangements for a meeting with Freya."

"Appreciate it," Dash said, then turned back to the Rin-ti. "I have another little favor I'd like to do for you. Although it's not really a favor, it's more making amends."

Vynix cocked his head, curious. "Making amends? For what?"

"Remember how I got you guys out of your vac suits by cutting them apart? I've asked Custodian to fabricate new and improved ones for you." Dash grinned. "So, how about we head back to the shuttle, go back to the Forge, and then go shopping for some new clothes?"

TIKKA AND VYNIX just gaped all around, their dark, beady eyes wide as they took in the Command Center. They'd already tried out their new vac suits, variations of a new design created by Custodian, with input from Ragsdale and Viktor, incorporating better life support tech, a longer endurance, and integrated body armor. The plan was to eventually equip everyone with them.

Harolyn and Ragsdale lingered nearby. Dash excused himself from the Rin-ti for a moment, letting them continue looking around the Command Center, and sidled up to Ragsdale.

"I saw a couple of your people aboard the *Greenbelt*," Dash said, his voice lowered. "You don't need to shadow the Rin-ti, so let's just drop the tail, okay?"

Ragsdale returned an undeterred look. "I have security concerns, Dash. We still have some unanswered questions about these Rin-ti—"

"And we'll get them answered." Dash sighed. "Look, I appreciate your diligence. Let's just not be so obvious about it. I'm trying to build up trust here, and having a couple of beefy guys lurking nearby, with obvious pulse-pistols stuck under their shirts, isn't exactly trust-building."

Ragsdale held up his hands. "Just remember you're paying me to stay on top of such things."

"Why does everyone think I'm paying them? I'm not paying you guys—"

Harolyn leaned in. "Uh, Dash, you have an audience."

Dash turned and saw Tikka and Vynix both looking at them. "You are concerned that—Ragsdale, correct? That Ragsdale is keeping close watch over us," Vynix said.

Dash sighed. "You overheard that, huh?"

"We Rin-ti hear things very, very well," Tikka replied. "Smell, as well."

"Okay, look, I'm sorry, but—"

Vynix held up a paw in a surprisingly human gesture. "Don't be. We understand. You are fortunate to have someone as diligent as Ragsdale seeing to your security." He opened his mouth in that odd Rin-ti shrug. "Honestly, our people watch you just as closely."

"We're just less obvious about it," Tikka put in. "That's the advantage of being able to hear and smell much better than you do."

"Fair enough," Dash said. "So let's aim to get to a place where neither of us feels the need to keep watch over the other."

"Agreed," Vynix replied, pulling his lips back in a feral smile.

"Glade we're all on the same side about this," Dash said, offering his best diplomatic smile. "Now, Custodian, could you put up the big star map?"

The wall-sized image appeared, depicting the galactic arm, with the Forge at the center.

Dash walked up to it then turned back to the Rin-ti. "Okay, so you have a split, I guess, among your people. The other group, for lack of a better word, live closer to the galactic core, right? Anyway, I know this might be a bit of a sensitive subject for you, but any information you could give us would be helpful."

"It is not especially sensitive," Vynix replied. "We simply don't discuss it much because we have few to discuss it with."

While he'd been talking, Tikka had been craning her head upward, swiveling it side-to-side, studying the big map. Finally, she pointed off toward the left side of it. "Can you make an area over there the center of the map so we can see more of the core?"

Custodian shifted the map as requested, pushing the Forge off of it, toward the right. The shift brought more of the galactic core into view, although even that faded into little more than speculation, even by the Unseen. The increasing density of stars in the core just made for an increasingly hostile environment, to the point that life of any known type simply couldn't survive. And beyond that, in the very center, lurked what was still marked on human maps as *Sagittarius A*, the supermassive black hole at the heart of the galaxy. More popularly known as *The Beast*, this vast hole in the fabric of space and time had the mass of millions of typical stars. The black hole was a source of unimaginably intense radiation, horrific spatial and temporal distortions, and rendered the innermost core entirely inhospitable to life.

Tikka continued to study the star map then pointed up and slightly to the right. "There. Zoom in there."

The image expanded, more and more detail appearing as it did. Dash saw that a diffuse band wobbled its way across the image now; as the zoom increased, a multitude of stars began to appear within it.

"That's enough," Tikka said. "There. That is the Cradle."

"The Cradle." Dash narrowed his eyes at it. "Looks like a nebula? But much longer and skinnier than any nebula I've ever seen."

"It is a stellar nursery," Custodian said. "A linear zone of concentrated dust and gas, almost seven hundred light-years in length. The Creators conducted a cursory survey of it, but it is a complex environment and really required more time and effort than they were prepared to invest."

As he spoke, a window popped open, depicting a breathtaking view of vast, billowing columns rendered in pastel shades from pink to pale blue. Each column was, Dash knew, light-years long; any movement of material within them was, at this scale, utterly undetectable. Searing points of light were scattered among them, a multitude of hot, young stars.

"It really is a stellar nursery, isn't it?" Harolyn said. "All those stars, being born from that dust and gas."

"Shockwaves from supernovae propagating through the material trigger the formation of new stars," Custodian said. "So, indeed, stellar nursery is an apt term. This image contains four thousand visible stars; there are at least one hundred times that many in total, but the vast majority are veiled by gases and dust clouds."

"Which is why these columns are so beautifully lit up like that," Dash said. He admired the striking image for a moment, then he turned to Tikka. "So, this Cradle—how does it relate to your people?"

"It is a boundary. Or, more correctly, a barrier," she replied.

Vynix nodded. "Many decades ago, when our systems were becoming overpopulated, a faction chose to leave and enter the Cradle, believing an ancient legend that there were Rin-ti living on the other side of it."

"There is a flaw in that reasoning," Custodian said. "Virtually all of the stars in the Cradle are far too young to have planets suitable for settlement, at least by lifeforms similar to yours."

"We know," Tikka said, the tone in her voice hinting that she'd be rolling her eyes if she could. "They pushed on, through the Cradle, and found habitable systems on the other side, some of which were, indeed, populated by other Rin-ti."

Vynix nodded. "So our old legends were based in fact. In any case, at first we did maintain some interaction through the Cradle with the Far-Flung, as we came to call those already there, as well as those who had made the journey. Relations were amicable but, over time—"

"You had a falling out," Dash said, nodding. "Definitely not the first time we've heard that story. Just ask Kai about it."

"We did," Tikka went on. "Over time, differences grew between us. New customs developed among the Far-Flung, while old traditions were shunned. Eventually, the ideological gulf was simply too great."

"We had become two peoples," Vynix said. "We are the same beings physically, but in terms of what we believe and how we think, we are strangers to one another. Eventually, this led to disagreement, then tension and strife, and finally violence and bloodshed."

"It always does," Harolyn said, nodding.

"In recent years, the situation has improved," Tikka went on. "But only because we have little interaction anymore. The Cradle is a difficult environment to traverse. We have sent probes, but they have simply vanished. We have also tried dispatching reconnaissance forces—"

"You mean spies," Ragsdale said, smiling. "Not that I'm judging. It's exactly what I'd do, too."

Tikka grinned. "Yes. Spies. However, they, too, have simply disappeared."

"Is that because you're losing them when they try to cross the Cradle," Dash asked. "Or because these Far-Flung are intercepting them and just *making* them disappear?"

"We assume the Cradle itself is the culprit," Vynix replied. "After all, we do not see any similar incursions from the Far-Flung to our side of it."

"It could be that, or it could just be that the Far-Flung are better at doing it, and you're just not detecting them or catching them in the act," Ragsdale said.

Tikka and Vynix exchanged a look. Dash immediately raised a hand. "I don't think Ragsdale meant to be insulting—"

"No, it is not that," Tikka said. "Ragsdale has just voiced a concern that some among us also believe to be true."

"Tikka and I, and others, have raised this possibility with the Over-Burrow," Vynix added. "That is similar to a—" He stopped, apparently at a loss for the right word.

"It's your government," Dash offered. "Your leaders, your ruling body."

"Yes. That's correct. Anyway, we have brought this possibility to the Over-Burrow—"

"And they have categorically rejected it," Tikka cut in.

Dash caught the venom in her voice; clearly, this was a sore subject for the Rin-Ti. He was tempted to just let it go. But he couldn't. This was too important a matter to just leave hanging when it came to a new ally; moreover, they needed to know what relationship, if any, existed between the Far-Flung and the Golden.

"Understandable, I think," Harolyn said. "Accepting that your breakaway cousins are outmaneuvering you like that would be hard for any leader to admit."

"I know I wouldn't be happy with it," Dash added.

"Yes, true," Vynix shot back. "But it does not change the fact that we are not doing the things we should: securing our borders, stepping up patrols, increasing surveillance…" He looked at Ragsdale. "I suspect that you understand."

"Oh, absolutely. I've run into the same thing myself, more than once. It's one of the things I like about this Cygnus Realm gig—the leadership doesn't automatically brush off concerns like that."

"That's because the leadership is still stuck on the verge of having no idea what it's really doing and is more than happy to have the experts speak up," Dash replied.

"If only the Over-Burrow were so…enlightened," Tikka said. "In some ways, I understand the frustration of the Far-Flung."

Vynix gave her a sharp look, but she shook her head. "I said I can understand them, not that I accept or agree with them."

Dash looked around the group, his eyes narrowed in contemplation. Yes, obviously a painful subject for the Rin-ti—but also one that couldn't just be left hanging.

"You know what I think we need here?" he finally said. "A second opinion. And I know just who should be able to deliver it."

14

Dash had made some long flights in the Archetype. One of the longest, in fact, had been shortly after he'd originally found the mech, a flight of days duration that had taken him beyond the edge of the galaxy and into the beginning of intergalactic space. He'd wondered just how far the mech could travel and asked Sentinel about it.

"Assuming there was no combat and, therefore, no resulting damage, then the Archetype has no theoretical limit to its endurance. The quantum singularity power source will continue operating until the latter stages of the universe's evolution. Of course, its structure would have failed long before that—"

"A long, long time, then," Dash cut in. "Meaning it could travel a helluva distance."

"Descriptive, and entirely subjective, but yes. A *very* long time."

Fortunately, this flight was only a few days long. But a few days was still a few days, and even with the Archetype's uncanny way of dealing with Dash's biological needs, it still left him staring at a heads-up portraying a whole lot of nothing.

And Leira sucked at chess, so they'd finally settled on poker, a game she decidedly did not suck at.

"So you owe me, huh—just under a million credits," she said. "Dash, tell me again how you used to swindle people out of their money with this game?"

"It's too soon, woman."

Leira laughed.

Eventually, Sentinel announced that the translation part of their trip was about to end. "We will be dropping back into real space in five minutes," she said. "That will place us on the near-side edge of the Cradle."

"Okay. Per the plan, we want maximum stealth. Leira, you and Tybalt got that?"

"Well, it's only the tenth time you've said it, so I'm not sure. We want maximum what now?"

"We're on high alert here. Enough sass."

"Surrrre." Leira's snort was barely audible, but it made Dash smile.

It was just the two of them. They'd decided to keep their initial probe of the Cradle, and the space beyond it, small and self-sufficient. Benzel had brought the bulk of the fleet forward to Point: Mathilde, so it was close enough that Dash could call it forward for help, or fall back to it if things got too exciting. In the meantime, Benzel would oversee their first efforts to rebuild the captured Waunsik station into a secure outpost of their own.

"We are returning to real space now," Sentinel said.

Dash blinked as the heads-up transitioned from nothing, to—

Glory.

It was the first word that came to him, and it barely fit.

Soaring columns rose like billowing storm clouds from a broad, diffuse band of light that extended to the limits of the heads-up in every direction. All of it was lit in soft, neon shades of mostly pink and blue, but here and there Dash caught splashes of other colors, especially variations on purple and the occasional, lurid swirl of green or yellow. And the stars—so *many* of them, most glaring as fierce, hard pinpoints of dazzling bluish-white, others more muted, and still others just fuzzy spots of glow, depending on how far they were inside the Cradle's titanic veil of dust and gas.

"I—wow. I feel small," Dash said.

"Yeah. I've seen stellar nurseries before, but nothing like this," Leira replied. "It's—yeah, I've got nothing better than *I feel small*, myself."

"Messenger, I have detected an anomaly."

Dash raised an eyebrow. "Isn't this whole thing basically one big anomaly? It sure isn't typical Milky Way galaxy, that's for sure."

A new layer of data appeared on the heads-up, a multitude of bright red dots. "Those are Dark Metal signals. There are thousands of them. Eleven-thousand, nine-hundred, and sixty-two of them, in fact."

Dash's other eyebrow lifted. "Eleven thousand Dark Metal signatures? Leira, are you seeing that?"

"I am. Tybalt just confirmed that he and Sentinel have compared data, and they have pretty much an exact match. So it's not a faulty detector, it's—"

"An anomaly, for sure." Dash glanced at the threat indicator, but it was dark. "Okay, well, before we translate across, let's take time to find out what the hell's going on. Because if there are eleven thousand-odd ships or installations in there, then we are absolutely screwed."

FROM THE INSIDE, the Cradle was both more and less spectacular.

More, because the soft, neon glow completely surrounded them, with more of the young, hot stars that were, from a stellar perspective, newborns. Less, because there were none of the billowing cloud-like columns, rippling waves, or other structures visible—just a diffuse glow in all directions, shot through the fierce glare of infant stars. It was still absolutely gorgeous, in an ethereal, almost magical way.

But Dash wasn't feeling awe or wonder—or he was, but it was overlain by something else.

Dread.

And he wasn't even entirely sure why. It was just a hint of feeling, something gnawing at the back of his mind.

"Sentinel, we're as stealthed as we can be, right?"

"We are. Non-essential systems have been placed in stand-by mode. The Archetype's shield has been modified to absorb as many incidental emissions as possible, then radiate them away at the slowest rate possible—you're worried, Dash. Why?"

Dash frowned. "I'm not sure."

"So, yet another feeling."

"Yeah, but a bad one."

They'd wanted to keep their mission signature as small as possible, hence only the two mechs, and both rigged to run as silently as possible. The Swift was actually better at it, being designed more with stealth in mind, but the Archetype wasn't too far behind. As long as they weren't using active targeting scanners and were keeping their other emissions to a minimum, it would be extremely difficult to detect either—especially while immersed in this colossal sea of dust and gas, and with all of these extraneous Dark Metal signatures around.

"That's it," Dash said.

"That's what?" Leira asked.

He didn't answer, instead just letting his mind do its own thing.

"Dash, are you there? Are you okay?" Sudden worry tightened Leira's voice.

"He is worried about something," Sentinel said. "He has not yet specified what, however—"

"Sentinel," he cut in. "Take us to the nearest Dark Metal signature."

"Dash, I thought we wanted to stay away from those as much as possible," Leira said. "At least until we knew more about what's going on."

"That's the trouble. I *do* think I know what's going on. Sentinel?"

"Course plotted in the nav. Translation time is twenty-seven minutes."

Dash nodded and spooled up the translation drive.

"Dash, what the hell are you thinking?" Leira said, the Swift's drive powering up. "What's going—?"

"Just bear with me here, Leira, for another twenty-seven minutes. I just want to let my brain run with this for now."

Leira made no reply, but as they began translating, the empty void of unSpace washing away the glory of the Cradle, he knew she wanted to, and was probably almost literally biting her tongue.

They'd intended to stay well away from the Dark Metal signatures, and had even plotted a course that would thread their way among several hundred of them, keeping the maximum possible distance from each, while still getting close enough to learn something from the passive sensors. The dust and gas of the Cradle, although spectacular on a massive scale, was rather unimpressive close up—only three to five times denser than the typical interstellar medium. Still, it was enough to significantly degrade sensors; that made it helpful for keeping the two mechs concealed, but it left them relatively blind in turn. They'd hoped that by gathering even some information about many of these Dark Metal signals, they could assemble a coherent picture and figure out just what was going on.

Now, though, Dash drove the Archetype directly toward one of the Dark Metal occurrences. As the range decreased, the signal steadily strengthened.

"Okay, Dash, you seriously need to tell me—"

"It's wreckage, Leira," Dash said. "See? This Dark Metal signature is wreckage."

Sure enough, the smashed remains of—something, a ship, a station, it wasn't really possible to discern which—solidified in the passive scanners. A few tens of meters long, it showed battered hull plating still attached to sheared-off structural members. All of it had been rendered into a matte dullness, probably by thousands of years of abrasion from the tenuous gas and dust of the Cradle.

"So it is," Leira replied. "But what does that mean? What are you thinking happened here, Dash?"

"Just a second, Leira. I promise that I'll tell you everything I'm thinking as soon as Sentinel answers two more questions."

"Which are?" Sentinel asked.

"First, are there any more structures like the Cradle, say, closer in toward the galactic core?"

"Yes. At least two. There are few details available in the current data, but—"

"That's okay. Second—how old are these stars? The ones that have been born here, inside the Cradle?"

"They are—"

Sentinel fell silent, and Dash nodded.

"Yeah. They're young, aren't they? Like, really, really young? In fact, I'll bet you're finding that they're, oh, not even two-hundred thousand years old, right?"

"How did you know this?" Sentinel asked. "The amount of time normally required for hydrogen fusion to be initiated in a proto-stellar cloud is measured in millions of years."

"Yeah. It's like this whole thing, this entire Cradle, is less than two-hundred thousand years old, isn't it?"

"It is, and that is itself anomalous. A nebula-like structure of the size and complexity of the Cradle should take a much longer period of time to form—ah, I understand your thinking."

"I don't—" Leira said. "Wait. Maybe I do. Dash, are you thinking that—"

"This is a battlefield. The whole Cradle. It's what's left of a battle that happened during the last war between the Golden and the Unseen. The dust, the gas, the stars, all the Dark Metal—it's *all* wreckage. *All* of it."

A LONG MOMENT passed in silence so thick, Dash felt like he could reach out and actually touch it. Finally, though, someone spoke.

"Holy shit."

But it wasn't Leira. It was—Sentinel?

Dash gaped at the heads-up. Hearing the AI use some casual profanity somehow shook him even more than the realization they'd just found the unimaginably vast remnants of a battle that no single word—not colossal, not titanic, not stupendous—even came close to describing.

"Dash," Leira said, her voice quiet. "Did I just hear Sentinel say—"

"Yeah, you did. And if that doesn't get across how big a deal this is, nothing will."

"Okay, anyway, how could a single battle have done this? A whole fleet of these mechs—hell, a whole fleet of *Forges*—wouldn't be enough to do this."

"Maybe not by themselves, no. But how about a fleet of Archetypes, each armed with a Lens?"

"Okay, I'm with Sentinel. Holy shit."

Dash thought back again to that time he'd first left galactic space aboard the Archetype, when he'd been chasing a Clan Shirna ship. In the midst of that, a slug of historical data had been unlocked, showing an ancient battle underway. He'd seen violence on a galactic scale, the stars themselves exploding. But he'd just let it slide into the deeper recesses of his mind—not forgotten, but not really *real*, either.

But the Cradle was real. It was *here*. It was a battlefield, one in which the stars themselves had been weaponized.

"It stands to reason, then, that the numerous Dark Metal signals are wreckage similar to this," Tybalt said. "All of it is the debris of that ancient battle."

"Yup, that's it exactly," Dash said, though it took him a moment to find the words. Being faced with something so *big* left him feeling very, very small, despite piloting one of the most fearsome war machines in the galaxy.

"So, Dash, Vynix, and Tikka said that the Rin-ti who wanted to cross the Cradle did so because of an ancient belief that there were Rin-ti living on the far side of it," Leira said.

"Yeah, that's right, they did." Dash narrowed his gaze. "So their civilization was split in two by this battle, which means they were either innocent bystanders in the war, or they were involved in it."

"Dash, I have been examining the various Dark Metal signals," Sentinel interrupted. "Indeed, your conjecture that they are debris seems sound. However, there is one, approximately point-seven-five light years distant, that is unusually large and complex."

"Let's see it."

A window opened on the heads-up, showing a fuzzy series of splotches of various sizes against a monotone grey background. Dash recognized a neutrino scan, the only proven way of detecting Dark Metal.

"Okay, that doesn't look like anything to me," Dash said after a moment. "But you're right—there are either a bunch of Dark Metal fragments there, or one thing that's more complicated." He sniffed. "Sentinel, plug the numbers into the nav and let's go take a look."

"THAT'S AN ARM," Leira said.

"And a big one," Dash agreed.

Sure enough, among a cloud of metallic debris was a massive mechanical arm, spinning slowly. It vaguely resembled the Archetype's right arm but was larger—about twenty-five percent larger, in fact. It was also more heavily armored and seemed to be colored a dull red, but whether that was the color of whatever composed it or something added later, Dash couldn't tell.

He zoomed in the image, and the big arm filled the heads-up. "Is that writing or something on it? Right there, on the armor on top of the forearm?"

"It is some type of pattern that is likely writing," Sentinel said. "But there is nothing like it in the available data."

"Okay, let's gather as many images and as much data as we can, and send it back to the Forge. Get Custodian to ask Kai if he and his people can work it out."

"Understood."

"In the meantime, I'm going to take a closer look at this," Dash said, applying gentle thrust and nudging the Archetype toward the disembodied arm. "Leira, watch my back."

"You're worried that you're going to be attacked by an arm?" Leira asked, a teasing note dancing through her words.

"Hey, after some of the stuff we've been through, would that really surprise you?"

"Good point, and no, it wouldn't."

When he reached the arm, he grabbed it with both of the Archetype's hands and halted its slow spin for what might have been the first time in two thousand centuries.

"Sentinel, can you tell who made this? Was it the Unseen, or the Golden?"

"I am unable to tell for certain. It has attributes of both, but also features that do not correspond to either—"

"Okay, there's another of those pauses of yours that tells me you've just come up with something interesting—or dangerous. I'm hoping the former."

"It is, at least at the moment. I am detecting a faint power signature from the arm. Some system within it is in a low-power state."

Dash frowned. "Huh. We've only seen that sort of life out of a power source when it comes to something big, like the Archetype or the Forge, or with power cores. Is that what it is? A core?"

"No, I am detecting no power core here. Rather, it would seem that power is being obtained from vacuum energy. Essentially, whatever system is drawing it is doing so from the fundamental background energy of space-time itself."

"I've heard of that," Dash said. "But hasn't that always been kind of a fantasy, more than something real?"

"I remember running into a guy on Passage who was hocking what were supposedly vacuum energy batteries," Leira said. "He was, needless to say, full of shit, and he left in a hurry when the station magistrates started to get interested."

"The amount of useful power that can be derived from vacuum energy is extremely small," Tybalt said. "It would be sufficient to maintain, for instance, a memory core in a low-power state."

"And that seems to be the case here," Sentinel said. "I am detecting a memory core in the forearm. Moreover, it is actively processing data."

"Wait, what?" Dash asked. "You mean there's something actually running in this thing?" He glared at the arm. Was the damned thing actually about to attack him, like in some cheesy story about a disembodied limb wreaking a terrible revenge from beyond the grave?

"Yes, but you do not need to be alarmed. There is otherwise no power source, so none of the intact actuators or other systems will function."

"So what is it, then?"

"I would speculate that it is an AI," Tybalt said. "Although that is by no means certain, the pattern of power distribution and utilization in the physical component drawing the power does suggest it."

"An AI? Why would a single arm require an AI?" Leira asked.

"It's probably a backup, a redundant system," Dash said. "I've never really thought much about where Sentinel *is*, but I'm assuming there are components in the Archetype that *contain* her. And it shows how much I've got used to thinking of Sentinel and Tybalt and the other AIs that I've never even considered where they actually are." He looked thoughtful as he added yet another item to his growing list of things to learn. "Anyway, it would make sense that you'd have backups of your AI, right?"

"That is correct," Sentinel said. "There are redundancies built into me so that I can continue functioning despite anything but truly catastrophic damage to the Archetype."

"Hey, is there a backup copy of you somewhere?" Dash asked.

"A mirrored version of me exists on the Forge. It is kept continuously synchronized, at least to the extent possible."

"Huh. Have I ever talked to her?"

"Many times."

Dash shook his head. "AIs are weird. Anyway, let's retrieve this one. We might be able to learn a lot from it."

"Or it could be hostile, Dash," Leira said. "I'd really think twice before downloading a completely foreign AI into the Archetype."

"I'm not going to download it. Sentinel, that arm looks too big to stow, and I don't want to lug it around with the Archetype. So, let's figure out how to retrieve the data module, or whatever's holding it, and keep it powered up, but totally isolated from the Archetype's systems. Leira, I'll need you to do some more overwatch. This place makes me twitchy."

———————

THEY LEFT the arm where they'd found it, tumbling slowly through the cold emptiness among the newborn stars of the Cradle, and resumed their journey core-ward. They did it in a series of translations, jumps of just a couple of light-years at a time, to ensure their navigation remained reasonably accurate, and to gather data. They also remained as stealthy as they could, which meant relying primarily on passive scanners.

Dash frowned at the data summary Sentinel had put on the heads-up. They'd dramatically extended their knowledge of the Cradle, but beyond the narrow lane they'd traversed through it, that knowledge became even more fuzzy and rife with uncertainty. They'd also marked at least two dozen large Dark Metal signatures and were able to visit two along the way. Both were the lonely wreckage of massive, ancient ships, their original purpose a mystery. The only point of interest was their value as salvage, given the size of each silent hulk. They didn't match anything in the data available to Sentinel and Tybalt, and Dash wasn't inclined to spend a lot of time trying to learn more.

They'd finally begun what should be the last translation through the Cradle; their next return to real space should put them close to, or on, the core-ward margin of the vast stellar nursery. It was another half-day of hanging in the Archetype's cradle, passing the time by reading, listening to music, and trying to persuade Leira to play something other than poker.

"But I win at poker," she said. "I'm up...I don't even know how much. Ten million credits? A billion?"

"Yeah, yeah. You've just been lucky. *Extremely* so."

"Like, seventy-five games in a row?"

"Damn right."

"Dash," Sentinel cut in. "We are about to return to real space."

"Back to business," Dash said, limbering himself up in the cradle, making the Archetype's limbs and head twist and turn in response. "Okay, looks like we're dropping out in thirty seconds. Leira, you ready?"

"I am. Kind of excited, too. We might actually get a decent look at the galactic core."

"Actually, the core itself will remain veiled behind voluminous dust and gas clouds—" Tybalt began, but Leira cut him off.

"It'll be more core than I've ever seen before, and that's good enough for me."

With the characteristic explosion of stars from a central point, the heads-up flicked from featureless nothing to incandescent glory.

"Yeah, the only word I have for that is wow," Dash said.

Tybalt had been correct; the galactic core itself was invisible, lurking behind intervening clouds of dust and gas thousands of light-years across. But it was there, a swelling luminosity beyond the glowing veils, some of which were themselves apparently ancient battlefields like the Cradle. The brightest part of the glow must be the core itself—or, rather, the searing multitude of stars crowded around The Beast, the supermassive black hole at the galaxy's heart. Even for someone who'd seen countless celestial phenomena—some of them truly spectacular—Dash found the view humbling.

Sentinel's voice cut through his amazed reverie. "Messenger, I am detecting a star system with at least one planet, approximately two light-years distant. Moreover, there are signals emanating from it with the organized nature and modulation suggestive of comm traffic, rather than natural emissions."

Dash pulled his mind away from the awesome spectacle on the heads-up. "Wait. A planet? How could there be a planet? Aren't these stars all way too young to have planets?"

"Since we are on the edge of the Cradle, it is possible that this star system actually predates its formation—if, as we surmise, the Cradle itself is an artifact of ancient battle."

"Ah. Good point." Dash whistled as he looked at the local star chart Sentinel had brought up on the display. "If there was anyone there when the battle actually occurred, they must have had one *hell* of a view."

"One hell of an utterly terrifying view," Leira said. "Imagine watching stars exploding in the sky, some of them pretty close, and wondering if yours was going to be next."

"Yeah, no thanks. Just imagining that gives me battle fatigue. The question is, who is it?"

"Well, it must be the Rin-ti," Leira replied. "Their Far-Flung, as they call them, right?"

"The signals are not conclusive, but they do not match Rin-ti communications," Sentinel said. "Moreover, I just detected a brief spatial anomaly in the system, suggestive of a ship translating into it."

"So there's someone there, and they—or someone, anyway—has interstellar flight tech," Dash said. "I guess I know where we're heading."

"I have found a medium-confidence match for the patterns in

the comm traffic radiating from the system," Tybalt said. "It is decidedly not Rin-ti in origin."

Dash narrowed his eyes at that. "Okay, who, then? Golden?"

"No," Sentinel replied. "The signals do not match Golden comm signatures, either."

"Then whose?" Dash asked.

"Again, it is only a medium-confidence finding—"

"I don't care. Who's broadcasting from that system?"

"The signals appear to be of human origin," Sentinel said.

15

"ONE PLANET ORBITING A——THAT'S an awfully small, hot star," Dash said. "You sure it's not one of the weirdly new ones? I mean, we are still technically inside the Cradle."

"Despite its size and temperature, this star's spectrum shows it to be quite old—a main-sequence, Type A white dwarf star approximately two hundred million years old. Such stars commonly have at least one large gas giant; the fact that this one doesn't suggests the catastrophic forces that formed the Cradle may have knocked such a planet out of orbit, and the single planet we now see was originally a moon of that long-gone body."

"And there are humans down there," Leira said.

"The comm emissions are, indeed, of human origin," Tybalt replied. "Or at least who- or whatever is on the planet is using comms in a way that suggests they are human——"

"Another ship just dropped out of unSpace," Sentinel said.

Dash watched the tactical display closely. Sure enough, a bulky ship had just translated into this enigmatic system and was now accelerating toward the planet. Another similar vessel had just departed and seemed to be outbound, intending to translate away.

"Busy place," Leira said.

"Yeah, it is," Dash replied. "Those look like freighters, which means this seems to be a stop on a trade route—plus, it's right on the edge of the Cradle, which implicates it, at least indirectly, in the war, or at least its aftermath." He gave the image of the planet a narrow-eyed stare. "We need to know more."

"It is called Almost," Tybalt said.

Dash's eyes went round. "*Almost?* That's the planet's name?"

"So it would appear. I have been able to decrypt some of the comm traffic, and although it is generally of a routine nature, that would seem to be the planet's name."

"So, on top of all this other mystery, the place has a strange name," Leira said. "I mean, Almost *what?*"

"Well, we've got lots of questions," Dash said. "And now we need answers to them. We're going to have to go and pay a visit to Almost."

"Just the two of us?" Leira asked. "Isn't that a little risky? And by *risky*, I mean *dangerous as hell.*"

"Not this time, I don't think. If we stay in the mechs, then diplomacy might be a problem. But if we dismount, then it's just the two of us against who- or whatever is down there on Almost." Dash shook his head. "No, I think these mechs are just too blunt an instrument in this case. I'm going to call Benzel forward, and we'll make planetfall here in force."

"It's going to take them a few *days* to get here, Dash. Are we just going to float around out, hiding, in the meantime?"

"Hey, it'll give me a chance to win back a few million of those credits I owe you."

———

Dash gave the tactical display one more scan. All four mechs were lined up, with the *Herald*, the *Snow Leopard*, and two more ships taking up the rear. All were showing as ready.

"Okay, people, let's go make ourselves known to the good people of Almost."

A private comm channel opened. "You sure, Dash? Sure you don't want to try and win back a bit more of your money?"

"Shut up."

Leira laughed.

As one, the Cygnus mechs and ships smoothly accelerated and began powering their way toward Almost.

As they emerged from the halo of rocky debris roughly defining the system's Kuiper Belt, the threat indicator lit up with a single contact.

"Okay, looks like they've lit us up with search scanners," Dash said. "So they know we're on our way."

"No comms yet, though," Benzel said. "You'd think they'd be asking us who the hell we are."

Dash nodded but didn't respond. He kept his gaze flicking between threat and tactical, waiting for any hint of hostile action.

But there was none. They were simply kept illuminated by active search scanners as the flotilla fell into orbit over the planet. There were still no comms, either.

"This is weird," Dash said. He examined the planet scrolling by beneath. Almost was clearly a dry, almost arid world, somewhat reminiscent of Penumbra, Conover's home planet. There were a few bodies of water, but they were isolated from one another, closer to the poles, and generally shallow and very, very salty. Rugged mountain ranges erupted from the sprawling deserts like exposed bones; there were a few patches of green, mainly clustered around circular impact craters that must have come from objects smashing deep into the crust.

"Not a very hospitable looking place, is it?" Amy said.

"Well, it's hospitable to someone. And there they are. The comm traffic seems to originate from a settlement just now rising over the planet's horizon," Dash said. "Sentinel, are you detecting any other habitation down there?"

"Various outlying installations and outposts, apparently related to activities such as mining and forestry. All are isolated and relatively remote, and they are centered on the main settlement now in view, which appears to also be named Almost."

"Okay, then. I really don't want this to look like an attack, and since whoever's down there doesn't seem inclined to talk to us by comm, we'll do our first contact here this way. We'll bring all four mechs down on the edge of that crater, a few klicks east of what I guess is called Almost. We'll land near that water purifier. Benzel, I'd like you to bring down a couple of squads of your people in shuttles and land right after us."

"And what then?" Benzel asked.

"And then, we'll wait. We'll make it clear we're not here to cause trouble or threaten their settlement, but also that we're interested in meeting with them."

"Incidentally, we have just received a message from Kai on the Forge," Sentinel put in. "He and his followers have thoroughly gleaned the available records and can find no reference to this settlement."

"Huh. Well, that's too bad, but it does tell us that whoever this is, and how they got here, they've probably been here a long time, and records of it have been lost."

"There is another possibility, Dash," Conover said. "This settlement might have been placed here more recently, and secretly."

"Yeah, that's a good point."

"More than that, Dash, if this was done in secret, it might be related to the Golden," Benzel said. "Whoever this is, they might be collaborators, humans working *for* the Golden."

Amy groaned. "Ugh, I hope not. I'm losing track. We've got Clan Shirna, the Bright, the Verity, maybe some of the Rin-ti, possibly the Waunsik, we already know we've had some human Golden agents— it would suck to find out these guys are just more of them."

"More for them than us," Dash said, his voice hardened by the prospect of collaborators. "A *lot* more for them."

DASH SHADED his eyes against the glare of the white sun, watching as the second of the *Herald*'s shuttles grounded in a billowing cloud of dust. The first was already unloading, Wei-Ping leading a squad of Gentle Friends—although they were no longer just Gentle Friends, because more and more refugees were finding the Forge and joining the Cygnus cause. Benzel remained in orbit aboard the *Herald* to provide top cover for their landing party.

Of course, their landing party also consisted of all four of the mechs which, Dash had to admit, looked pretty damned imposing lined up along the edge of the shallow crater, towering against a flat, hot sky that shimmered like molten lead.

"Looks like we've got company, Dash," Leira said, cradling her pulse-gun. Amy and Conover stood with her, staring across the crater's floor. Armed as they were, and decked out in body armor, he had to admit that the three of them—indeed, all of the Cygnus personnel—looked pretty damned impressive, too.

Dash followed Leira's gaze. A pair of vehicles raced toward them, billowing plumes of dust rising behind them. They sped up the slope from the crater's bottom, an incline made gentle over time by the steady chew of erosion from wind and whatever rain might fall here. Scrubby vegetation—clumps of bush, stunted trees, and thick-bladed grass—filled much of the bottom of the crater, hinting at the aquifer filling the rock beneath it, probably in the void spaces shattered by whatever ancient impact had formed it. It explained the water purifying plant hunkered on the edge of the crater, pipes snaking off to pumping stations scattered among the olive-grey foliage.

The two vehicles, big armored trucks on balloon tires, rolled to a stop. In one, a man—very definitely human, and clad in dusty body armor—stood in a cupola sporting a light autocannon, a slug-rifle held at the ready. In the cupola of the other truck was a smaller figure who was also armed and armored.

A Rin-ti.

Dash kept his pulse-gun pointed at the dirt. He glanced at Leira. "A human and a Rin-ti, together, on this side of the Cradle, well core-ward of what we know as the inhabited arm. I am *really* interested to find out just what the hell is going on here."

"Pretty sure we all are," Wei-Ping said, joining Dash and the other mech pilots. The two squads of Forge troops hung back in the slug-proof cover of the mechs.

Both the man and the Rin-ti dismounted and walked forward, and they stopped about ten paces away. The man, who was probably in his forties, had the lined and leathery face of someone at home in the elements, with severely brush-cut hair and mutton chops. He kept his slug-rifle aimed downward, mirroring Dash's lowered pulse-gun, but the Rin-ti raised its weapon.

With a barely audible whisper of alloy and actuators, the Archetype took a step forward, at the same time deploying its power-sword. The massive blade rose over the two trucks, crackling with sudden discharge. A teeth-aching hum filled the air.

"Okay, *that's* cool," Amy muttered.

The Rin-ti gaped at the sword, the blade of which was easily ten times as long as it was tall, then lowered its weapon. The man shot his companion a glare then turned back to Dash.

"Sissik has a suspicious nature," the man said. "And you have to admit, having all this drop out of the sky without warning is kind of suspicious."

"I'm sure it is," Dash replied. "But we're not here as aggressors. Doesn't mean we won't fight, but we'll do so only if we have to. So, that out of the way, I'm Newton Sawyer, but everyone calls me Dash, which is the name I'm most likely to answer to."

"You have others?" the man asked.

"I'm also called the Messenger, and I lead the Cygnus Realm. That's these ships and—others."

The man nodded. "I'm Curbon, and I'd rather not fight if I can avoid it, either." He glanced up at the towering mechs. "And, given the circumstances, I think avoiding a fight is definitely in *our* best interest." He looked back at Dash. "Who the hell *are* you people? And what the hell is the Cyg…Cygnal, whatever realm?"

"Cygnus Realm. We're fairly new and on the other side of the Cradle, so I'm not really surprised you haven't heard of us." He went on to give Curbon and Sissik a brief summary of who and what they were, and how they'd come into being.

"So these are the mechs, the best example we've got of Unseen tech aside from the Forge itself. The one that pulled that sword on you is the Archetype, which I fly. Sentinel, say hello to these folks."

Her voice boomed out of the external speaker. "A pleasure to meet you. I am glad I did not have to kill you."

Curbon just gaped for a moment then shook his head. "Not as glad as I am, believe me."

"Okay, my turn," Dash said. "How in the hell did you guys end up here? You guys, as in, humans? The Rin-ti I understand, but—"

"We're traders. Or we were, anyway. We'd started trading with the Rin-ti on the other side of the Cradle—sorry, the other side relative to us, here—and then got the bright idea to cross over and try to open up trade with the Rin-ti on *this* side."

"Didn't you know that the two groups of Rin-ti didn't get along?" Leira asked, eyeing Sissik. The Rin-ti glared back at her.

"Yeah, hate to admit it, but I think that was part of the reason we did it. I was just a kid at the time; my father was part of the trader's compact that owned our ships, and my mother was chief engineer aboard one of them. Until we got here, my feet rarely touched anything that wasn't the deck of a ship. Hell, I was born in unSpace during a translation."

"They sought to deal with both sides during the strife between our peoples," Sissik said, her voice a hard rasp. "When that strife erupted into outright war, they were trapped here, paying the price for their opportunism."

Dash shrugged. "You're far from the first traders to try and play both sides. Let me guess, the plan was probably something like selling better weapons to one side, then better defenses against those same weapons to the other, over and over, as many times as you could get away with it."

Curbon raised a hand. "Again, I was a kid. But yeah, it was something like that." He gestured around. "Instead, we ended up stuck here because it was just too dangerous to try and cross back through the Cradle. And once we'd been here a year, well, my father and the other traders with him started doing business on this side, and after a couple of more years, business was good. So, here we are."

"And here you are," Dash said, nodding. "Which means you, Curbon, have been here—what, twenty years or so?"

"About that."

Dash glanced at Leira and Wei-Ping. "Looks like we've found the right people to tell us what's happening on this side of the Cradle."

"You have," Curbon said. "But I've got a couple of questions first. Or, actually, only one question—"

"Why are we here," Wei-Ping said.

Curbon gave a thin, hard smile. "You have to admit, you people come dropping out of the sky in these…mechs, that's what you call them, right? Anyway, you show up with some of the most *impressive* alien tech I've ever seen. First, it raises some eyebrows, and then it makes you wonder, what do they want?"

"Have you ever heard of the Golden?" Dash asked.

The leathery creases on Curbon's face deepened as he frowned. "Some hostile race we've heard about, yeah. Kind of xenophobic."

"Kind of?" Amy muttered.

"We haven't had much to do with them, though," Curbon said. "In fact, to be honest, I don't think we've ever encountered them here."

"Count yourself lucky for that," Leira said.

"My people know of them," Sissik put in. "They have apparently contacted other Rin-ti. But I know nothing more than that."

Curbon gave Dash a curious look. "They're really more like interstellar boogeymen than anything else. Why are you asking about them?"

"Because they're an ancient race of aliens who are determined to slaughter all sentient life in the galaxy," Dash replied. "Two hundred thousand years ago, the Unseen fought them to a standstill with tech like these mechs here—and much, much more."

"We think the Cradle was one of their battlefields," Leira added. "It was formed when they turned the freakin' stars themselves into weapons."

"And now, they're back, rising again," Dash went on. "And so far, the Cygnus Realm and our allies have been the only thing really standing in their way."

"So you came here looking for the Golden?" Curbon asked.

"In part. We also just wanted to get an idea of what was coreward of the Cradle, since the Golden seem to have a bigger presence the closer you get to the core."

"Okay, so you find the Golden. Then what? You take them on?"

"Damned right. We're going to eliminate the Golden and every single one of their allies and collaborators."

Curbon stared at Dash for a moment then gave a slow nod. "You really mean that."

"I do."

"He suspects that we might be *collaborators*," Sissik snapped. "That is why he has brought his people here."

Dash let go of his pulse-gun, letting it hang from its sling, and spread his hands. "I'm all about being open-minded. What I'd really like to do is establish a diplomatic relationship with you guys, open up some mutually beneficial trade."

Curbon turned to Sissik and made a *let's talk over here* gesture with his head. The two of them withdrew back to their trucks.

"So what do you guys think?" Dash asked.

"That Rin-ti is really suspicious of us," Wei-Ping said. "Notice the way she kept brushing her finger? If that's what it's called when it's on a paw? Anyway, she kept almost touching the trigger on that slug-rifle."

"And that's after seeing the Archetype whip out a power-sword bigger than one of their trucks," Amy put in.

But Conover shook his head. "I was watching them pretty closely while you were talking, Dash. They seemed genuinely unaware of anything you told them about us. You'd think that if they were Golden collaborators, they'd have been more ready for us."

"They could just be really good actors," Amy replied. "Or the Golden might not have told them about us deliberately, so they didn't give anything away."

"They *could* be Golden in disguise," Leira countered. "They *could* be lots of things. We can only go by what we can see, though."

"And what do you see?" Dash asked her.

She shrugged. "A human who grew up in space and ended up

stranded here, living alongside Rin-ti who are deeply suspicious of anyone from the other side of the Cradle. If they're more than that, then they're not showing it at all."

Dash nodded. "Yeah, I agree. I think these guys are genuine——"

"Dash," Conover cut in, nodding. Curbon and Sissik were walking back.

"Sissik and I are just patrol commanders," Curbon said, then gestured at Dash, his people, and the mechs. "All this is way beyond us. And since you didn't just show up and start shooting, we think there's at least a pretty good chance you're telling us the truth."

"But it's not certain," Sissik said, her beady eyes gleaming at Dash.

"Anyway, we're going to take you to Almost and let you speak with the Guilds," Curbon went on. "It'll be up to them where to go from there."

Dash nodded. "Sounds good. We'll bring the mechs closer to your settlement, but we'll still keep them out of sight as much as we can. Wei-Ping, you keep your people with the mechs—I think showing up in Almost with two squads of troops might send the wrong message." He turned to the others. "Meantime, we're now officially a diplomatic mission."

"Guess that means it's time to smile!" Amy said, her grin bright.

———

DASH MADE sure to not quite land the mechs somewhere out of sight of Almost. He had Sentinel get the AIs to lift them high into the hot-metal sky west of the settlement, and then land them where anyone who wanted to look off to the west would *just* be able to see them.

214

"Subtle," Leira said to Dash, a coy smile playing on her face. "Why didn't you just have them put on an airshow while they were at it?"

"I considered it," Dash replied. "But I figured that might be a little too on the nose."

They followed Sissik, who strode ahead of them, her shorter legs scissoring but her pace unflagging. Curbon walked with them, playing tour guide.

"So this is Almost," he said, gesturing around. "It's not much, as settlements go, but it's home."

Dash took in the cluster of drab buildings that seemed to be crowded around the junction of two roads. One road ran west, away from the big water-bearing crater where they'd originally landed. The other tracked north thirty klicks, ending on the shores of one of the broad, shallow salt-seas that splotched the otherwise arid planet. Other trails originated here as well, winding off into the surrounding wilderness.

"Reminds me of home," Conover said, and Dash nodded. Penumbra, Conover's home planet, was another desert world with more dust than comfort. For some reason, Dash thought, desert worlds spawned these generally ramshackle, thrown-together-looking settlements, made of disused cargo pods, cast-off spaceship components, and miscellaneous junk. It almost seemed to be an unwritten rule among settlement builders.

"Uh, okay, I've been trying to figure out how to put this delicately, but—," Leira started to say to Curbon. "

"What's that stink?" Curbon asked, grinning.

"Yeah, I was wondering that, too," Amy added. "I mean, I know I'm supposed to be diplomatic and all, but that smells like shit. Seriously. And sorry!"

Curbon's grin became a laugh. "Don't be. You're smelling nebula fish."

"Let's pretend for a moment that I have no idea what you're talking about," Dash said, trying to breathe through his mouth rather than letting the eye-watering reek into his nose. "What are nebula fish?"

Curbon gestured for them to follow him, and he led them into a crowded warren of stalls, kiosks, and little shops run out of converted cargo containers. "This is the Fair," he said, stopping among a crowd of people either chattering among themselves or gawking at Dash and his companions. "Almost is run by two guilds. One is the Gravel Guild." He grabbed a rough gemstone off a nearby table and held it up so it scintillated in the hard sunlight. "This is sun stone. It's pretty, but it also has superconducting properties."

"That would be useful," Conover said.

"It's one of the things the Gravel Guild mines and uses for trade."

"So, unless that stink is coming from some of these rocks, I assume that would be related to the second Guild."

Curbon nodded and led them further along, then he stopped and pointed at strips of greasy, pinkish-tan meat hanging from a rack in the full glare of the sun. "That's nebula fish, the main commodity of the Scalers Guild."

Amy scowled at the drying fish. "Fancy name for a stinky fish."

But Curbon just laughed. "That's just its meat. This is why it's called nebula fish," he said, picking up a piece of what looked like leather from another stall, while the proprietor watched them warily. Curbon held it in the sun, and Dash's eyes widened.

Leira said, "Oh, my."

What had looked like a drab piece of leather suddenly came alive with a shimmer of color right across the spectrum, from deep reds to somber purple, and every possible color between.

"Okay, that's gorgeous," Amy said.

"It really does look like one of the more spectacular nebulae, doesn't it?" Leira added.

"It is, and it does," Curbon agreed. "And it fetches a damned good price, because it's not just beautiful, but it's tough and durable, too. The Scalers catch nebula fish in the Broad Sea—that's that big salty body of water north of here."

Dash opened his mouth to reply, but Conover cut him off, leaning in close.

"Dash, I just caught someone behind us talking about a Rin-ti ship that was apparently forced down about ten klicks east of here."

"Forced down?"

"That's all I caught, although the crew are somewhere here in Almost."

"Oh. Well, if the crew are alive and in town, it must have been an emergency landing then, not them being shot down."

"Unless they're prisoners."

"Yeah, that's a good point—"

"Excuse me, you are the Messenger?"

Dash turned, already expecting to see a Rin-ti, from the way it was pronounced, *Mess-in-jurrrr*. And indeed it was, except his one was neither armored nor obviously armed, unlike Sissik, who stood nearby. Instead, this Rin-ti was dressed in respectable clothes that made Dash think of a merchant or a politician.

"This is Cavax," Sissik said. "He is a representative of my Burrow Leader, and the head of the Gravel Guild, the esteemed Narvex."

Dash nodded. "Pleased to meet you, Cavax. What can I do for you?"

"I am here to extend an invitation to meet with Narvex. She is most anxious to make your acquaintance. Off-worlders are rare here, and therefore very interesting when they do show up."

Dash smiled. "Word gets around fast, I see. We've only been here a short time—"

"I informed Narvex of your arrival," Sissik said flatly.

"Ah. Okay, then."

Curbon grinned. "Narvex just wants to meet you before anyone from the Scalers Guild manages to grab you."

"I gather there's some, uh, competition between the two Guilds?"

"Even though they really don't seem to be competitors at all?" Leira added.

Curbon's grin became a chuckle. "Everyone's a competitor, as my father used to say. And the most competitive are the ones who claim not to be."

Dash nodded at that. "Your dad sounds like a man after my own heart." He turned back to Cavax. "We would be delighted to meet with your boss. Please, lead on."

Cavax gave an enthusiastic nod and began leading them through the crowds packed around the stalls and shops. The stink of the curing nebula fish faded, thankfully, but it was a short-lived respite; there were a lot of fish vendors, so the reek just kept coming back.

Leira moved close to Dash. "Ugh. I don't know how these people put up with this smell. I can practically taste it."

"I guess they get used to it."

"What a horrible thought, getting used to this." She snorted and shook her head. "Anyway, aren't you a little concerned about going to meet this Rin-ti in some unknown place? I mean, if these people really are collab—"

"Let's not use that word too openly, okay?" Dash said. But he released a sigh that, yes, tasted of nebula fish stink. "But you're right. Sentinel?"

"I am here," she replied over the comm.

"I have a little job for you…"

16

Dash paused at the entrance to Narvex's surprisingly stately house, an arch opening through a stone wall and revealing a squat, sturdy building beyond. Cavax stopped as well and gave him a curious glance.

"Is there something wrong?" the Rin-ti asked.

"Nope, just waiting—ah, there we go," Dash said, shading his eyes as he peered upward.

A massive shadow rolled over them, as the Archetype settled down just a few meters away from the wall enclosing Narvex's walled estate. Although the mech rode silently on its grav repulsors, it still raised a swirling cloud of dust as its massive bulk touched down. Dust seemed to be the order of the day, rising from their footsteps in little clouds, swirling in the occasional dust devil along the street, and just generally coating everything with a fine, gritty coating of dreary beige.

"Well, that's certainly attracted some attention," Leira said. Dash glanced around and saw people frozen on the porches of scruffy buildings or gaping through dusty windows. The looks, he saw, ranged from wary awe of the Archetype to equally wary suspicion of them.

"Precisely the point," Dash said. "I mean, I fully expect that our dealings with Narvex will be amicable..." He let his voice trail off and turned a beatific smile on Cavax.

The Rin-ti looked up at the towering menace of the Archetype, then back to Dash. "Of course, of course!"

They carried on, through the arch, across a small courtyard of gravel—probably specifically to defeat the pervasive dust—and stopped at a door of riveted alloy inset with a cluster of what must be sun stone, arranged in three, concentric circles. These sun stones had been cut and polished, so they threw back the hard daylight in a ripple of colorful sparks that completely changed with the slightest shift of the head.

Cavax knocked, and the door opened. A suspicious Rin-ti gestured them inside, letting Cavax guide Dash and his party along a corridor, around a corner, and into a sumptuous sitting room. Yet another Rin-ti was sitting on piled cushions before a low table, while a lone figure lurked in the background, silhouetted against the glare of an open set of doors, a small garden beyond them.

"My friends, greetings," the Rin-ti said. "I am Narvex, former captain of the Standoff Fleet of the Rin-ti Star Alliance, lately head of the Gravel Guild here on Almost. Please, be seated. Cavax will see to some refreshments."

Feeling more than a little awkward in his body armor, Dash settled himself onto the cushions across the table from Narvex, Leira to his right, Amy and Conover to his left.

"So you are the Messenger," Narvex said.

"I am," Dash replied. "And might I say, you speak my tongue like you were born to it."

Narvex offered a slight bow, presumably of thanks. "It was a challenge learning how to pronounce certain sounds in your language. The Rin-ti mouth was not designed, I'm afraid, to easily deal with *m's*, and particularly *f's*. But I appreciate your kind words."

Cavax returned with the Rin-ti who'd opened the door for them laying out a tray laden with cups holding a rich, amber-colored liquid of some sort, along with what looked like strips of dried meat wrapped in leaves of such a dark green that they were almost black.

"The liquor is a brew native to Almost," Narvex said. "It's made from a—I believe you would call it a cactus. We call it *quaff*, which is a word meaning to drink, I believe, yes? And these are nebula fish wrapped in another native plant species called glare frond, as they only grow under the full light of our star."

Leira gave the fish wraps a narrow-eyed look. "All due respect, but we encountered nebula fish in your Fair, and it—"

"Smelled like ass, is the way I believe many describe it," Narvex cut in, pulling back her lips in a grin.

Leira laughed. "Uh—well, since you put it that way, yeah. So if it tastes anything like it smells—"

"Try it."

Leira glanced at Dash, shrugged, and said, "Okay, I'm going in." She picked up a wrap, gingerly bit into it—

And then her face lit up. "Holy crap, that's delicious!"

Narvex's smile widened, and then she turned to Dash. "Now, as you refresh yourselves, we may talk."

Dash nodded, but he'd been studying Narvex, as well as the man who'd simply remained standing in the background. His eyes had adjusted to the contrast between the cool gloom inside and the hard glare outside, so he could make out more details. Narvex seemed typical for her species, if perhaps a little on the chubbier side, suggesting a relatively affluent life. The man was tall, with a short, neatly trimmed beard, a shaved head, and dark eyes that gleamed with a keen intelligence.

Dash considered saying something to the man but decided to take a different tack instead and just ignore him completely. His gaze fixed on Narvex, he sipped the quaff—which was also very good, somehow smooth, sweet, and satisfyingly bitter, all at once. Then he smiled.

"So, you wanted to see us—presumably before the Scalers Guild could."

Narvex again offered a slight bow. "You are a to-the-point sort, I see. Of course, I shouldn't be surprised, since you made quite the show of landing your fearsome war machine just outside my house."

Dash maintained his diplomatic smile. "I find it's useful to put all of the cards on the table. That one happens to be my ace. Sorry, I'm not sure if you recognize the—"

"Analogy of poker? Absolutely. Unfortunately, I am not very good at the game," Narvex replied.

Dash chuckled. "Exactly what someone who's very good at the game would say."

"I'm not very good either," Leira muttered, and gave Dash a sweet smile.

He ignored that, too.

"In any case, I am told that you intend to wage war against the Golden, who you have declared to be more than just a vague menace, but an actual, and very clear and present threat," Narvex said.

"They are, believe me."

"And your intent is to not merely defeat your enemy, but to destroy them utterly."

"That depends on who the enemy is," Dash said, idly looking at his hands.

"Ahh. And you believe my people are such an enemy," Narvex said.

"*Your* people? Have you been elevated since our visit began?"

"I am but a humble trader and speak only for my Guild. By my people, I only refer to the Rin-ti generally. I actually have scant influence with those on this side of the Cradle, those known as the Far-Flung, who are allied with the Golden. And yes, I know the Golden are more than a vague, distant menace. However, I do have concerns beyond my own pockets, as well as an eye for what might come next if—excuse me, when—you win your war," Narvex said.

"You mean *our* war."

"True. But we are one planet. Just one."

"And yet, you control this area of space. Why?"

"Because no one wants to be here," Narvex said. "This place is—"

"A graveyard?" Dash asked.

Narvex gave Dash a keen look. "Indeed. How do you know?"

"The Dark Metal signatures, the lack of life. A vast expanse of dust and gas from exploding stars, but new stars that are too young for what they are. This is a battlefield, and a big one. For some reason, the Golden have left this place to you, and to the Unseen, should they return," Dash said.

"I hope the Unseen *do* return," Narvex said softly.

"Why?" Dash asked, hoping to flush out more of what Narvex might know about the enigmatic aliens. But it was the bearded man who finally stepped forward, clearing his throat.

"Because the Unseen are the only chance for life to go on." His voice was deep, his face grave.

Dash frowned at the sweeping statement then shook his head. "You're wrong about that. Or you're right, but not in the way you think you are."

"Rausch doesn't speak often," Narvex said, "but when he does, he's almost always right. That is why he's my closest advisor."

"I know what the Unseen left behind," Rausch said. "I know what they left unfinished."

"Really? Because I *am* what they left behind." He gestured at Leira and the others. "*We* are what they left behind. We might not have asked for this, but the Cygnus Realm will finish what the Unseen started," Dash said, his tone flat and factual, because it was true—absolutely true.

Rausch nodded. "Then you've come here for a reason, and it isn't merely to conduct trade, or to free the Rin-ti of their endless war."

"Everything that Unseen left us, and that the Golden have done, keeps leading us closer and closer to the galactic core. We think that's where the Golden are, and if the Rin-ti on this side of the Cradle are their allies, then they're in my way." He looked back at Narvex. "That means your people's war is now my war and, like I said, our war—because you're here, right on the way to the core and in the middle of it all. So help me with this, and we can end the Golden threat once and for all."

Narvex nodded. "Very well. We must start with something called the Shroud."

Dash resisted a glance at Leira and the others, and just gave a slow nod. "We've heard about it."

"We don't know what it is, only that it is located between the Cradle's Edge and another massive gas cloud called the Maelstrom. The Far-Flung send sortie after sortie to claim it, but all of their ships die. And they blame us, accusing us of war because of it, but we have done nothing of the kind in that area. We don't have the resources, and even if we did..." Narvex trailed off, waving her hands in frustration. "All we know is that—well, show him."

Rausch gave Narvex a doubtful look, but she nodded. He sighed, turned, and opened a wall safe. From within, he removed a small, black data drive, festooned with cable openings. "We found this among the flotsam out there." He handed the item to Dash, who turned it over in his hands.

"Looks like a Golden data module," he said, showing it to Leira, Amy, and Conover, who all nodded agreement. He then noticed a small, circular inset. "Huh. Looks like a button. Anyone try pushing this?"

"No," Rausch said flatly, taking the item back. "We don't press buttons randomly. Especially on tech that's older than civilization itself."

Dash nodded, but he'd turned thoughtful. He saw a path forward and sent a message to Sentinel, telling her to find the feature called the Maelstrom based on coordinates given by Rausch. After locating the Maelstrom, she was to scan it and alert the fleet.

A moment passed, then Sentinel replied, "I have alerted Benzel to marshal the fleet. And I have scanned the supposed Shroud, to the extent it is possible to do so at this range."

"Supposed Shroud?"

"It is much larger than what we know as a Shroud, based on its

Dark Metal signature. It is also surrounded with a ring of debris, suggestive of working defenses. It is impossible to discern more at this distance."

"Then we'll go in carefully," Dash said. Turning to address the room, he gave a tight nod. "We're going to the Shroud."

"That's suicide," Rausch said.

Dash grinned. "If I had a credit for every time someone told me I was going to die." His grin faded. "But I have a plan."

"So THAT's what's been killing the Rin-ti ships here," Dash said, studying the Archetype's tactical display. "Three defensive platforms, all stealthed up."

The Archetype's display showed them clearly, however, thanks to their own Dark Metal signatures. The Rin-ti apparently lacked the means of detecting Dark Metal, so they had no way of locating Golden weapons until it was too late.

"What I don't get is why, if these Far-Flung Rin-ti are allied with the Golden, they're attacking this place," Leira said. "Isn't this a Golden facility?"

"Who knows," Dash replied. "Maybe there's another breakaway group of Rin-ti."

"Oh crap, I hope not. This is complicated enough as it is."

"Or maybe lots of things," Dash went on. "But it doesn't matter. This Super Shroud, or whatever it is, doesn't currently belong to us. All I care about is changing that." He switched to the general fleet comm channel. "Alright, everyone, time to launch. Let's go get ourselves a Shroud."

The battle was brief but intense. The lurking defensive platforms launched missile barrages that must have immediately over-whelmed the Rin-ti, whose ships were now the halo of debris tumbling around the Super Shroud. But the Cygnus Fleet's counter-measures limited the damage to mostly superficial, with only one solid hit on the *Herald*. The Cygnus ships brought missiles and point defense systems to bear in milliseconds, something the Rin-ti could not do. The Cygnus weapons, delivered from long range, pounded the defensive platforms; there was no need to maneuver, since the Golden installations were essentially fixed. In less than thirty minutes, it was over, and they were able to get in close and evaluate their prize.

And a prize it was.

"It manufactures Q-cores," Dash said, his voice quiet. "That's what the scans are telling us. It makes Q-cores, and it makes them quickly—a lot faster than our version of the Shroud ever could."

"So put this together with all the Dark Metal debris in the Cradle, and we've got..." Leira said, but her voice just trailed off at the implications.

"Sentinel, send word to Custodian to start making plans for a bigger fleet," Dash said. "Then get me every salvage ship you can find and bring them here."

"You sound excited," Sentinel observed.

"Damn right I am. This isn't just a battlefield. It's a gold mine, one bigger than I think we could have imagined."

17

Dash watched with satisfaction as the Cygnus fleet deployed, taking up station in strategic locations around the Super Shroud. A flotilla of salvage ships worked the intervening space, gathering as much raw material—especially Dark Metal—as they could, before taking it, and the Super-Shroud itself, back to the Forge. And as for the Forge, it was now underway as well, pushing toward the Cradle to join them.

"Okay, Benzel," Dash said. "I'm leaving all of this in your capable hands and heading back to the Forge. We've got a delegation of Rin-ti who want to meet me there."

"Got it, Dash. We'll have every molecule of Dark Metal in this volume of space scavenged in no time."

"And if the Golden, or any of their lackeys, show up in the meantime—"

"If we need you, we'll call you. You go do what you need to do."

Dash signed off and launched the Archetype back to the Forge.

DASH WATCHED as the Rin-ti delegation boarded their shuttle to return to their ships. They'd been suitably impressed but, like Vynix and Tikka, had been particularly charmed by Freya. They'd also been excited by the new hydroponic systems that were being adapted aboard the *Greenbelt* to produce fish of the types that made up their staple diet.

"So, those Rin-ti are...allied with Almost?" Harolyn asked.

"That's right. I know, it gets complicated. They're a pretty factious race," Dash replied. "Narvex put them in touch with us. They were suspicious, but it looks like we've won them over."

"So that means we've got the Rin-ti on the rim-ward side of the Cradle, plus Narvex and *some* of the Rin-ti on the core-ward side now friendly with us," Ragsdale said. "The other Rin-ti on that side are—"

"The Far-Flung," Dash put in, nodding. "The ones allied with the Golden. We can expect them to be not so friendly, yeah."

"Messenger," Custodian interrupted. "I have a message from Benzel for you."

Dash frowned. Was this the *we need you* call? "Put him on. Benzel, what's up?"

"The salvage op in the volume of space we identified around this Super Shroud is almost done. We've started dispatching salvage crews deeper into the Cradle to claim Dark Metal. Custodian says we're going to need a *lot* of it, because this Super Shroud is going to be especially hungry for it."

Dash relaxed a notch. "That's great. Any problems?"

"One encounter. We had a Rin-ti cruiser show up and start nosing around one of our salvage ops. Amy, together with Viktor in the *Slipwing*, were able to intercept it. We wondered if it might be friendly, but it wasn't. And now, it's more scrap to salvage!" He sounded positively gleeful, probably the privateer in him rejoicing at the sheer size of their haul.

Dash glanced at Harolyn and Ragsdale. "Unfriendly Rin-ti, so they were Far Flung."

"We're going to have to be really careful to come up with some sort of identification, a friend-or-foe system to ensure we don't end up inadvertently fighting the wrong Rin-ti," Ragsdale said. "Friendly fire isn't very friendly at all."

"Good point. Can you work with Custodian and Benzel on that?"

Ragsdale nodded. "Happy to. I've got some relevant experience."

"Sounds like there's a story there."

"There is, but it isn't a happy one."

"Benzel, as soon as you're good with towing that Super Shroud back here, let's do it. Next time it might not just be a single Rin-ti ship that comes snooping around."

"Will do, Dash."

"Messenger," Custodian said. "Since it would appear that you have some time available, might I prevail upon you to meet with myself and the other AIs? We have a matter we wish to discuss with you."

Dash gave an inquiring glance at Harolyn and Ragsdale, who both looked mildly surprised. "Sure. I could use a shower and a bit of down time, anyway. We'll speak in my quarters."

D<small>ASH</small> <small>TOOK</small> the long way to his quarters, detouring through the fabrication level to check in on the work being done there. As they had been for weeks now, the fabrication systems were running flat out, producing ship components, weapons, and miscellaneous ancillary stuff, like more of the upgraded and armored vac suits.

The Forge's fabrication capabilities had further expanded. Now, in addition to making and repairing armor and weapons, Custodian had been able to make standard power cores, apart from those produced by their smaller version of the Shroud. They still could only produce single Q-cores, though, and very slowly at that; getting more of them meant enduring the raw hazard of diving into gas giants and retrieving them from Golden caches. Of course, the Super Shroud would change that.

They could even develop entirely new AIs, according to Custodian, and repair existing ones. It just took Dark Metal—of course, because it always took Dark Metal.

He left the mechanistic bustle of the fabrication level behind and retreated to the quiet solitude of his quarters.

After a shower, Dash took a moment to luxuriate, wearing nothing but a bathrobe. He sprawled in a chair, a glass of chilled plumato wine in his hand, and sighed.

"Okay, Custodian, you've got my undivided attention. What's up?"

In answer, a holo image appeared against the far wall. It showed the Archetype.

"Okay, so what am I—"

A second image appeared alongside it, of another mech—similar, but bigger and more imposing. It was armored in plates that were shades of blue and grey, and a deep red similar to that of the disembodied arm they'd found in the Cradle.

Dash sat up. "Okay, what *am* I looking at here?"

"This is the next iteration of the Archetype," Custodian said.

"Oh. Alright." Dash stood and padded close to the image, studying it. "Looks like it'll take a whole lot of Dark Metal, and a bunch of new cores, too. That's nice, but—"

"You don't understand," Sentinel said. "This is not a new mech. It is an upgrade to the existing Archetype."

Dash blinked. "Really? It looks *larger*."

"It is. Some existing components of the Archetype will be replaced, and new ones added. But the core systems will remain."

"That includes you, Sentinel, right?"

"It does." After a pause, she added, "Why, would you miss me?"

Dash laughed but nodded. "Yeah, I would. I've gotten used to working with you."

"And I you."

"As soon as you are able, Messenger, bring the Archetype in for these upgrades to begin," Custodian said.

"I will for sure."

"I would also request your final authorization to begin work on the system of sub Forge stations we discussed some time ago, the Anchors. The first self-assembling hub for the Anchor is now finalized and construction can begin. I would only point out that it will diminish the Forge's fabrication capacity by almost twenty percent to do so, as it is a major task."

Dash, his eyes still on the upgraded Archetype, gave a slow nod. "We've got the Super Shroud now, so making Q-cores shouldn't be a problem. And Q-cores means *more* capacity, right?"

"It does. The only limitation will be—"

"Yeah, I know, Dark Metal." He sniffed. "We're looking at material needs beyond anything we could ever imagine—even with the

Cradle, it might not be enough. Not for an entire Realm. Well, we'll just have to destroy a whole bunch more enemy ships and harvest what we need from them, right?" He walked to the viewport and looked into space, at the *Greenbelt* majestically sprawling across the star field. "Go ahead. Start work on that hub. Let's get these Anchors underway so we can start solidifying our territory—especially now that we're moving the Forge toward the galactic core."

"Understood."

Dash waited for Custodian to go on, but he didn't. He might simply be finished, but Dash had the feeling he wasn't. He'd said all of the AIs wanted to talk to him, but he had only heard from him and Sentinel.

"Was there something else?" he asked.

"Yes. I, along with Sentinel, Tybalt, Kristin, and Hathaway request a favor from you."

Dash put his plumato wine down. A *favor*?

"Okay, what sort of favor?"

"Survive."

Dash blinked. "Oh. Sure. Surviving is good." He shook his head. "Where is this coming from, this sudden concern for my welfare?"

"As a group, we have decided that you are indeed worthy of the title Messenger, and we are glad that you have come to fill that role."

Dash surprised himself by getting a little choked up. "Well, thank you. I—" He shook his head again, swallowing hard. "Just, thank you." He smiled. "Anyway, don't worry. We'll all be fine."

As he got dressed, Dash reflected on what he'd said, *we'll all be fine*. He truly did believe it; it was really the basic philosophy that had gotten him through life so far.

As he left his quarters to return to the war, though, somewhere in the back of his mind, he knew that it might not always be true.

HIS FIRST STOP took him all of twenty klicks from the Forge. He brought the Archetype into station-keeping mode a klick away from their newest build, the carrier that Custodian had discussed with Dash and Leira. It was actually beginning to look like a ship, and a damned fine one. Benzel was already making noises about moving his flag aboard it when it was complete.

"It needs a name, though," the engineer supervising construction, a wiry, restless man named Sumner, said over the comm from his construction shuttle. The man had come to them from the Local Group, reputedly one of their top engineers. And Dash could believe it; although he found Sumner irritating, he had to admire the man's intuitive grasp of such a massive project, and yet his full attention to the finest details.

"A name. Hmm." Dash frowned in thought. "You know, the first thing that comes to me is *Relentless*. Because that's what we are. We're not going to stop until this war is won, so Sumner, you are building the *Relentless*."

"The *Relentless*. Good name. Got it."

"So how much longer until the *Relentless* is complete and ready for her first space trials?" Dash asked.

"At the present rate of construction, about a month. Which is pretty bloody amazing, considering something like this would have taken us months and months, probably a couple of *years* to build in the Local Group shipyards."

"A month." Dash had been hoping it would be sooner, but

Sumner would know. "Okay, well, work with Custodian regarding weapons, Q-cores, all that. Once we get the Super Shroud here and running, we should be able to beef up production quite a bit."

"Got it."

Dash took a last, admiring look at the big ship now named the *Relentless*, then powered up the Archetype and headed for the translation point that would take him back to Almost.

"So we're calling the new carrier the *Relentless?*" Leira said. "That's a good name."

"A *damned* good name," Benzel put in.

Dash looked at the heads-up, at the Swift, and the *Herald*, keeping station with the Archetype in orbit around Almost. The towing operation to get the Super Shroud back to the Forge was underway, under Wei-Ping's supervision, with Amy and Conover providing an escort with their mechs. Dash had all of them on the comm, though.

They spent the next half hour or so reviewing tactical updates. Then, Dash added a briefing regarding the fabrication priorities of the Forge. When he got to the potential upgrades for the Archetype, every face in the room was bright with interest. Everyone was in general agreement about fighting through the Far-Flung segment of the Rin-ti, and either destroying or otherwise neutralizing them in the process. It was the next logical step in their ongoing campaign to bring the war to the Golden.

"I am convinced that the Golden are out there, core-ward of us, hiding." Dash said.

"Dash," Benzel cut in. "We might have a problem. We have a

salvage ship that's gone offline. She's not responding to any comms at all."

Dash watched the data that came up on the tactical display. The salvage ship, the *Striker*, was a compromise between warship and freighter, trading some of the attributes of each for the capabilities of the other. That meant she could fight if she had to but was intended to be fast enough to get away if she couldn't. If something had happened to her, and it wasn't just an accident, then she'd run into something too big and fast for her to deal with.

"Okay, we've got her last known location," Dash said. "Amy, Conover, you guys seem to be close enough to the Forge that we can pry you away from your escort duties. Meet Leira and me at these coordinates Sentinel's sending you. Benzel, detach the *Slipwing* and a couple of corvettes to accompany us, and let's find out what's going on."

DASH FLICKED his gaze to the tactical display, ensuring everyone was where they were supposed to be. He had Leira at his side, Amy and Conover behind, and the *Slipwing*, flown by Viktor, keeping company with the pair of fast corvettes.

Satisfied, he turned his attention back to the visual imagery on the heads-up. There, at the base of a soaring column of dust and gas, was the icon marking the *Striker's* position. She'd activated her transponder in distress mode, which was a good sign, but they still couldn't establish comms with her.

"Okay, Viktor, you're the reserve. You hang back with the corvettes. Leira, Conover, Amy, we'll go in, in our usual pairs, you guys following us. Let's go."

As one, the Cygnus ships smoothly accelerated, each falling without question into their part in the plan.

As they approached, the distress signal grew stronger; at the same time, the scanner returns resolved more fully. Soon, Dash could start making out details on the heads-up imagery—the Striker slowly tumbling through space, surrounded by debris. Not all of it was hers.

"Messenger, I am detecting small quantities of Dark Metal. Some of the wreckage is clearly from the *Striker's* attackers—the remains of a missile carrier, and parts that appear to be from a Harbinger."

"Good for you, folks," Dash said to the image. "She looks mostly intact."

"Indeed. However, based on scans, her reactor is offline, and approximately sixty-five percent of her hull integrity has been lost."

"So she does still have some life-support working aboard."

"She does." A threat indicator lit up while Sentinel went on. "Three contacts, inbound at high acceleration. Their signatures make them Harbinger-class."

Dash looked over the tactical situation. There was no way they could rescue the *Striker's* crew, much less recover the ship, in the time available. Gritting his teeth, he held back a curse. "Okay. Let's tear these incoming guys a new one. Leira, Amy, Conover, weapons free. Viktor, you and the corvettes cover the *Striker*, get her surviving crew off, if you have a chance."

"Will do, Dash."

Dash flung the Archetype ahead, racing to intercept the incoming Harbingers, the other three mechs racing along like a pack of dogs on the scent.

THEY WEREN'T JUST HARBINGERS. Or they were, but just as Custodian had revealed upgrades to the Archetype, it seemed the Golden were doing the same to their own tech. These were bigger and more heavily armored, reminiscent of the disembodied arm he and Leira had discovered deeper into the Cradle.

Dash threw the Archetype aside, dodging the worst of the blast from a chest-cannon, then responded with paired nova-gun and dark-lance shots. Dash had fallen into the habit of leaning on the dark-lance, a weapon that had been installed on the mech since he found it; the nova-gun, a more indiscriminate weapon, had been added more recently and he hadn't used it much since.

He'd resolved to change that, though, after an arm-waving argument with Benzel and Leira over a little too much plumato wine, and had found quite an effective combo with the two weapons. At longer ranges, he'd fire both together. The nova-gun, which essentially squirted a plasma charge through the Dark Between, effectively became a zero time-of-flight weapon; its blast would saturate the target's shields an instant before the dark-lance beam hit. He did that now and watched with grim satisfaction as the dark-lance beam ripped open the Harbinger's torso.

"Got it," Leira shouted, firing her own nova-gun. Its blast erupted around the stricken Harbinger, tearing through its guts and leaving it spinning helplessly, trailing glowing streams of molten metal.

"Dash, one of these bastards has slipped by us!" Conover shouted. "Viktor, it's heading for you!"

Viktor's reply was as calm as ever. "I see it."

Dash spun around. Amy and Conover rolled and dodged

around one of the remaining Harbingers, but the other had broken off and raced toward the Striker and her protectors. Dash saw the *Slipwing* accelerating to intercept it, while the two corvettes fired salvoes of missiles.

"That's not a fair fight. Leira, let's go after that asshole."

"After you."

The two mechs raced after the Harbinger, but they were a good three minutes behind; the Golden mech ignored them and drove straight in for the *Slipwing*.

"Viktor, you're not up to a head-to-head fight with that thing," Dash said. "You—"

"I've got it, Dash," Viktor replied.

Dash held his breath as he watched the distance narrow between his old ship and the Harbinger. The alien mech struck out at the missiles launched by the corvettes, giving Viktor time to get in a few shots that slammed into the Harbinger, doing some damage. But as the last missile erupted into fragments from a point-defense hit, the Golden mech turned its full fury on—

The *Striker*.

Dash could only watch in horror as it loosed missiles then fired its chest-cannon at the helpless ship. Viktor flung the *Slipwing* into the path of the missiles, switching his fire to them, while the corvettes added the weight of their own shots. They managed to take down all the missiles before they struck, but against the chest-cannon blast, there was no defence except shields—and the *Striker* didn't have any—and armor. And her armor wasn't enough.

The massive blast hit the *Striker* squarely, blowing her to chunks of debris.

"Oh, no," Leira said.

Dash growled and threw the Archetype into combat overpower.

He'd catch up, deploy the power-sword, and personally dissect this son-of-a-bitch.

Viktor threw the *Slipwing* back into the path of the Harbinger. Now the two vessels raced toward a collision that was only seconds away.

Fury became raw alarm. "Viktor, break off!"

"Damn it, Viktor," Amy shouted. "No, please, just break off!"

But he didn't. He drove the *Slipwing* in at full acceleration, apparently determined to destroy the Harbinger even if it killed him.

Dash shook his head in helpless frustration. "Viktor, no!"

The two ships met.

After a series of explosions, the Harbinger emerged, battered, one arm spinning away, trailing debris and sparks. Of the *Slipwing*, there was no sign.

Then the *Slipwing* reappeared, racing away from the blasts.

Dash gaped. He had to try twice to find his voice. "Viktor?"

"Right here."

"How the hell—"

"Your Fade system. Remember that? I've been toying with a few ideas about how to use it. Turns out firing missiles point-blank, then kicking in the Fade right before you collide, works pretty damned well."

"But—the safeties. The missiles shouldn't have even armed."

"Oh, I just deactivated the safeties."

"So you were flying with live warheads."

"I was. And sorry for not explaining myself, but timing is every-thing, so I was kind of preoccupied."

"That's crazy. And brilliant. But mostly crazy."

"Yeah, but it didn't save the *Striker*." Now genuine sorrow flattened Viktor's voice.

"None of us managed to do that," Dash said, watching as the two corvettes pounced on the damaged Harbinger and began to methodically blast it apart. In seconds, it was wreckage, like its two fellows.

"Sentinel," Dash said. "How many aboard the *Striker*?"

"Nine personnel."

"I'd like to see our records on all nine. Pics, too."

"I understand."

Dash felt his eyebrows raise a little at that. Her voice echoed the same sorrow as Viktor's.

"I believe you, Sentinel," he said. "Yeah, I believe you *do* understand."

18

Dash dismissed the holo image, leaned back, and picked up his glass of plumato wine, but he just put it back down again. The final report of the battle had been good news; not only had they recovered hundreds of kilos of Dark Metal, but they'd also retrieved three somewhat intact Harbinger frames, complete with their upgrades—and one of them still had an intact AI.

"So, Custodian, can you decrypt that Golden AI? Hack it?"

"It is, by definition, intelligent. It can therefore choose what to reveal and adapt itself to any attempts made to subvert it."

"So, no."

"It can only be decompiled and analyzed at the source-code level. That would provide valuable information about the nature of the underlying programming, but the AI stores most of its information dynamically, in the continuous interactions between its components. It is similar to how your brain does not store information passively, but does so in the neurochemical—"

"That's okay, I get it. No."

Dash closed his eyes. He abhorred torture. But torturing an AI for information? What were the ethics of that? Was it even possible?

"It should still be possible to extract some useful information," Custodian said. "Some data is stored passively—mainly anything accessed only rarely. That is encrypted and will take considerable time to decrypt—and much of it will be largely irrelevant."

"I don't care. Do it. And if it happens to make the AI…let's say, uncomfortable, so much the better."

"You are angry—"

"Damned right I am! That bloody AI, that machine, made a specific decision to attack a helpless target. That, right there, tells me everything anyone needs to know about these Golden assholes."

"Then you will be satisfied to learn that I have already extracted and decrypted a considerable amount of information from the AI just retrieved."

"You what? Wait, how?"

"The AI you and Leira recovered previously provided a template. It had degraded to the point where it could provide little useful information, but I still learned much about the underlying operations."

"Why didn't you tell me that right up-front? That's great!"

"Sentinel suggested that providing bad news, and then following it with good news regarding the same subject, elicits a stronger positive emotional response from humans."

Dash had to laugh. This time he did take a slug of his plumato wine. "So you guys are working with the old, *do you want the good news first or the bad news first* thing, huh?"

"I am not familiar with the reference."

"Doesn't matter, Custodian. You guys just keep being awesome like this."

He finished the plumato wine and licked his lips. He'd been putting off a trip to the fabrication plant because he really didn't feel like seeing anyone right now. But although the sting of losing nine good people remained, having the AIs now seeming to be looking out for their *feelings* just made him smile.

DASH GAVE the mech a bemused stare. He'd never seen a mech like this one before.

For one thing, it was less than a meter tall.

Leira grinned at it. "It's adorable!"

"Now all we need is a pilot about five centimeters tall and we're all set," Dash said.

"It is only a model—" Custodian began, but he stopped as both Dash and Leira broke into laughter.

"Yeah, we know, Custodian. That was humor—or at least an attempt," Dash said. "Seriously, you made this to, uh, *try out* some ideas for the Archetype?"

"Yes. Holo imagery has its limitations; most notably, the images are not truly three dimensional, or interactive in a tactile sense, the way this scale model of the Archetype is. Sentinel suggests that humans are very tactile creatures, so this is a good compromise."

Dash glanced at Leira. "I don't know what I find more amusing —that Custodian is getting advice on how to deal with humans from Sentinel, or that she's offering it."

"Hey, it could be Tybalt."

"I believe that my insights regarding humans are perfectly sound," Tybalt said.

Leira rolled her eyes, and Dash laughed again.

"Okay, Custodian, you've got a model here, and a bunch of 3D-printed components that we can apparently swap out. How do you want to do this?"

"You may simply add, change, and remove armor. Should you choose to alter weapons, and other systems, all of that can be done with a mere command. As you make changes, the implications for the offensive, defensive, flight and other attributes of the Archetype will be displayed in the accompanying holo-image. The updates are instantaneous."

Dash gave a wry grin. "Playing dress up with an Archetype doll Or action figure, as one prefers." He glanced at Leira. "You must have had dolls, right?"

"Yeah. I'm really girly like that." She snorted with laughter. "What do you think?"

"Yeah, I take it back. You probably spent your time as a kid threatening other kids for their stuff."

"*Now* you're onto something."

For the next hour, Dash and Leira swapped armor components, weapons, and ancillary systems on and off of the basic mech framework. They also tried changing some of the structural components, making the mech taller, shorter, bulkier or more slender, and all the while watching as the specs changed on the holo-image.

Dash finally paused, holding a piece of armor. "Some of these remind me of the armor we've seen on the upgraded Harbingers."

"Some of these new component designs are based, in part, on pieces of the scavenged Harbingers, yes. It seemed only sensible to adapt sound concepts for our own use," Custodian said.

"Good point."

Finally, they reached a point where the various stats for the mech seemed to be at their optimum. Dash stepped back and looked over their new creation. It was still clearly the Archetype, but it also wasn't. It was something bigger and better.

"So, what have we got now," he said, his gaze flicking between the model and the display. "Arm-mounted railgun that should penetrate most armor and shields at close range. Still have the dark-lance and nova-gun. I won't give up the blast or distortion cannons since they're so effective in certain situations, and we've got room. I'm keeping the sword. It's too useful for high-speed passes and close work."

"Better shielding, and this cool new hexagonal armor that looks like it can take another ten percent damage before failing," Leira said. "Those are excellent."

"Agree. Unfortunately, we've lost some of the point defense. And we need another Q-core to power it all." He glanced at Leira, who nodded emphatically.

"I like it."

"So do I," Dash said. "Let's do it, Custodian. As soon as we can pull the Archetype into the shop, we'll get these upgrades done.'

"Understood."

"You should put this thing on display in your quarters," Leira said, nodding toward the model.

But Dash shook his head. "I see lots of the Archetype already. Not really excited about it being the last thing I see when I go to sleep and the first thing when I wake up."

She nodded again. "Yeah, I get that."

"Custodian," Dash said. "One other thing. Can you extract any star map data from those AIs? Anything about the area core-ward of the Cradle?"

"I have managed to retrieve a partial star chart. Unfortunately, the Golden AI was able to activate a kill switch and wipe itself before I could recover any further data. A copy of the AI remains in an isolated backup, but I am reluctant to attempt anything with it until I can determine how to deactivate the kill switch function. I cannot guarantee that further copies will be possible."

"You're the expert for sure," Dash said. "Let's see what you did manage to retrieve."

The holo image changed to a star map, a new one that Dash had never seen before. It showed a small expanse of the region beyond the Cradle—just enough to show the volume of space controlled by the Far-Flung.

"Sixty systems," Leira said, her eyes narrowed at the image. "That's a lot of space to fight through."

"We don't need to fight through all of them," Dash replied, and pointed at the edge of the image where the data petered out. "Here. It looks like this stretch is part of a series of defended systems— maybe a line of them, though we only have data for this bit. But it looks like somebody considers this the edge of their territory, and it needs defending." He glanced at Leira. "Now, I wonder who that might be?"

"The Golden."

"Yeah. Or at least I hope so. I'm tired of their minions. Anyway, we don't need to occupy all of the Far-Flung's space—we just need to neutralize their fleet then push through to this border. Taking the Golden out makes their allies a lot less relevant."

"So we need more data, more intelligence," Leira said.

"Yeah. Custodian, can we add translation capability to the stealth drones we've developed? Carry them as close as we can by ship and then launch them? I'd rather not send ships and people into what might be Golden space, if we can avoid it."

"It is possible, yes. I will develop schematics. It will require freeing up some fabrication capacity, however. I would suggest that we currently have enough armored vac suits, because we are now only making spares of those."

"Sounds good, yeah, these drones have priority. We'll start deploying them as soon as we can." He crossed his arms and looked at the map. "Somewhere in there, we're going to pick a new central point for the Cygnus Realm, and start getting settled in."

"Right on top of the Golden?" Leira asked.

"Damned right. Make them lose space and resources while we increase our own."

"Messenger," Custodian said. "I have an incoming transmission from Almost. The system is under attack."

Dash and Leira exchanged a wide-eyed look, then both, without a word, hurried off toward the docking bay holding their mechs.

———

THE CYGNUS FLEET translated into the middle of a one-sided battle.

As they raced in to relieve the planet, Dash could see the telltale signatures of weapons discharges around the planet. Hissing in anger, he drove the Archetype on at full combat overpower, the other three mechs matching his acceleration. The *Herald*, *Retribution*, and all of the other ships that could be mustered followed on their own fast trajectories.

"Sentinel, anything from the *Vicious*?"

The *Vicious*, a light cruiser, had stayed on station in the Almost system, along with a frigate, two corvettes, and a minelayer. He could make out transponder signals from all of them, and none were in distress mode. But repeated calls for a sitrep went unanswered.

"The plan's simple," Dash said over the general comm. "Straight in and kill everything that isn't us or Almost."

Assents came back, followed by silence as the range steadily diminished.

Finally, the threat indicator switched from a general warning to specifics.

"That's a mixed bag," Leira said. "Two Verity ships, three Bright, three Rin-ti corvettes, and two unknowns?"

"Yeah. Advanced weapons, armor, and systems of unknown design," Dash replied. "Similar to the *Herald*."

"Golden," Benzel put in. "Has to be."

"I think you're right—and we're now in long range. Here we go..."

Dash loosed the one-two combination of nova-gun and dark-lance at the nearest of the probable Golden ships, and was rewarded with a powerful blast that tore a chunk out of her flank. The other Cygnus ships opened up, firing missiles, dark-lances, and their own nova-gun shots. As the range decreased, pulse-cannons threw their weight of fire into the battle. Smaller ships, like the *Slip-wing*, raced ahead and tore into the enemy formation, dodging, spinning, and weaving as they snapped out close-range shots.

As he swung the Archetype aside, dodging the questing beam of a petawatt laser array towed by one of the Rin-ti ships, he saw Viktor use his missiles up close on a Verity cruiser, blasting its bow and bridge to glowing wreckage. The *Snow Leopard* wheeled around and pumped hyper-velocity railgun shots into the ravaged hull; the rods punched out the other side with dazzling flashes and long trails of glowing debris.

Dash somersaulted the Archetype, avoiding another laser shot, then fired the dark-lance, blowing the towed laser array apart. The

Rin-ti corvette towing it burned hard, trying to pull away, but Dash muttered, "No freakin' way," and raced after it. He fired the distortion-cannon, the gravitational pulse yanking the light corvette through a quarter turn, exposing its entire length to him. A series of fast dark-lance shots slammed into it from stern to bow left it dead in space.

Dash looked for another target. He saw the *Herald* rake a Bright destroyer, its pulse-cannons tearing into the bow and inflicting what must be horrific carnage along the ship's entire length. But aside from the two probable Golden ships, which were retreating at high speed, none of the enemy ships remained operational, much less generally intact. He considered chasing the Golden, but they were on a hard acceleration curve, and Dash wasn't ready to chase them through unSpace back into their own territory.

"Let them go," Dash said, sending a rally signal to the fleet. "We'll see them again."

"They are Golden ships," Sentinel said. "The scans confirm it."

Dash nodded at the two receding ships. "Yeah. And I'm sure there are Golden on board." He gave a thin smile. "Looks like they're finally taking us seriously enough to come to battle themselves. Well, boys, believe me, it's going to get a whole lot worse."

DASH LANDED the Archetype near Narvex's house. Like nearly every other building in Almost, it had been damaged but not destroyed.

"That's thanks to the *Vicious* and her consorts," Dash said to Leira, who was remaining mounted in the Swift as cover. "Because of them, this place isn't a smoking crater."

"Well, believe it or not, Benzel says they had some wounded, but no dead. The *Vicious* needs some serious repairs, though."

He dismounted from the Archetype and stepped into the hot glare of Almost's sun. At once, he was struck by a wall of stink—hot metal and burned plastic. Smoke fumed the air, hanging over the settlement like a shroud. Chunks of debris—fragments of stone, pieces of structural alloy, ragged shreds of cargo-pod hull—lay scattered about. Further down the street from Narvex's house, a blast crater had swallowed an entire building.

Dash picked his way through the rubble, into Narvex's house. Cavax met him at the front door and led him inside. He found the Rin-ti lying in her sitting room, her right arm and leg swathed in bandages. Much of the fur on that side of her body was either singed, or simply gone, revealing angry, red flesh.

"She received a flash burn during the attack," Cavax said. "She will recover."

Narvex's eyes opened. "Damned right I'll recover. Dash, I'm so glad to see you. The ships you left here saved us."

Dash sighed. "Wish they could have done a better job."

"If it hadn't been for them, you would have found nothing of Almost but smoldering craters." She reached out and touched Dash with her good hand. "Thank you."

Dash looked around. "Where's Rausch? I was hoping…" He trailed off.

The Rin-ti's faces, despite their inhuman form, answered his question.

"After you left, he began examining the Golden artifact he showed you. Ironically, he believed that having you as an ally gave new life and purpose to his belief in the Unseen and sought to—"

She stopped wincing. "He thought he could learn something of it, something that would help you."

Dash remembered what might have been a button on the device. Had Rausch succumbed to temptation and pushed it? Or done it accidentally?

Narvex nodded at the thoughts obviously playing out on Dash's face. "Yes. The irony is that he may have provoked this, brought the Golden down upon us."

Dash released a breath then pulled a data-pad off his belt. "Narvex, we extracted some data from a Golden AI we cracked. It's a star chart—or part of one." He tapped the pad and it lit up with the cracked star map. "Can you tell us anything more about this? Is this accurate? I'd really like to corroborate it before we start basing any plans on it."

Narvex lifted herself slightly, wincing again, and studied the chart for a moment. Finally, she nodded. "Yes. These systems are controlled by Rin-ti—mostly the Far-Flung, although there may be other factions." She gave Dash a faint smile. "My people are fractious like that."

"And what about beyond that space? We've only got a bit of data."

"Beyond, toward the galactic core—it is there that the Far-Flung are finding allies. We only just saw that. At least one of the ships that attacked us was theirs." She settled back. "If the Golden are anywhere, they will be there."

19

Dash crossed his arms and tried to stay out of the way. He felt out of place on the *Herald's* bridge; the spacious compartment actually felt *wrong*, being far larger than the cockpit of either the *Slipwing* or the Archetype. But, after considerable discussion, he'd reluctantly decided to leave the Archetype at Almost, operated by Sentinel; the reasoning was that its surveillance capabilities and firepower were more than enough to replace that of the settlement's defensive satellites, all of which had been lost. It was only a brief trip, anyway, to meet with the Rin-ti delegation from Vynix's and Tikka's Burrow, who were apparently ready to be swayed to join the Cygnus cause.

Benzel looked up from a data-pad and scanned the tactical display, then he turned to Dash. "Everything that we can spare is either at Almost, or is underway from Point: Mathilde, and soon will be. That includes four Makos for top cover and early warning, all of B Squadron, plus the other three mechs. Four more Makos will be underway soon from the Local Group shipyards, giving us a total of eight. This'll be the first Local Group build for us, and they're keen to get them into service. Custodian has also done some reconfiguring on two of the construction tenders from the Forge, turned them into fabrication ships. As soon as they arrive, they'll start sending building materials and the like down to the settlement. Anyway, Leira and Wei-Ping are getting it all under control."

Dash nodded. "Excellent. Now, if we can get these Rin-ti on our side, that'll scale up our fleet even more."

"Well, you're about to get your chance at that," Benzel said, nodding toward the tactical display. "Three Rin-ti ships just translated in and are coming to intercept us, like Tikka said they would."

The Rin-ti bared her teeth in a smile. "This gas cloud we are approaching is a key resource for our Burrow. We harvest it for fuel and water. Accordingly, it is well-protected."

Dash nodded, glancing at the comm station as a transmission arrived from the approaching ships. "So I see." He made an *over-to-you* gesture to her and Vynix then stepped back. "I will leave you to deal with your people. If you need me to say anything, I'll be right here."

A window opened on the display, showing a Rin-ti in the same sort of vac-armor Tikka and her brother had been wearing when they were first captured, less the helmet. Still, Dash could tell the slender Rin-ti was young, and nervous, even for a species that resembled a twitchy ferret at the best of times.

"Surrender, prey!" the Rin-ti almost shouted. "You will be—!"

"Roxun, please—shut up and listen, or I'll burn your whiskers off with a maser," Tikka said casually. "*Again.*"

"How *dare* you—oh. Tikka?"

"Yes. And these are my friends, Dash and Benzel. Now, do me a favor before I get angry," Tikka said.

Roxun immediately wilted, his bluster gone. "Um, what's that?"

"Go get mom and dad. Tell them we have a war to fight."

Roxun rallied a bit, glaring out of the image and opening his mouth—but he snapped it closed again as Vynix took a menacing step forward. It was an empty gesture, of course; the two Rin-ti were tens of thousands of klicks apart. But it worked anyway, Roxun deflating again and nodding.

Dash leaned down toward Tikka. "Let me guess—little brother?"

Her whiskers twitched in annoyance as she nodded. "Yes. How did you know?"

Dash chuckled. "Call it a hunch."

Some things were truly universal.

DASH GLANCED around the *Herald*'s planning room, essentially a miniature version of the Command Center on the Forge. Since the *Herald* was intended to be a flag ship, she had the planning room as a place from which to run an entire fleet, while the ship's master fought the tactical battle from the bridge. Now, it was crowded with everyone. All of the senior Cygnus personnel were there, as were representatives from the Aquarian Collective, the Local Group, Katerina Vensic's outfit—all of the Cygnus allies. And this included their newest, the Rin-ti of Tikka's and Vynix's Burrow. They'd assembled everyone in orbit over Almost, in what was quite possibly the single most powerful military force currently in the galaxy.

The Rin-ti commanders—and the matriarch, Yerr, and patriarch, Hunox, of the Burrow—had just finished introducing themselves and giving an overview of their contribution to the fleet. A total of four light cruisers, four corvettes, and one missile frigate had arrived, everything they could spare from the defense of their own systems and people.

Yerr scanned the people crowded into the planning room. "Do you have questions?"

"Not a question, but a proposal," Dash said. "We are really grateful for your ships. However, they're a little under armed, compared to what they'll likely be facing. So how about we give you the bulk of our plus-light missiles—you should be able to install those on your ships with minimal setup. We can also spare a single shield generator for each of your ships and have some spare ablative armor pieces we can layer over vital compartments. It won't be pretty, but it'll work."

Yerr and Hunox exchanged a look. "That's very generous," Yerr replied. "But it also speaks to a difficult battle—one in which many may die."

"I'm not going to lie to you," Dash said. "Yes. It will be difficult, and it will be costly, and many will die. Everyone in this room understands that."

Virtually everyone nodded, and Leira spoke up.

"The alternative, though—"

"Is not good to contemplate, yes," Hunox said. "We understand that as well. Even so, your honesty with us is even more appreciated than your weapons."

"Offering hard truths is the ultimate show of respect," Yerr said. "Had you offered us pleasant lies instead, we would be leaving now."

Dash offered a nod then threaded his way to the front of the gathering, Yerr and Hunox moving aside for him. "Okay, so this is us," he said, gesturing at the tactical display, which switched to a schematic of the fleet. "This is everything we have to bring to the party, aside from the Forge itself."

"If only we could bring *that* into battle…" Wei-Ping said, just letting her voice trail off.

"That day will come," Dash said. "Meantime, though, it means we don't have to leave strong forces to guard the Forge, because it can take care of itself." He turned back to the display. "Anyway, this is what we have to work with." He called up the partial star chart taken from the cracked Golden AI. The chart had been embellished by Narvex, as well as Tikka and Vynix. More data had been added from the first telemetry sent back by their stealth drones. "And this is where we want to go."

"That's a pretty blank map," Benzel said.

"It is. And we're working on that. But I don't want to wait any longer than necessary. It's time for us to take the war to the Golden."

Dash had just settled himself into the Archetype's cradle, and was confirming the mech's systems were powered up, when the threat indicator lit up.

Brightly.

"Messenger—" Sentinel began, but Dash cut her off.

"I see it. Yeah, looks like the Golden decided to try and hit us first." The tactical display finally refreshed, showing numerous contacts, some of them big. He switched to the fleet comm.

"Looks like the Golden are here," he said. "Good. Saves us the trouble of going to them. So, everyone come with me and follow your orders. See you on the other side."

"Dash?" Leira asked over a private comm.

"Yeah?"

"I just saw the final casualty count for Almost."

"Yeah, so did I."

"I'm not normally an especially violent person, but—not one bit of mercy for the Golden. These bastards need to die."

Dash powered up the Archetype's drive and broke orbit, accelerating away from Almost and aiming the Archetype at the approaching Golden. The Cygnus fleet and its allies swung smoothly into formation behind him.

"Believe me, Leira, of all the things inside me right now, mercy isn't one of them."

20

Dash threw the Archetype into a tight, spiraling turn, its thrusters pushing hard as he tried to get a clear shot on the Harbinger. A Rin-ti frigate flashed past in the role of cannon fodder, clearly pressed into a charge by the Golden. He snapped out a dark-lance shot at the fleeting target and scored a hit on its conning tower that punched right through and blasted out the far side.

The Harbinger—the only Golden unit that had actually entered battle so far—spun around and, now facing backward, fired its chest-cannon at the Archetype. A quick jink caused most of the blast to miss and slam instead into the hapless Rin-ti frigate, blowing its aft end to scrap. Dash responded with his now-favorite tactic, the one-two punch from nova-cannon and dark-lance, catching the Harbinger at the waist and blowing it in two.

Momentarily unengaged, he scanned the tactical display. The Cygnus forces were getting bogged down in fighting the Far-Flung, leaving the three big Golden cruisers to stand off and pump missiles into the battle.

"Yeah, I don't think so," he muttered, then switched to the command channel. "Benzel, are you still unengaged?"

"Holding back like you wanted. Getting kind of tired of just sitting here firing missiles, though."

"Well, now's your chance. Bring the *Herald* and your reserve in and follow me. I'm going to blast a path through these Far-Flung to the Golden. Leira, you still with me?"

"I'm staring at your cute metallic ass right now."

Despite the desperate swirl of battle, Dash laughed.

He spun the Archetype toward the thinnest part of the Far-Flung line. That was where Yerr and Hunox had focused their own attack, putting their trans-luminal missiles to good use, wreaking terrible havoc among their rebellious kin. As Dash swept by their ships, though, he couldn't help seeing the gaping holes, battered armor, and streams of escaping atmosphere and plasma.

Well, he'd told them it would be a difficult battle—and, to their immense credit, their Rin-ti allies were still in the fight and showing no signs of backing down.

A trio of Far-Flung destroyers blocked the way ahead. Dash eased to one side, giving Leira a clear field of fire, then opened up, slamming nova-cannon and dark-lance shots into his targets, even while the Archetype's point-defense chewed away at missiles racing in from the big Golden ships. A Golden fighter raced in, firing, its pulse-cannon shots slamming into the mech's shields; a second later, it became a cloud of debris as Viktor wheeled the *Slipwing* in behind it and opened up. Dash stayed focused on the Far-Flung ships, though, and in minutes, all three were just battered derelicts.

Dash raced past them, the other three mechs, the *Herald* and her consorts, and the *Slipwing* all following.

He snapped out orders, coordinating the attack among the

Cygnus forces. He focused his own efforts on a big battlewagon of seeming Verity design, probably pressed into Golden service. It poured fire at him, and the Archetype shuddered under the barrage; Dash grimly pressed on, firing the nova-cannon and dark-lance in measured shots, then fully cutting loose when the range got close. Now the battlewagon loomed, filling the star-field; Dash fired as fast as the weapons could cycle, scoring hits all along the length of the enemy ship. Once past, he spun about and decelerated hard, to start another pass. As he did, he saw the Talon and Pulsar attacking one of the other Golden ships. Amy's mech was happily slamming shot after shot into it, its shields apparently having failed—and Dash saw why. Conover had hacked them and simply switched them off. It left the Golden ship fully exposed to Amy's fire, and now Conover joined in with the Pulsar's weapons.

"Good work, you two," Dash muttered, then turned his focus back to his own quarry.

The threat indicator sounded an alert; the third Golden ship, which was yet unengaged, was trying to target the Archetype with a battery of petawatt lasers. Dash dodged fast into the shadow of the Verity ship, using it as cover from the powerful, banked beams. Unleashing the power-sword, he whirled and flew back along the length of the ship, using the searing blade to tear the ship open from bow to stern.

The *Slipwing* flashed past, pouring pulse-cannon fire into the stricken Verity ship. More shots crashed into it from the *Snow Leopard*'s rail gun.

"Dash, we'll finish this one off if you want to take on that third Golden ship," Viktor said.

"Sounds good to me. Leira, Benzel, let's take out this third asshole."

Dash raced out from behind the Verity battlewagon and imme-diately began to jink, trying to throw off that massed laser battery.

A pair of Golden fighters swept in, firing. Leira threw the Swift toward them and, in an impressive display of fury, grabbed one. She flung it into the other, turning both to wreckage. Dash took an instant to appreciate her work—and it cost him. Even the brief distraction let the laser bank catch the Archetype full-on. The shield went black, then died a few seconds later, and the mech was suddenly awash in stellar heat.

Dash groaned as he *felt* the searing blast of energy through the Meld. The Archetype was immediately engulfed in a cloud of its own vaporized armor, which had the ironic effect of degrading the beam somewhat. He threw the Archetype into the hardest skid he'd ever tried, hearing, and even *feeling* the mech's structure groan under the shearing forces. But it got him out of the beam, leaving him a few seconds to take stock.

"Dash!" Leira shouted, her voice verging on frantic. "Are you—"

"Okay? No—dark-lance is out. Missiles are out. Shield's down. Shit, none of this looks like it can self-repair!"

"It can't," Sentinel said.

Dash sighed. Didn't matter. He had what he had—

A shape flashed by, a Mako. It was alone, its wingman gone; Dash watched as it pressed home the attack, taking hits as it closed. Its pilot drove in regardless, debris spalling away in the fighter's wake. Dash opened his mouth to order the pilot to break off—

But a tremendous blast engulfed it and the Golden ship. The pilot had triggered the Mako's powerful blast-cannon, and then just doggedly driven on, his battered fighter slamming into the Golden ship and breaking its back. The *Herald* swept by and began turning what remained into scrap.

"Sentinel," Dash said, his voice quiet. "Make sure to note the name of whoever was flying that Mako. We're going to remember everyone who died today—but that pilot especially."

"Done. They were very brave."

"Yeah," Dash said, swallowing hard. "They were."

Dash yanked his attention back to the battle and scanned the tactical display. The Golden ships Amy and Conover had been attacking had decided to break and make a run for it; now it accelerated as hard as its damaged state allowed, desperately trying to reach safe translation distance.

"No way," Dash said. "All units that can, fire at that fleeing Golden ship. I don't want it getting away."

A moment passed, and then a swarm of missiles erupted from the Cygnus ships, racing after the Golden escapee. It burned hard, but the missiles burned harder, and what had once been a powerful capital ship was soon a ravaged hulk.

Dash turned back to the Verity ship. It still snapped out desultory shots; Dash raced up to it, deployed the power-sword, and began cutting it apart. After a few strokes, a blast of escaping gas blew a suited figure into space. Dash caught it and looked at it.

A Golden. And it was screaming.

Dash closed the Archetype's fist.

EPILOGUE

Dash stared at the Archetype in awe. Even bereft of its armor, it loomed over him and Leira in the fabrication bay, an imposing presence made more imposing by the fact that the mech now stood taller, thanks to new structural components.

"I knew it would be bigger," he said, craning his neck up at it. "But not *this* much bigger."

"Yeah, that little model didn't really do it justice, did it?" Leira said.

"No it did not."

"The weapons have been rearranged, per your direction," Custodian said. "The new arrangement is both more effective and more efficient in terms of power utilization."

"Always a good thing," Dash said, nodding.

He turned to the other side of the bay, where the mech's armor plates had been racked, awaiting installation. The new ones were red, a color imparted by their particular composition; it would, Dash thought, make the Archetype look even *more* badass.

"Hey, Custodian, is that chest armor cooled yet?"

"It is safe to approach and touch, yes."

Dash walked across the bay and stopped at the massive plate that would cover the front of the mech's torso. As thick as he was tall, it still radiated a faint warmth. Tentatively, he touched it, and found it hot, but not uncomfortably so—certainly not enough to prevent him from doing what he did next.

He extracted a marker-pen from his pocket and began to draw on the huge armor plate.

Leira watched, her curious frown getting ever deeper as Dash scrawled on the ablative alloy. She said nothing, though, until he stepped back to admire his handiwork.

It was a reasonable facsimile of a Golden. And it had two kill marks after it.

"Custodian, can you machine that design into this armor and make it stand out in some contrasting color."

"If that is what you wish, certainly."

Leira took his hand in hers. "Can I assume that we're done with being stealthy?"

Dash looked at her hand and smiled, then he turned toward the opening to the fabrication bay and looked into the star-speckled blackness beyond it. He thought about their losses in the recent battle at Almost. Three Rin-ti ships had been lost. Their own fleet had lost two destroyers, a frigate, two corvettes, and a minelayer. One of the fabrication ships had been hit, too, and would have to be towed back to the Forge.

One hundred and sixteen dead in all.

Dash finally nodded. "Oh yeah. From now on, when we're heading into battle, I *want* the Golden to know it's me."

"They'll know," Leira said, her voice soft.

Dash gave a nod, and for just a moment, his features were hard —even cruel. Such was the cost of war. "Good."

DASH, SENTINEL, LEIRA, VIKTOR, and CONOVER will return in RADICAL DREAMER, available to preorder now on Amazon.

For more updates on this series, be sure to join the Facebook Group, "J.N. Chaney's Renegade Readers."

STAY UP TO DATE

Join the conversation and get updates on new and upcoming releases in the Facebook group called "JN Chaney's Renegade Readers." This is a hotspot where readers come together and share their lives and interests, discuss the series, and speak directly to J.N. Chaney and his co-authors.

https://www.facebook.com/groups/jnchaneyreaders/

He also post updates, official art, and other awesome stuff on his website and you can also follow him on Instagram, Facebook, and Twitter.

For email updates about new releases, as well as exclusive promotions, visit his website and sign up for the VIP mailing list. Head there now to receive a free copy of *The Other Side of Nowhere.*

https://www.jnchaney.com/the-messenger-subscribe

Enjoying the series? Help others discover *The Messenger* series by leaving a review on Amazon.

ABOUT THE AUTHORS

J. N. Chaney is a USA Today Bestselling author and has a Master's of Fine Arts in Creative Writing. He fancies himself quite the Super Mario Bros. fan. When he isn't writing or gaming, you can find him online at **www.jnchaney.com**.

He migrates often, but was last seen in Las Vegas, NV. Any sightings should be reported, as they are rare.

Terry Maggert is left-handed, likes dragons, coffee, waffles, running, and giraffes; order unimportant. He's also half of author Daniel Pierce, and half of the humor team at Cledus du Drizzle.

With thirty-one titles, he has something to thrill, entertain, or make you cringe in horror. Guaranteed.

Note: He doesn't sleep. But you sort of guessed that already.

Made in the USA
Coppell, TX
15 September 2021